AND

MARTIN DASH

Bonja Books

Published by Bonja Books Ltd

Moonwood, Cheddleton Road, Leek,

Staffordshire ST13 5QZ United Kingdom

www.facebook.com/AndyBaileyMartinDash

www.bonjabooks.com

Dedicated to my beloved Mum and Dad

Martin Dash is sitting on a bench in the park. It's a fine day with mere wisps of white cloud streaked across an azure sky, the yellow daffodils and green grass combining to produce a chartreuse riot. In fact the whole scene – as we look at it now – has a too perfect sheen that suggests a day in time when trouble is far away and the aims of creation have been achieved.

Martin is handsome; beautiful, even. His soft blond hair has recently been cut sharp but the front falls playfully across his forehead and high cheekbones underpin sapphire blue eyes that are gazing, without looking, across the Serpentine, that lies before him. Full feminine lips finish off a look that is celebrated more widely in some times than others but is never really out of favour.

Martin stood up and buttoned his coat – not against the cold (although it was, in fact, a chilly spring day) but because he thought employers liked to see a neatly-dressed candidate. He was on his way to a job interview with the legal firm Stone Rose and his whole outfit was calculated to give the right impression – regulation black Crombie over dove grey suit over clean white shirt, pattern tie and black patent shoes.

It's all about making an impression.

Martin Dash sits in Stone Rose's reception on one of the soft boxy armchairs beloved of swanky law firms throughout the land. He sits very still with an assured air; gazes through the glass walls at the street below; checks the lawyers and clients who pass through between the lift and the smiling receptionists. This public face has had all the care lavished on it that a firm must bring to bear if it wishes to project the requisite image of money and modernity – a lot of glass; the curved marble desk; the TV screen tuned to Bloomberg Business.

A door the other side of the desk swings open and Gerry Bild walks in, his eyes straight away spotting Martin; a quick check with the desk who nods, 'Yes, that's your man'. Martin has also registered that this is Gerry Bild (he's done his homework on the Stone Rose website). Affirmed, Gerry strides over to Martin and – in a courteous, professional manner – asks "Martin Dash?" with a proffered hand. Martin stands, extending his hand, in turn – "Yes, hello."

"I'm Gerry Bild, Martin. You're going to be seeing myself and Vanessa Carr – she's waiting for us." And with that he motioned back through the door to the meeting rooms beyond.

Gerry was a well-built man of medium height in his 40s with sandy hair that had been wavy until it started thinning on top and so was now trimmed to avoid the unseemly contrast that would be on display otherwise. His handshake, his gait as he strode in front of Martin now, his tailored camel suit, in fact everything about him, was designed to speak of confidence, strength and acuity and, as they passed the meeting rooms on both sides of the corridor, with the frosted glass façades so that you could see the shapes of the players inside (but not their faces), Gerry allowed himself the odd complacent smile, content with the buzz of business going on inside each cell.

Finally, he stopped at one ("Here we are"), tapped and opened the door to reveal Ms. Carr sat at a shiny black table that occupied much of the room. She had been working diligently at her laptop but now stopped and looked up, straight at Martin. With her large brown eyes, long auburn hair, and olive skin she looked vaguely Mediterranean but when she spoke it was with the standard received pronunciation generally encountered in these parts.

"Good morning Mr. Dash – oh, I'm sorry, that sounds rather formal; do you mind if I call you Martin?"

"Not at all – Martin's fine."

"Good – I'm Vanessa and you've already met Gerry. Please sit down."

Pleasantries ensued and the three soon got down to the business of trying to establish whether Martin's beautiful face would fit into the shiny world of Stone Rose – a solid, respectable legal firm just edging into the top 100 nationwide, with offices in London, Manchester and Leeds and currently doing as well as ever on the back of a long property boom that no-one thought would end.

"OK, Martin – so we're here to talk about a possible role for you in our Development Team – Gerry's team." Vanessa motioned abstractedly to Gerry. Martin looked at Gerry. Gerry smiled. Martin smiled. "I see from your CV that you've been doing predominantly development work at Chard Bone for the last four years. Cornel Vine has given you a very good reference."

Cornel had been Martin's boss at CB until six months ago, when he'd taken the job of managing Stone's Leeds office.

He was always full of praise for Martin's work at Chard and, when they'd met at a seminar – subsequent to Cornel's move – and Martin had spoken of his wish to work in London, he'd had no hesitation in recommending Martin for a job at his new firm's London office.

"Yes, Cornel has been very good to me," said Martin. "I enjoyed working for him at Chard and was sorry to see him leave."

"Is that why you want to leave now? – because Cornel's gone?" asked Vanessa.

"Oh no; Chloe - who's taken over – is great; I like working for her but, no, it's simply been my desire for some time now to come and work in London."

"Where the real action is?" interjected Gerry, jokily.

"Yes," laughed Martin, joining in on the joke.

Vanessa cast Gerry a look with upturned eyes and a smile.

Martin continued, "I've enjoyed the work at CB and some of it has been big, national deals but, at the end of the day, London is where most of those deals are done, is it not?"

"Yes, you're right, there's no doubt about it," said Vanessa. "80% of commercial property transactions in the UK, by value, are done here and many of those are international too. There's a definite buzz about working here – it is one of the world cities after all. And you want to be in on it?"

"Well yes, I want to test myself, I suppose."

Gerry beamed and nodded to Vanessa, as if to say: 'There, I told you so – he's what we want.'

Vanessa simply continued to pore over Martin's CV in her hand. "You've worked on the Wood Halls, the PFIs and for The Carter Group. That's an impressive track record – in Leeds too," the last comment smiling, with mock condescension.

"*Sophistication*? – he's *been* to Leeds," laughed Gerry.

Martin recognised the joke, from the Harry Enfield sketch about the northern businessman. He smiled, "Yes, there's plenty going on up there."

Vanessa continued, business-like, "And you've got no ties up in Leeds? It'd be no problem for you to up sticks and move down here?"

"No."

"Your CV doesn't say much about you personally. Not married?"

"No."

"No partner? Sorry, I'm not meaning to pry but we have taken people on before who've retreated back to prior entanglements after we've put considerable time and investment into them."

"No, none of that." This was firm from Martin and a slightly awkward silence followed, that pretty much brought to an end that line of questioning but Vanessa looked at Martin a little more intently. Then back at the CV – "You were in Bristol before Leeds and working as a security guard before starting your legal studies, it says here?" Vanessa looked up again at Martin but more quizzically now.

"Yes, a former life. That was my misspent youth before it dawned on me that I'd probably make a better living at law." This was slick from Martin and Vanessa recognised it.

"Did you choose the law just for the money then?"

"Yes." Martin's answer seemed abrupt and cast a slight chill over the proceedings for a moment (although a definite smirk could be seen on Gerry's face). Again

Vanessa regarded Martin intently and then she seemed to recall something and searched the document in her hand.

Having found what she was looking for she addressed Martin again, this time in a rather kindly, sympathetic way.

"Martin, you've included here – and I wouldn't bring it up but for the fact that you have sought fit to include it – a detail regarding a . . . a *medical condition* you have." This last phrase she enunciated rather gingerly.

Martin simply cocked his head slightly, as if he was unsure of what she was referring to. Vanessa ploughed on: "In the personal section you have stated that you suffer from a condition . . . aah . . . anhedonia. I've not come across that before but your CV says that it's a condition whereby you don't feel emotion."

Vanessa looked genuinely puzzled now. Gerry had been looking at Martin benignly but his eyes narrowed now. Martin, however, appeared unfazed and seemed only concerned to explain this, in a matter of fact way.

"Yes, I'm anhedonic. I realise that it may seem odd to include this in my CV but I've found that it's generally best that I'm upfront about this as it can cause confusion if people are unaware of it."

"I'm sorry . . . how do you mean?" Vanessa did now seem genuinely confused.

Martin continued, "Anhedonia is a condition that has been well documented for a long time now although it is actually quite rare. It's exactly as you say – an inability to feel emotion or pleasure or anything like that . . ."

He could see concern creeping across the faces of his interrogators, ". . . but please don't worry – it doesn't mean that I'm bad, or do bad things; no, I go about life in exactly the same way as everyone else: I sleep, I wake, I work – you know? It's just that all those things are somewhat mechanical for me. I do my work diligently, I understand perfectly well everything that is required of me – and do all that is expected of me – but, underneath, there's no enjoyment and I don't experience emotions, like sadness or happiness . . ."

". . . or love?" interjected Vanessa.

"No."

"Martin . . ." – Gerry now – ". . . could I ask why you tell us this? Actually, Cornel – who I know well – did tell me something of it but I must admit it didn't really register with me until now. I mean, if you behave just the same as everyone else in your daily life, presumably no-one can really tell and you could get away without mentioning it at all. Because, the thing is, by bringing it up – say, in a job interview" – this with a nervous laugh – "you might get people thinking there's something wrong with you. Sorry, I mean . . ." Gerry stumbled on his faux pas. "Sorry, I know you have something wrong with you" – now starting to dig a hole; quick, fill it back – "Sorry, not that this is wrong, I mean, but you know it's something that might appear to be to your detriment, like you're a depressive, say . . . but that you don't really need to bring up . . ."

Vanessa was scrutinizing Martin very intently by now.

"Well, I should say," said Martin, "that it doesn't mean I'm depressive or anything like that at all, almost the opposite in fact. The point is that I don't feel anything. So I never feel sad, or happy for that matter, or anything. In fact it sort of gives me something of an advantage – so far as work is concerned – because it means I'm ultra-dependable !" Martin said this smiling, trying to lighten the mood that had dipped to worryingly sombre (worrying, from the point of view of a candidate trying to impress potential employers) and, indeed, Gerry at least seemed to brighten at this.

"Basically, it means that I work without the sorts of distractions that afflict many people and slow them down – you know: break ups, fights, anxiety, that sort of thing."

"You've never had a partner?" This seemed a little intrusive from Vanessa and Gerry shot her a glance but Martin simply said "No", flatly.

"And it means that I don't take pleasure in eating, drinking, bathing . . . none of those things.   But I still do them because I have to. To get by as a normal person."

Another potential question from Vanessa hung in the air but, this time, was left unasked.

"However, there *is* a downside and this is why I now flag it up" – both Gerry's and Vanessa's ears pricked up at this. "Experience has taught me that it's often better to forewarn people because, otherwise, they might draw the wrong conclusions from how I act sometimes, if they don't understand."

"What do you mean, Martin – how you act?" – Vanessa again.

"Well, because of how I am I don't understand humour, for example – you know, if something is meant to be funny, I can miss that and often have to just follow others in laughing. I do at least understand that – that you're supposed to laugh if someone has made a joke. And I do." Martin smiled. "But if I'm on my own, and don't get a prompt, I might not react at all and it can be embarrassing. There are a few things like that and the accumulation of those things can, after a while, lead people to feel that I'm creepy, or whatever. And it has caused problems in the past."

Martin paused and both Gerry and Vanessa were caught with their eyebrows raised.

Martin continued, "But I've found that, if people are told of my condition, they simply take it into account and gradually get used to me. And soon I'm treated like anyone else. It's not really a disability – it's just something to be aware of."

Again, another pause while Gerry and Vanessa took all this in. Finally, Gerry: "Well, you've been commendably frank with us, Martin, and I have to admit this . . . err, what's it called again?"

"Anhedonia."

"Yes, anhedonia; this . . . err . . . thing is intriguing and, I imagine, something that can be hard to deal with?"

"It's just how I am – I'm used to it. And I find that I can function perfectly well, nevertheless."

"Yes, well . . . well done you. It does show a great deal of character that you don't let it stop you doing what you want to do."

Gerry seemed to have made his mind up on this one and to be relieved at that – "Yes, it's very good."

Vanessa appeared less effusive but still regarded Martin closely; she was clearly caught up in her own thoughts but, presently, she – and they all – returned to the more prosaic elements of Martin's CV and talked for another half an hour about Martin's experience in the field of commercial property development; about Gerry's team; how Martin might fit in and when he might be able to start if the job was offered to him.

They didn't particularly stray into more personal details, partly because there was little in the CV to give them a prompt but partly because they didn't now feel any appetite for that, nor that there was any call for it.

And, finally, the meeting was brought to a close with Vanessa and Gerry thanking Martin for his time and assuring him that they would get back to him soonest.

3

"Anhedonia?" was Vanessa's opening remark in the debriefing session she and Gerry were now holding in the same meeting room, after Martin's departure. "Have you ever heard of that before?"

"Well, Cornel did say something about it when he called me about Martin but, no, I'd not heard of it before. But, anyway, he says that he's a good guy; in fact, one of the best workers he's ever come across . . . recommends him highly."

"But what about the no feelings thing? Doesn't that strike you as odd? What did Cornel say about it?"

"He said that, if you haven't been told about it, you might not notice but, once you know, you do spot little things that give it away – but then you get used to it, get to know him and it's fine, no bother."

"Little things like what?"

"He did mention the humour thing; apparently, you do notice – *if* you're looking out for it – that, when he laughs, he only does it when someone else has laughed first; just a second after they've started laughing, like he's copying them."

"Also, he doesn't really have a personal life, at least not that Cornel could see. He does do the client entertaining stuff – very well, apparently. He'll wine and dine them, take them to the races, to the opera, whatever's needed but doesn't drink alcohol himself. I suppose there's no point really – if he has no emotions to enhance he'd only get the downside, the hangover."

"And no girlfriends?" said Vanessa, one eyebrow arched.

"No, none and apparently that does it for a number of the girls at the office – bit of a standing challenge to get him in the sack, you can imagine. And he is a good looking lad, you may have noticed . . ?" – this with a sly look.

"Piss off," Vanessa snapped, only half playfully.

"Although Cornel did say that some of the girls had said that they found it creepy and, in fact, there are some who, once they know about it, can't take to him. But he says that's just some people's prejudice – you have to remember this is basically a disability and once you think of it like that, see it for what it is, you have to have some sympathy for the guy. I mean, imagine how it must be – he can't experience happiness, joy, pleasure, love. It's a hell of a cross to bear when you think about it. And to cast him off because of it makes it even worse, doesn't it? Wouldn't that be cruel?"

"But he wouldn't feel any disappointment, would he?" Vanessa simply said this as it occurred to her but straight away caught Gerry's accusatory look and felt a twinge of shame.

"So that it wouldn't count, you mean?" Gerry had picked up on the same implication that was seeping through Vanessa's thoughts and there was a silence while this sank in for both of them.

"What if he's making it up? Have we considered that?" – Vanessa, a little hesitantly.

"Why the hell would he do that? He tells prospective employers that he has what is, basically, a personality disorder; it strikes me as a high-risk strategy and for what? To get sympathy? He doesn't need it; look – he's got all the skills, the track record and, you must admit, he is a bit of a charmer. He'll go far with that package without having to resort to some bizarre made-up condition. That just wouldn't add up, Van."

Finally, she said again: "It is odd."

"That aside, he's the best candidate we've had for the department in a long while. Look at the work he's been doing: all top-draw jobs. That development for Balloch in Huddersfield – Cornel tells me that he ran a team of six on that for nigh on two years. They all worked like billy-o for him; dealt direct with the CEO, Josh McGivern – do you know him? Yes, well you know what he can be like and, apparently, there was no problem at all. The whole thing went like a dream."

"I wonder if Josh knew about his . . . thing?" mused Vanessa.

"Yep, told him up front. Cornel reckons he was tickled by the idea of no feelings . . . "

"No scruples; yes I can imagine how that would appeal to Josh – he's a dream lawyer for a property developer !"

Gerry laughed and Vanessa had to smile too.

"Cornel reckons he's ready for partnership but he'd be coming here as just an Associate – he's an outstanding lawyer, Van, and we'd be getting him cheap !" Gerry laughed again at his own joke.

"For the time being" – Vanessa, in a more sardonic tone. "How long before Mr. No Scruples is clambering over our corpses?"

"If he's ambitious, so much the better. That's what always say we want in our young lawyers. He'll put the work and the time in – we need someone at that level. We need someone able to get onto that riverside job." One of Stone Rose's major clients – Grudge Developments – had optioned an entire swathe of Thameside real estate that had missed out on the initial wave of developments in that area in the 80s and were now building a whole new complex of offices and shops that would net millions of pounds, ultimately.

"I'm fronting it, of course, but I can't do everything and I need someone like Martin as my wingman. Since Charlie went, I've been right up against it." A perceptible cloud momentarily descended on the proceedings with the mention of Charlie Turner, the previous incumbent in the post of trusty lieutenant, now departed under something of a cloud of his own. However, Gerry was clearly in his stride now and it occurred to Vanessa that he'd put some thought into this Martin proposition.

"Or wing woman – what about Orla?" she challenged.

"Oh, Orla's all right but she's not got what Martin has, you can see that," sputtered Gerry. Vanessa raised that same eyebrow again.

Realising what he had said, Gerry waved his hand dismissively. "You know what I mean. Anyway, Orla's up to her neck with the Hammersmith job. Everyone's rammed out at the moment, you know that."

"Well, Martin could take that over from Orla and she could do Grudge" – Vanessa's last stab.

"I want Martin for that work. I just know he's the right man for the job," Gerry suddenly quite firm. So Vanessa called it quits at that point as she realised that, for whatever reason, Gerry had fixed on the idea of having this soulless smoothie as his personal protégé. "Very well, I can see you mean to have him but on your head be it."

4

Martin Dash is standing in the living room of his flat in Roundhay, Leeds, ironing some work shirts and listening to Radio 4. It's nine o'clock, Saturday morning, and the news is on. Martin keeps himself informed of what's going on; then, when conversations with colleagues or clients turn to politics (not often) or football (more often), he generally knows the subject and can converse.

Occasionally, he looks through the window of his flat out onto the park where the odd perambulator ambles along the tarmacked paths splitting the carpet of green laid between the railings, trees and bushes and a group of kids are playing football in the far corner. It's a dull cloudy day outside and in.

Martin had taken the tenancy of this flat not long after he'd arrived in Leeds (having spent the first few weeks simply renting a room in a B&B) and had renewed it six-monthly ever since. His flat was on the first floor of the middle of a row of three-story 60s blocks just a couple of miles from Chard Bone's offices in the centre. This was convenient as it meant he could cycle to work, take the bus or, even, walk as it might suit him (although he was not like the 'Two Jakes' at work – Connery and Twemlow, respectively – who jogged to and from work, religiously).

The blocks were in a perfectly respectable neighbourhood and populated with young professionals like himself; shopkeepers; firemen; chauffeurs; beauticians; pensioners; and some families (most of them the single parent variety) – normal people, basically. The pale, sandy brickwork and the bright green and blue doors all trimmed with brilliant white panelling meant that the blocks presented a pleasant aspect to the park-goers passing by and the occupants (Martin excepted) were duly pleased.

His own flat was rented through an agency in the town acting for an unknown owner (in fact, he had seen their client's name on some original tenancy documentation – a Mr. Clough or Clowes or some such). It had been in good condition when Martin took it on and he had maintained it as such since then. It was also furnished, which was another reason it had suited Martin at the outset. This avoided the need to go out amassing furniture and the fact that it represented someone else's taste was of no concern, particularly as the décor was neutral, like Martin.

There was very little in the flat in the way of personal possessions, the things that ordinarily give a clue to someone's personality – CDs, books, DVDs, magazines, booze, clothes, food even. When, on the one occasion that a colleague from work had actually been in Martin's flat (one of the Jakes, in fact – Connery), he had explained this lack frankly – in the context of his condition – by pointing out that he didn't really listen to music on his own; there were two CDs he had acquired almost as a mere fact-finding exercise, to hear what was in the records that were being released that seemed to stir people – Girls Aloud: Chemistry and Coldplay: X&Y. Similarly with DVDs, he had The Bourne Supremacy and Saw.

He had a few more books but even these tended to relate either to his job (there were textbooks on Property Investment and Contract Law) or current affairs; he explained that he felt it important to be able to exhibit some understanding of what was going on in the world when conversing with successful and influential clients. In fact, he advised that much of what he knew was gleaned from television, in any event. Jake had left with the distinct impression that, apart from sleeping and eating (the kitchen's contents were equally perfunctory), Martin didn't really do much, on a permanent basis, aside from watching TV.

Or iron his shirts, as now.

He heard the clack of his front door letter box, sat the iron back on its haunches, and went to retrieve the missives – a bank statement and an envelope which, he saw straightaway, was from Stone Rose. Inside was a letter, signed by Gerry Bild, confirming that he had got the job.

Heralding a new start.

Martin Dash walks along Rheidol Terrace on his way to Angel Tube station. It's his first day at work for Stone Rose and he's had a lie-in as he's not due there until 9:00 am to meet the HR Director to begin his induction. It's a bright summer morning, June 2006, and he's just walked out of the door to his new flat at number 23. This was probably not the most convenient place to live, given that Stone Rose's offices were in Mayfair but neither was it the most inconvenient – a short walk to the Tube, one change, and then the Piccadilly Line straight down to Hyde Park Corner. The point was that Cornel Vine owned the Islington flat – basically as an investment – and, conveniently, had it coming vacant at the point when Martin was finishing his notice period at Chard Bone. He'd offered it to Martin to rent, without hesitation. He knew he'd have no trouble with him as a tenant, so it suited. He was beginning to look like Martin's full-time sponsor and Martin was duly grateful. In any event, Islington is a perfectly nice place to live, with its mix of solid Georgian houses and laid-back vibe.

Sunshine bathes the area and it's warm already. The weather has been great since Martin arrived at his new residence on Saturday lunchtime. A number of the houses he passes have window boxes holding splats of colour – purple and yellow pansies, red carnations, blue chrysanthemums – that brighten the scene, happily and confidently.

There are quite a number of people on the pavements and cars on the road, all hurrying to their work at the start of a new week; many – like Martin – scurrying to the Tube station or bus stops; most – like Martin – to get to the offices in the city centre, throbbing in the distance, to play their roles as accountants, bankers, brokers, consultants, financiers, and lawyers. They are dressed well – in fashion – and Martin blends in perfectly, with his Hugo Boss suit, Thomas Pink shirt and Alden shoes. In fact, you'd probably have to say that he stands out; with that shock of bright blond quiff and moody blue eyes, you might imagine (or, rather, he might be doing the imagining) that he is being (secretly) filmed or, at least, (secretly) observed but he doesn't have the air of a dandy seeking attention (and yet you will, if you are sufficiently heedful, spot an admiring glance here and there from the women – and some men – who become aware of Martin in the crowd). In fact, you'd almost say that he looks as though he feels awkward or at least self-conscious. His gaze appears to be fixed almost exclusively on the grid of paving slabs as they pass under his feet down below. He looks as though he's thinking.

In any event, he's now moving down Upper Street – the High Street of Islington – with the rest of the mass; past the wine shops, flower shops, bars and cafés and the fresh morning light twinkling on the car mirrors, shop windows and motorbike chrome; the clap-clap-clap of the multitude of footsteps on the pavement like a muted applause for the strivings of Man, echoing the tide on the shore animating smooth pebbles to chat, chat, chat in a syncopated babble; the babble of shore and the squeak of shoe.

It's the hub-bub of city life, an alien horror to most country folk but a comforting blanket to those accustomed to it; written afresh at the start of the new century but repeated through the ages of urban history.

Martin's ice cream hair bobs along like a fleck of foam on the dark river of North Londoners being drawn into the vortex of the great financial centre that is London. Down the plughole that is the Angel Tube station, into the underground of pipes that rumble through the substrata. Down there with the sewers and drains, the mighty worm holes channelling the food to the belly of the beast.

Susan Sachs is sitting in one of the firm brown leather chairs at the back of Café Nero in Curzon Street, reading The Guardian as she sips at her espresso and chews on her Milanese Panini. She could read it online on her laptop but a certain cussed streak in her means that she continues to get her news from the inky, dirty, rustling thing. She feels it's more authentic.

Susan loves old film noir, 40s glamour fashion, and basically aches to be Ava Gardner in The Killers. She dresses accordingly, although women's fashion has, by now, gone through so many permutations it's reached the point where almost anything can appear to be up-to-date and most of Susan's contemporaries would reference a look like hers to Dita Von Teese rather than the Hedy Lamarr image to which it's actually directed. So she is now wearing a figure-hugging, knee-length cerise dress (on a figure designed for hugging), with rather boxy shoulders and tight sleeves that cling all the way to the bases of her thumbs; maroon three-inch heels; and her auburn hair, glossy and wavy, laps down to her shoulders where it curtains an alabaster throat. Everything about Susan is soft yet firm; everything glistens; everything has been thought through and executed and, to be fair, the result is a job of work. The finishing flourish is a coat of vibrant crimson lipstick applied to full pouting lips, just to make sure you get the picture.

Her violet eyes flick across the pages of the paper and occasionally she glances at the rest of the café when she turns another page and, at one such point, she sees Martin Dash enter from the street. Her immediate instinct is to catch his eye and wave him over but something makes her hold back, at least for the moment, so that she can observe him, undisturbed, for a little while.

Gerry Bild had introduced Martin to the team the day before and it looked like she was going to be working with him. He had intrigued her straight away. Firstly, the way he looked – the outright near universal consensus amongst the girls at the office was that he was lush, i.e. gorgeous, fantasy fodder. That baby soft blond hair, the high cheek bones, shimmering blue eyes and sulky full lips ticked all the boxes. He had straight away reminded Susan of someone but she hadn't been able to pin down who it was. Then, as she watched him at the counter (happily, he hadn't noticed her skulking behind her newspaper in the gloom at the back), she suddenly recalled who it was – John Fraser as Bosie in The Trials of Oscar Wilde.

Susan was a film buff and had spent a large part of her young life gazing intently at the stories unfolding before her on the small screen and big screen (she didn't mind which). Initially, as a girl, she had simply watched what everyone else watched – Grease, Titanic, Footloose – but then gradually honed in on films which bore a certain mark that she considered her favourite style – mostly noir, classic or modern, but really anything that had a germ of real originality, something different (and she would always consider such things as, essentially, noir anyway). So Double Indemnity, Body Heat and Gilda but also Daughters of Darkness and The Trials of Oscar Wilde. She loved the latter mostly because of John Fraser's Bosie; he was just so achingly beautiful, and bad . . . and she couldn't quite believe that a facsimile had been plonked right in her lap like this.

Added to which was the double whammy of this anhedonia thing. Gerry had briefed everyone in a team meeting before Martin's introduction because, as he put it, "the lad's behaviour might otherwise appear a little odd." Peoples' ears had pricked up immediately and they listened intently as Gerry explained that this was a condition that was essentially only a problem for the unfortunate subject and in no way meant that anyone was at any more risk of harm from the sufferer than from the average man in the street – from Gerry himself, say.

"Oh God, we're in trouble then," joked Davey – Davey Hood, the other solicitor in Gerry's team, who was at a similar level as Susan, in the second / third year of 'proper' employment after their two years as trainees. With the other associate, Howard Harvey, the two secretaries and the current trainee, this amounted to seven people in Gerry's team (including Gerry), now upped to eight with the arrival of Martin. Vanessa's team of eleven was also in the meeting as the two teams often worked together and were dealt with, administratively, as one unit.

Gerry explained that Martin was happy for his condition to be disclosed – and, indeed, had asked for that – as he felt it was not something he had to or ought to hide. Maisie, the younger secretary in Gerry's team, asked quizzically, "So . . . he has no feelings?" It was apparent that she was struggling with this idea, as were a number of the group, to be fair, although it was always a good bet that any question from Maisie wouldn't be entirely innocent, nor delivered without a degree of mischief.

"That's exactly it," said Gerry, adopting a matter-of-fact tone, as though he were telling them which University Martin had attended. "It's a psychological condition that means the sufferer can't enjoy any of the normal things that the rest of us take for granted, like the taste of food, the sound of music, sadness, laughter . . ."

" . . . or love," Maisie finished, smirking.

"Yes, I'd got money on you being the one to bring that up," said Gerry wearily but good-naturedly. Vanessa looked less indulgent and actually appeared properly cross.

"Maisie – all of you," she retorted with a definite note of irritation. "We realise that this is a little unusual – I mean, the fact that we're disclosing a person's medical details at all – but, as Gerry says, it's something that Martin feels is important to be out in the open and, in fact, as a firm we feel that it's part of our duty of care – as employers to a new starter – that he not be placed in a position where his behaviour, or rather his demeanour, could be misinterpreted in any way. We want this group to carry on functioning just as well as it's always done and the fact is that Martin is a thoroughly personable young man and, more importantly, is damn good at the job. He's come with a very good record and references from Chard Bone and we think he'll be a valuable addition to the team. As everyone knows, we're all run off our feet and desperate for good people. Martin looks to be just the sort of person we need to fill Charlie's shoes and do the liaison – with Gerry – on the Grudge account."

"In that event, Susan, you'll be working closely with Martin, going forward."   Maisie gave Susan a raised eyebrow which suggested she hadn't taken on board one iota of the admonishment from Vanessa. Word had got up to the Sixth Floor from the girls in Reception that Martin was a bit of a looker and, so far as Maisie was concerned, this meant that the game was on. The fact that the boy in question was apparently the Ice Man himself simply meant a greater opportunity to show what she was really made of. Maisie frankly liked men, or rather men's attention, and her exertions in the field over a number of campaigns meant that she had come to feel confident that she could actually break the resolve of any man she wanted, if she just put her back into it. She had come to know that every man – virtually – was programmed to react to certain stimuli, if you just knew where the buttons were to be pressed.

In any event, Martin might as well have had 'CHALLENGE' stamped on his forehead. The runners and riders to be the first to get Martin into bed had lined up before the end of that first meeting and Susan had concluded that she was in pole position as a matter of absolute fact.

She studied Martin round the side of her newspaper. It was lunchtime and she could see that he was ordering coffee and a sandwich. After Martin's introduction to the team, she'd only exchanged a brief word with him as he was spending his time, initially, in the various induction sessions that new recruits were put through – HR, IT, PR. However, he'd been allocated the office next to hers, so she'd expected that they'd be acquainted soon enough.

He was having to wait a moment while others before him were being served so this gave her the opportunity to scrutinise him, as long as she could remain undetected behind the newspaper. There were the two things that hit you again – the striking good looks but also the knowledge of his ... *condition*. The whole thing struck Susan as very odd. Hearing Gerry talk through the thing, it didn't sound right to her at all and she was sure – not least from the faces of the people she knew around her (many of them hard-bitten, naturally sceptical lawyers, after all) – that she wasn't the only one. The possibility of a person literally having no feelings, no pleasure, no nothing, had never really occurred to her before and yet she had googled 'anhedonia' at home that evening and, sure enough, there it was: 'noun – psychology – lack of pleasure or the capacity to experience it.'

Further reading disclosed that the term was first used by a French professor of psychology, Théodule-Armand Ribot, at the turn of the 20th century, to pair off with analgesia (the inability to feel physical pain, not the same thing ...); that there is a distinction to be made between lack of motivation or desire to engage in an activity ("motivational anhedonia") and the level of enjoyment of the activity itself ("consummatory anhedonia"); that it can present in various forms, such as social anhedonia and *sexual* anhedonia; and that it can be characteristic of mental disorder like schizophrenia, which can be caused by stressful life events, whereas more recent research had raised the possibility of a genetic component, even highlighting a particular gene – the Disrupted in Schizophrenia 1 (DISC1) gene – as a possible culprit.

"DISC1?! – WTF ?!" thought Susan, who – when reading all of this – was enjoying the distinct experience of a visitor to a wholly alien land in a dream where all the signs are unfamiliar and perturbing. Indeed, reading this had given her a decided sense of unease and foreboding which had trailed into her sleeping dreams that night.

However, she felt she had overcome those emotions as she now sat spying on Martin in the comforting surroundings of the coffee bar. After all, he appeared perfectly normal (just setting aside for the moment the looks thing) – ordering his sandwich, picking up the purse for the lady who dropped it in front of him and handling it to her with a smile. Yes, there – with a smile. So he can't be that bad. But the knowledge of what he was – or, at least, what she had been told he was – somehow undermined that presentation of normality in her thoughts: 'I mean, he wouldn't make something like that up, would he? And even if he'd made it up, that would be at least as weird, wouldn't it?'

So the fact is, here he stands, apparently the same as everyone else but she knows that, beneath that benign carapace, there is something that is most definitely not the same. She starts thinking of what it must be like to have *no desire*, to *not want anything*. She'd read somewhere that Buddhism teaches that desire is the root cause of mankind's suffering – was Martin a Buddhist then? Had he achieved Nirvana? In that case she should feel happy for him or envious but, somehow, her overriding feeling was that there was something enormously sad about Martin and she felt sorry for him. After all, the Buddhists might have got it wrong . . .

Her musings were brought to an abrupt halt when he turned to look straight at her. She nearly flipped the newspaper back across her face (which would have been shameful) but, fortunately, had the presence of mind to simply smile and beckon him over. When he'd seen her, she noticed that he flinched slightly, disconcerted, and then he'd gathered his composure, simultaneously with her, in a telepathic choreography.

He smiled also – a charming smile – and brought over his sandwich and coffee.

"Mr. Dash, how are you?" she started the conversation.

"Fine, thanks – and you?"

"Yes, just keeping abreast of world affairs."

". . . and fashion tips?"

Susan, who prided herself on being always on her mettle for vigorous badinage – à la Hepburn and Grant – was momentarily caught off balance by this. But she saw that Martin was ironically appraising her modish outfit, so she smiled, "cheeky," and laughed. And Martin laughed.

"You didn't strike me as a typical Guardian reader," he continued the costumery theme. "I thought they were all sandals and duffle coats."

This was a not unpleasant surprise for Susan but, at the same time, somewhat disconcerting, given that she had, at least subconsciously, been prepared for a conversational style that would be . . . well, stiff at least. But then she remembered what Gerry had said in conversation with her, late on yesterday: that, while Martin apparently had no real appreciation of humour, it was a sign of his innate intelligence that he had studied its anatomy and learned how to get by with banter, often taking his cue to laugh from others around him (although his timing apparently went awry sometimes – when he wasn't concentrating closely enough – and his chortlings would kick in after too much of a delay behind the rest of the group and that was the sort of occasion that would make people look again at Martin and wonder). Which, again, was why he felt the need to apprise people of his condition, so that they'd then understand why he might sometimes appear out of synch with others.

But was that not a self-fulfilling prophecy? thought Susan. Was it not the case that Martin having put this knowledge in people's heads was what made them scrutinise his demeanour in a way that they wouldn't otherwise? If they hadn't been told that he was an actual medical freak, wouldn't they have hardly noticed such little quirks at all and, even if they did, just put it down to one slightly odd facet of his nature, like the multitude of facets that most people had?

Such murmurings were rumbling away at the back of Susan's mind even as she tried to put them aside for the sake of an admittedly agreeable encounter with this beautiful (there was no other word for it) young man who was sat with her, giving her his undivided attention, apparently flattering her.

"There's a lot you wouldn't know about me, mate . . . you're not the only one whose appearance is deceptive, you know."

'He got that one all right,' thought Susan as a shadow of grave seriousness suddenly passed over the scene. 'My god, we've jumped right in here, haven't we?' she mused. He looked momentarily . . . hurt? (but he couldn't, could he?) and she wondered if she'd gone too far.

"Ah . . . Gerry told you of my condition?"

"Yes, he briefed the whole team yesterday."

"Good – I asked him to."

A silence.

"What was the general reaction?"

"Err . . . a little bemused, I reckon. It's not really something that any of us had come across before, I don't think. It is a bit out of left-field, you must admit?"

"Yes, it's . . . err . . . not common, I agree."

"How long have you had it?"

"Always."

"Since you were born?"

"Yes."

Another pause.

Susan looked at Martin and Martin looked at Susan. She was staring into his eyes, trying to catch a glimpse, through those ocular windows, of what was actually going on in that singular mind, and Martin stared back, knowing she was doing this, allowing her some time to let her curiosity roam. While she was doing this she was also getting a tingle of something else and she reddened slightly and Martin saw this too.

"I know it's difficult to understand and I could just keep quiet about it but, over time, experience has taught me that not telling people about it – people I work with, for example – can cause more problems."

"Why?"

"Well . . . because . . . I don't feel anything and that has consequences for how I behave and if people don't know about that they take it to mean that I don't like them or that I'm malevolent in some way."

This sounded like a rehearsed speech that he'd trotted out many times.

"Behave how?"

As a background to their conversation, mugs clacked and the coffee machine swooshed but they didn't hear them. At least Susan didn't. Martin sat perfectly still as he spoke to Susan, occasionally taking a bite out of his sandwich or sipping his coffee.

"It's difficult for me to describe because I've never felt any different, so I can only tell you what I've heard people say."

"To your face?"

"Sometimes . . ." His eyes flicked past her and then back to her.

"People have said that they get nothing back from me, that I don't respond – at least in the 'normal' way. I mean, I can 'turn it on', if you like. I've learnt enough over the years by watching and listening so that I can engage people; I'll question them and show interest and flatter them. But I can only do that for so long and then I run out of steam and revert to type. Whereby I don't show any interest. Because I don't have any. I really have no interest in what people do or think or feel and, after a while – mostly, not a long while – people usually realise this and they get to feel that I was just play-acting initially and then they'll feel that they've been conned and, before you know it, they're feeling quite hateful towards me."

Martin was looking straight into Susan's eyes again.

The inevitable question: "So you're play-acting now? You've no real interest in talking to me?"

A moment passed and then Martin smiled and laughed.

"There, you see how quickly it can happen? You're feeling aggrieved already. So I learn to manage my time with people."

He was right, she had felt a definite twinge of ill feeling towards him.

But she pressed on: "You're being very candid about all this."

"I'd say it was a decision I took but, actually, it was really forced upon me because of the way things kept turning out, as I've said; I found that explaining it was the only way to deal with it, really."

"You must have had some funny responses?"

"To be honest, it's not been a massive problem, most of the time. You'd be surprised how accepting people can be."

"Most of the time? You've had some who don't believe you? Think you're making it up?" – this just a little pointed.

Martin look directly at Susan again.

Not smiling this time.

"Why would I make something like that up? Expose myself to ridicule. Cut off any hope of a relationship. Why would I do that?"

"Don't you get angry at all? Or does your condition stop you feeling that too?"

"I don't feel anything." With that he took a bite from his sandwich and a look around the interior of the place.

Susan took this as a sign to move on and the conversation took a turn into the safer avenue of work.

After a pause to munch some more of her sandwich and take a sip of her cappuccino, which left a wee moustache of froth on her upper lip, which she wiped off with not a little embarrassment and which was followed by her sitting purposefully back into the chair, crossing her legs and giving her hair a quick flick, she embarked on a fresh line of enquiry.

"So what are you going to be starting on? At work."

"There are a few things, I think, but Gerry's talking about the Grudge Group principally. Or, at least, in the first place."

Susan pulled a face, "Barry Rogers."

"Does he?" This childish joke response from Martin, with a big cheesy grin to boot, brought Susan up with a start. She pursed her lips and gave him a mock indulgent look but she had still missed a beat, nevertheless.

Anyway, she expanded: "You may joke but the guy's a complete arsehole," she said this with some feeling but, remembering where she was, gave a slightly nervous glance around, as though to check that Barry Rogers – a *valued client* – wasn't sitting behind them.

In a (slightly) quieter tone: "He owns the group with his sister, Joan. Well, I say 'sister' . . ." Her tone darkened and, again, her eyes fluttered around; she was aware she was being indiscrete.

Martin screwed his eyebrows together to ask the question.

Susan shook her head, "Nothing – no, nothing" and, moving on: "They're friends of my father; well, I say 'friends'."

Martin looked even more puzzled and Susan realised she was being cryptic. "You've not come across them?"

"No."

"Oh. Because they've got property all over. I thought you might have."

"No."

"Well, anyway," she was leaning in more now, anxious not to be overheard, and Martin leaned a little towards her, in turn. "They've clawed their way up the greasy pole together over the years. Properly ruthless, completely vulgar," she was into her stride now, contemptuous but trying to make it appear casual.

Martin appeared to be smiling while she was conducting the character assassinations. "So they're sort of friends of your father?"

Susan snorted at this, "Barry just wants what he can take from my father and Daddy puts up with him for the sake of the money."

"Why, what does your father do?"

Susan looked taken aback for a moment, genuinely surprised at Martin's ignorance. "You don't know?"

Martin seemed a little piqued, as it appeared that there was something he obviously should have known but didn't. "No, I don't."

"My father is the Secretary of State for Defence – Jimmy Sachs," she announced flatly; obviously not something she was any longer proud of, if she ever had been.

But Martin's eyebrows involuntarily shot up. He clearly hadn't made the connection. "Well I've obviously heard of Jimmy Sachs but I didn't realise that you're his daughter."

Susan scrutinised him through narrowed eyes for the dreaded sign that he was suddenly more interested in her than before. That was the sort of thing that really set her against a person and Martin caught this just in time.

"Well, that's interesting, of course," looking for the words – she was still watching his reaction.

"I mean, it must be fascinating seeing that level of politics up close." Surely that sounded like a reasonable proposition that she couldn't take amiss? She merely snorted half-heartedly but did, at least, relax back into her chair.

"Fascinating? Yeah, that's one word for it. Fucking abysmal, there's another. My father's 'friends'" – at this, she popped up her fingers in the inverted commas sign – "are the vilest bunch of people you could wish to meet. They come round to the house and it's like you've let a bunch of lizards in – they *slither* about the place." Martin raised his eyebrows and smiled but she pressed on: "No, they do – they *slither*. All eyeing each other up and down, flattering you one minute and stabbing you in the back the next. It's nauseating to watch."

Susan seemed to be getting genuinely angry and Martin was now looking at her quite intently. She suddenly realised that someone else was too: a couple who were at the next table had clearly stopped talking – probably when they heard the bit about Susan being Jimmy Sachs' daughter – and now found themselves caught earwigging.

Awkward.

A thunderous glare from Susan prodded them into a flurry of activity, shuffling magazines on their table, grabbing their coffees, a few hurriedly marshalled words to fill the silence.

Martin brought her back, "So the political life doesn't attract you?"

"You must be joking," she spat, now a little less vehement.

And after another short moment while her temperature lowered. "No, it doesn't attract me. It did. When I was younger." She caught Martin raising his eyebrows and they both smiled. "Yes, I sound like an old woman don't I? But I mean when I was much younger, more naïve, before I'd seen what I've seen since."

Martin smiled again, "Come on, you're hardly over the hill. I know you're not supposed to ask a lady her age but you're no more than . . ." slight pause (minefield territory, Susan mock-narrowed her eyes) ". . . well, 21?"

"Piss off," Susan laughed and rolled her spine, neck, head back into the chair. "I'm 27 . . . and a half !" She laughed again. And then Martin did too.

Susan noticed this again and, once more, it brought her up. She considered Martin and, just now, felt the first intimation of what had happened with his former friends who had come to dislike him or, rather, his lack of sincerity.

And she scrutinised him afresh. They had been talking away quite intently and you wouldn't have thought there was anything between them that was different from any other young couple, feeling their way with each other, but now she was sure he'd noticed her pause.

So what the hell was going through his mind? Did he not feel *anything* for her? How could anyone live such an act *all the time*?

It was true, she had seen plenty in her still young years. She had been 18 when the Labour Party had come to power in 1997 with her father riding the wave and all the optimism that came with it and, in the nine years between, she had watched his every twist and turn and the wretched humiliations along the way.

Jimmy Sachs was considered an interesting case by most astute political observers. His father was Walter Sachs – Harold Wilson's Industry Minister in the 60s – and, whilst there was always something of the champagne socialist throughout the line, there was also a palpable sense of conscious public obligation that Jimmy had inherited and it was a source of considerable interest to many commentators to see how the myriad triangulations and dysfunctions of Tony Blair's government would impact upon Jimmy's shape-shifting character.

Those who knew him or could read such things knew he had the serious impulses – to do the right thing, to make a positive difference – but that he also had the fatal craving for action, to be at the centre of things, to accumulate money; in other words, he had an ego. That had to be fed. And the battle between these two shouldered angels was something that fascinated many who could discern such things.

It also periodically manifested itself in capricious behaviour that provided considerable entertainment for many more who could appreciate the spectacle without necessarily divining what was the underlying motor that drove it. He'd appeared on Newsnight one evening, red-faced and obviously 'tired', and got into an horrendous slanging match with Jeremy Paxman – live on air – over Kosovo, which culminated in him appearing to start to get out of his seat to advance on the pompous presenter only for a hasty cut to another piece just in time to deny the nation the undoubted pleasure of hearing Paxman described – at full decibel – as a "spineless cunt." Rumours of this denunciation got about and it was recorded on tape but, somehow, it hadn't (yet) appeared on YouTube. That sort of thing generally swung in his favour (much as John Prescott's impromptu right hook on a member of the public had done for him).

The sort of thing that swung against him – and meant him losing his cabinet seat for a time and having to sit out a two year purdah – was the less savoury revelation of his obviously venal forays into dodgy property investments (cue Barry and Joan Rogers), the most disastrous of which (at least politically – all involved, including Jimmy, actually made a tidy killing on it) was the now infamous Sunny Glades complex at Newbury, a chalet development copying the Center Parcs model that had all but destroyed an ancient woodland for the sake of pseudo-bucolic getaways for the stressed middle classes in the face of furious opposition from the environmental and heritage lobby.

Yes, it was true – she'd seen all the ugly innards of high stakes political machinations (and had hardened in the process) but she'd not come across anything like Martin Dash.

That made no sense.

7

Martin Dash is sitting at a large table in one of Stone Rose's meeting rooms to the left of Gerry Bild who, in turn, has Barry Rogers diagonally to his right. They are all poring over a large plan of the Crack Harbour complex.

Barry is mid-50s, lean, with a slightly crinkly face, lightly tanned, thinning tawny hair that is now whitening, well-dressed in expensive-casual; trendy spectacles; Rolex watch (natch). All round, the very picture of your successful middle-aged property developer, which is what he is. The contours of his face are such that he appears to wear a perpetual smile but this can be misleading – sometimes he is smiling but other times he isn't and, if people mistakenly think that he is and that his 'smile' bespeaks a genial benevolence, they can get a nasty shock when he suddenly turns on them, snarling and spitting. And this happens fairly frequently because Barry is no-one's fool. And he knows that to survive – and prosper – in the world he inhabits, you've got to snarl. And bite. Because, if you don't get them, they'll get you. If you appear weak, they'll take the piss. So you get your retaliation in first. Despite his apparently genial visage, Barry is, in fact, a deeply unpleasant individual.

The meeting rooms, site huts and Council chambers of solicitors' offices, building sites and planning authorities all around the country sullenly attest the imprints of split heads, bruised egos and warped sanities inflicted by the marauding shitheap of self-interest and vileness that is Barry Rogers.

But today he is in one of his good moods (when he lightens up a bit and his acolytes do their best to keep him in that happy place) and this is due to a number of things. Firstly, he's at Stone's to finalise the plans for the latest stage of the Crack Harbour development – his company has now delivered its residential phase (high-end apartments that are already sold to foreign investors, City titans, and heavyweight celebrities) and is accordingly due a cool £20m from the investors; £20m to share among the Grudge shareholders – basically himself and Joan plus a select few, hand-picked when the project needed start-up funds, including Jimmy Sachs MP (or, at least, his Swiss-fronted trust company).

And, secondly, he's got someone new to show off to. For some reason – and this has Gerry absolutely beaming whilst also wondering, slightly concernedly, exactly what is at the bottom of it – Barry appears to have taken a shine to young Martin. Gerry has introduced Martin to Barry as the one to get his contract structure in order ready for the big pay-out in a month's time. The paperwork wasn't in a mess as such but Stone's business was booming, clients were riding the crest of the wave, and Gerry was finding it hard to keep all the plates spinning. This was exactly the sort of job Martin had been brought in to deal with – a mountain of contracts, bonds, options and due diligence that needed a proper slogger to shift it but a slogger with a safe pair of hands and a cool head that wouldn't get bogged down with the inevitable difficulties that would arise to, potentially, jeopardise the whole project.

Gerry knew that Martin had successfully completed this sort of stuff numerous times for Chard Bone and was convinced that he was the right man to work with Barry on this one. It needed someone with a fairly robust outlook to be able to cope with Barry (and Joan . . .) and Gerry felt that Martin's unique brand of composure would be the perfect salve to apply to Barry's festering ego.

In fact, Gerry has apprised Barry of Martin's affliction which was, perhaps, risky as Barry might easily have taken against the idea of someone with a mental illness being entrusted with his assets. But, ultimately, he hadn't (Gerry had anticipated correctly there) and, in fact, Barry had appeared quite intrigued by the idea of having a lawyer who literally had no feelings. In fact, he'd been more than intrigued – he appeared quite delighted by the idea. And if you understood Barry's character you'd grasp why.

The concept of bloodless, unfeeling lawyers was hardly new, of course, and, for many people (people like Barry, in fact), the cachet of your very own lawyer being infinitely more vicious and venal than the rest was considerable and here, landed in Barry's lap, was an experienced streetwise young lawyer . . . who was actually certified remorseless by doctors ! Excellent ! This Barry found truly piquant and the fact that the boy was also the possessor of killer looks – who could ensnare men and women alike, simply as a prelude to rebuffing their attentions with an absolute indifference – was merely the icing on the cake.

Martin's condition was not, however, talked about between the three of them, at least on this occasion. Gerry had previously told Barry about it; Barry had assimilated the information; and decided that it probably wasn't right to bring it up as a matter for conversation in a meeting like this. At least, it probably wouldn't serve his interests to do so. Barry only ever calculated decisions on that basis and that basis alone. Barry fully intended to quiz Martin in due course – the whole thing fascinated him – but he would wait for the right time and circumstances and environment or, rather, *engineer* the right time and circumstances and environment.

No, they were discussing the intricacies of the Crack Harbour development at this point in time and Barry was perfectly happy to do so. This one he had been planning and building for years and it was now coming together. His boat was most definitely coming in.

It was a huge development sprawling across an irregular area that sat between the river on its south side and the High Street on the north, comprising a compact marina overlooked by three high-rise apartment blocks which in turn backed onto a 200 bed hotel on top of 20 shops and restaurants all catering for the City's hoi polloi of Russian oligarchs, Arab sheiks and British aristocracy. The idea was an oasis of wealth and opulence where those of sufficient means could reside in their convenient Chelsea pieds-à-terre overlooking the sparkling ripples of the Thames; cruise up and down that historic channel on their boats moored in the marina; shop in the new Prada, Burberry and Kenzo; and eat in the finest restaurants of the new breed of celebrity chefs.

It was a project riding on the wave of the longest-running boom in history that seemed as though it would never end. The country was indulging in an orgy of borrowing and spending that defied all logic and spawned 'entrepreneurs' like Barry and Joan...Their company, Grudge Developments, was the chosen partner for the investors, Atlas Court, to deliver the project and Barry had worked tirelessly for five years to get to where they were now – the marina and residential just completed and the retail and leisure on the High Street at the back well on their way. The agreement with Atlas meant phased payments for Grudge at fixed stages and this very stage meant a tidy sum of £20m for Barry and Joan.

Nice.

The project had not been without its difficulties and controversies but nothing out of the ordinary so far as Barry was concerned – the usual snide allegations of planning committee palms being greased, funny money being washed clean, etc, etc. Each obstacle was met with a belligerent ram that ploughed on, remorselessly, come what may. This was money, this was serious, and now came the payoff.

Gerry Bild had nursed the legals along for Barry from the start back in 2001 when the first options on the site – at that point, an ageing government complex – were secured for Grudge. He'd put a large part of his working time into this job, with his team behind him, but he had many calls on his time and it was now time to hand over the steer to another – Martin.

The really hard work was behind them – identifying the right location; massaging the planners into line; winkling the options out of curmudgeonly land owners; juggling the funding and the costs – so that it ought now to be a question of simply docking the ship in a safe harbour. But it still needed a safe pair of hands to do that and it would be perfectly possible for an inexperienced hand to crash it into the quay. So when Gerry had initially proposed to Barry the idea of handing over the reins to a new guy – albeit with Gerry still keeping an eye on things from the back seat – Barry was, at first, distinctly unimpressed but Gerry persevered and had arranged this meeting with the three of them. And to Gerry's surprise (and relief) it had gone so much better than he could have hoped for. It was when Gerry had briefed Barry on Martin's story that Gerry could see Barry's interest was hooked and Barry's first encounter with Martin at this meeting simply sealed the deal. Barry was flattering Martin, joking around as Gerry had never before seen him, and generally behaving with such a totally un-Barry-like gaiety that Gerry actually started to find it rather unsettling.

He did wonder if it were possible that there was anything more than professional admiration on the part of the middle-aged businessman for the handsome young lawyer; after all, there had been persistent rumours for many years regarding Barry Rogers' personal peccadillos (and – worse – the true nature of his relationship with his sister). But, quite frankly, such were really of no interest to Gerry – Barry paid his bills (mostly ...) and kept bringing the work in; Gerry would only become concerned if personal entanglements – and the wreckage of same – threatened that cherished income stream.

Martin, for his part, was doing what Gerry had noticed him doing during his first few weeks at the firm – with clients, with the staff, with his peers: playing the part. Note perfect. He oozed charm. Flattered Barry back. Dropped in astute suggestions at apposite points. Demonstrated that he'd briefed himself thoroughly on the complex labyrinth of the Crack legal and financial structure. Laughed at Barry's jokes. It was real textbook stuff on how to conduct such a meeting. Gerry was delighted. Barry left the meeting convinced afresh what a wonderful chap he was (Barry, not Martin. Although Martin came a close second).

They had finished off with the details needed for money transfers and the like – £20m to come to Stone Rose's client account on the issue of the latest phase completion certificates. "And that will come from Atlas Court's lawyers?" asked Gerry of Barry.

"No, it'll be coming from an associated company – Ad Jalal."

"OK," said Gerry.

"OK," said Martin.

8

Late afternoon – in the summer – on Mayfair's gilded streets. The capital had been enjoying a prolonged spell of warm – no, hot – weather which, as ever, buoyed the populace into thinking they led happy lives. Accordingly, early tipplers were spilling out of the wine bars and cafés onto the pavement forming lapping puddles of multi-coloured (but mostly black and white) chatting, laughing, slurping office workers high on (a) the working week being done with (b) living in one of the world's (still) great cities (c) being amongst the best paid and best fed in that city and (d) being young (mostly).

The light still fell on them and warmed them where the street aligned with the sun's descent into its evening bough and it was possible to think that history's course had attained a new plateau at this time and this place and bestowed on its denizens a joyful and carefree mien borne of nothing more than pure, simple entitlement.

Martin stood amongst the group milling around the pavement tables outside 'The Hop House', a drinking establishment that had stood on the spot since the 17th century and was currently fitted out in such a manner as might allow it to bathe in the reflected glory of all of those years of history and intrigue and passion and drunkenness.

He had tried to avoid coming with the group from work when Maisie had first broached the subject. Martin had been at the firm over a month now and they hadn't yet managed to get him out for a drink but Martin's clear steadfastness on the issue only made her more determined. Maisie was only 19 but might as well have been 30. The basic blond bombshell proposition. Sassy. Mae West. With a carefree, lively persona that was hard to resist. Unless you were Martin. Lusted after by all the men at the firm (especially the older ones). Except Martin.

She was not far from turning, so far as Martin was concerned. She was becoming inclined to take Martin's repeated rebuffs to her advances as a personal insult and unpleasant smears and accusations were beginning to seed in the darker recesses of her mind. Only 19 but with years of experience behind her, she had got used to the idea that it was her divine right to pluck any man she wanted, when she wanted and, working at Stone Rose, she had begun to formulate the first inklings of a vague plan to entrap a wealthy client – single or otherwise – so that she would, in due course, get her hands on the wherewithal to match the sense of entitlement. Maisie still lived with her mum and dad and two brothers in the East End and, although she loved them all deeply, didn't want to stay there indefinitely. She had other ideas.

Martin didn't fit the marriageable magnate template (he obviously didn't have the requisite fortune for a start) but, underneath the scheming and self-serving, Maisie did have feelings – desire – and something about Martin (basically his stunning good looks and studied indifference) stirred her, and his total failure to reciprocate only made her want him more. The situation was beginning to tarnish her standing as the premier man-eater of the firm.

Obviously, she could not stand for this and could not believe that there was a red-blooded man alive who wouldn't react if a boy's wet dream such as herself was served up on a plate to them. Her pneumatic chest (always exposed enough to draw the eye), tight skirts, blond curls and bright red lips sent a simple, and irresistible, message ('This is what you want') that, in her considerable experience, rarely went unheeded.

Martin wasn't gay – she knew that, she could tell – but bad thoughts were beginning to gestate in her musings as to why he appeared to have no desire. Yes, she had listened to Gerry's discourse on anhedonia but she couldn't accept or believe that. The thing was, he appeared so normal in every other way – he laughed and joked with people and even charmed them when he needed to and yet he didn't have any feelings? No, she couldn't really believe that.

No, she was having a full go tonight, make no mistake. But this might be his last chance. If he didn't bend to her will, he was quite likely to feel the darker side of her passion. And the nasty edge of her tongue.

But he had taken some persuading and, in fact, it was Gerry who had swung it with the advice that one of their most esteemed clients would be at the pub and it would be a good opportunity for him to get acquainted with Martin. At this, Martin acquiesced. He always made himself available for work detail. Social carousing with over-sexed secretaries was one thing, schmoozing valued clients was quite another.

Gerry had allowed the team out of work early so they'd been at The House before 5:00 – it was now past 6:00 and the first few drinks were doing the same warming job as the late afternoon sun. But Martin wasn't drinking. And was being lightly teased about this by Maisie.

"You mean you've never had a drink in your life?" she asked, incredulous. She was very close to Martin by this point and was getting closer so that her boobs were nearly touching his shirt. Electricity crackled between them. At least in Maisie's mind.

"I had it once when I was younger, but it did nothing for me except make me sick." Martin tried to smile to make light of the issue but he looked uncomfortable.

"Well, that's the same for everyone – you get used to that, Marty !" she laughed, throwing her head back and taking the opportunity to plant her hand on his shoulder. Martin laughed with her and took another sip from his fresh orange juice. Maisie appeared to be the only one who'd adopted his shortened soubriquet but Martin didn't seem to take umbrage.

"I never get used to it," said Davey Hood, also standing in the group. "Bloody awful hangovers every time ! You're best out of it, mate," Davey's hand plonked onto Martin's other shoulder.

Davey had, fairly quickly following Martin's arrival, decided that he was going to look after Martin – to be his wingman. Davey was most definitely on the side of the angels generally – a nice guy. Helpful. Liked a drink. Good fun. Not a bad word to say about anyone.

Davey had taken Martin's story entirely at face value right from the off – unlike some such as Maisie, who always seemed to be trying to test it, to pull it apart. So far as he could see, Martin was to be pitied, and to be helped. He took it exactly as read that Martin suffered from a recognised condition that meant he had no feelings, no desire and couldn't, therefore, engage with the stuff that coursed through most people's haphazard lives. And Davey felt sorry for him for this.

"Imagine what that must be like," Davey had said to Maisie after Gerry's résumé of the position. Maisie had simply sniffed, "I'll make him feel all right." Cue blushing and head-shaking from Davey.

Anyway, Davey had, from that point, looked out for Martin and felt an almost paternal concern for his new mate, even though Martin was some four years older than Davey and his superior at work.

"Yeah, well – you're just a pisshead," laughed Maisie, but with affection. "You'll be collapsing while Martin will be up all night on his orange juice." Maisie drooling at Martin, lasciviously. And getting closer still. Martin could now

46

feel the pressure of her breasts against his chest. Her arm now wrapped around his shoulder, shoo-ing Davey's hand away.

Maisie had sunk three big shots already and had got to a more advanced position in the proceedings rather earlier than she ought to have. But, in any event, the whole crowd was amicable as amicable be. This was very much a work hard, play hard slice of society and things did generally tend to get pretty risqué pretty quickly. The high-pressure demands of the job necessarily and beneficially forged a familial bond between them all that could sometimes lead them to forget the ties to those left at home and the potent mix of big-money, high-profile deals; long nights and weekends of adrenaline-fuelled, head-butting negotiations; and the celebratory blow-outs that followed, had too often proved too much for many a conflicted partner's marriage.

Gerry was a good example. Married to his former trainee, Debbie; she now at another firm in the City (after a fall-out with Vanessa Carr); debate ongoing as to whether they should try for a child; Gerry seeing his two boys when his first wife (now back at the ancestral home in Sussex) decreed. Debbie had come over to Mayfair for a drink with Gerry and his team and was chatting with him by the door. They looked across and smiled indulgently when Maisie shrieked a particularly high-pitched wail at being grabbed by Davey, the pair of them apparently fighting over Martin.

Some of Maisie's drink spilled onto her chest (how inconvenient) and she looked archly at Martin – "How am I going to get that off?"

"Don't worry, Maisie – he isn't interested in the drink or what's under it !" shouted Judith, Maisie's fellow secretary and fellow slapper.

More shrieking and Martin looking increasingly uncomfortable in the middle of it. But Maisie took it in good part and merely sidled up closer to Martin – "Well, we'll see about that . . ." – she was definitely pissed by now.

"You'll need to get a gallon of this inside him first, Maisie" – this from Howard, the other associate in the team, waving his pint of lager in the air.

Howard's nose had rather been put out by Martin's arrival and apparent assumption of the number two's role. Previously, he'd jockeyed with the now departed, unmourned Charlie (former holder of Martin's post) for that gig and, when Charlie had suddenly disappeared (in slightly mysterious circumstances, it had to be said), he'd rather hoped that the question had been decided definitively. And was thus considerably peeved when Martin arrived, all handsome and charming and – even worse – clearly good at the job. At least with Charlie there were regular screw-ups and indiscretions to bring to Gerry's attention (and Howard never missed the opportunity) but Martin appeared to be a machine – everything was done by the book, efficiently and professionally, and he had proved adept at charming the clients. The way through to the next partnership appointment had, in Howard's mind, seemed clear but was now blocked by this blonde interloper . . . with a mental illness !

The injustice of it was eating away at Howard and, although he thought he was hiding it well (too proud to allow that he was being bested), his regular demeanour gave him away; albeit that snide remarks, involuntarily sneers, and general haughtiness were, in fact, Howard's stock-in-trade with most people (except those who might offer advancement), so Martin was actually not alone in receiving this treatment.

Howard's little quip brought him a warm glow of smug satisfaction, striking – as it did – simultaneously at two of his most immediate objects of loathing: Martin (for the reasons just stated) and Maisie (for the reason that she had rebuffed him on one particularly drunken occasion when Howard had unwisely allowed vanity to overcome his natural and rational caution in his dealings with women and lunged her; and she had done so with such obvious satisfaction). So he decided to follow it up, thinking to simultaneously prick what he saw as Martin's pomposity (with all his miserablist bullshit) and to suggest, slyly, that Maisie's alleged appeal for men wasn't actually all that it was cracked up to be.

"Yeah, come on Martin – a few lagers might release the inner beast in you – you might even get to fancy Maisie."

But this was getting tricky and, before he knew it, Howard had blundered into quicksand and suddenly found that it was he who was fixed in the glare of opprobrium; once more failing to appreciate the level of people's distaste for him, that they did actually understand him.

In fact, it was Martin's reaction that swung the pendulum back at him. If one had not known that Martin was medically incapable of anger, one might have thought that the look he gave Howard suggested that he'd been stung by the remark. He almost looked as though he had glared at Howard. But that wouldn't be right, would it? This, for a moment, was the obvious point going through the minds of the group as they scrutinised Martin, loving the action that had suddenly flared up; smelling blood; minds fleetingly cast back to school days when the shout would go up: "Fight! Fight!" – often enough a shout of provocation as of reportage and some hapless sap would be dragged into a beating for the mob's delectation.

But that odd look – which, if it wasn't anger, was perhaps something even more menacing – passed just as quickly as it had flared, Martin seeming to catch himself and revert to the usual bland smile. And in any event, the moment was at the same time broken by Davey:

"Yeah and *he* might even stand a chance of getting her, eh Howard?"

Everyone knew of Howard's embarrassment at Maisie's hands and they now roared in the joy of seeing Howard skewered on his own hubris. Howard turned puce, his eyes suddenly smarting with humiliation and, in the chemistry of his rancid psychology, his hatred of Martin ratcheted up another notch.

It was at this point that Susan – who had been on the edge of the group, increasingly irritated at the vulgar display of tedious egos (as she saw it) – swooped to rescue Martin from what was quickly developing into a potential car crash situation.

"Come on, Martin – I'm short of a drink and it's your round. I'll come to the bar with you."

Maisie couldn't help herself but look most put out; nevertheless, Martin scuttled gratefully after Susan towards the pub's front door, having taken a check of everyone's requirements. There were fewer people inside the pub and it was darker and cooler. The Hop House, like a number of its kind, was done out to suggest a direct link to the golden era of the city's pre-eminence in commerce and money and power, with thick beams all around, painted black and gold, and plain wooden tables and chairs all designed to put one in mind of the taverns of the past, where men of influence plotted the course of the empire's trajectory and their own allied prospects.

"Thank you for rescuing me," said Martin as they stood at the bar. Susan smiled to say, 'No problem.'

"I don't think Howard likes me," he continued.

"And maybe Maisie likes you a little too much," replied Susan, with one eyebrow raised. Martin smiled, but didn't blush.

"I reckon Maisie's got plenty of men to choose from."

"But she can't have you. Which is what's riling her."

Which prompted nothing but the stock inscrutable smile, as usual.

"I'll take these out to them. Wait here if you like and I'll come back in." Martin nodded his grateful assent while he was paying for the round.

Presently, they were sat together in a corner booth at the back of the pub.

"I don't blame you for avoiding these nights out," said Susan, clinking her glass against Martin's.

"You don't enjoy them?"

"Oh, it's all right but it can get a little repetitive after the first hundred. They're a nice crowd, really (yes, apart from Howard), but there's only so many times you want to hear Davey's lament for his lost love, Julie, or Maisie's roll call of scalps amongst the great and the good."

"Really?"

"Oh yes, she's been busy, has our Maisie. If she chose to dish the dirt on the married barristers, bankers and clients she's shagged there'd be chaos."

"You're kidding?"

"I'm bloody not. She'll go far that girl, I'm telling you. But to be honest, I think that, underneath it, all she really wants is to be loved . . . by just one person . . . like the rest of us really."

The conversation halted at this point, with Susan looking at Martin, intently. While Martin looked back, apparently not intently. And then she noticed him glance across the pub and then look away again, smartly. She quickly shot her eyes to where he'd looked, to catch a glamorous woman in a red dress and resplendent jewellery, gazing at Martin; clearly taken by him and unable (unconcerned?) to hide it.

Susan looked back at Martin who appeared to be trying to appear to be trying to find something interesting in the food menu on the table before them. Pretending he hadn't noticed that he'd been so obviously lusted over.

"I've noticed you get a lot of women hitting on you, Martin."

Martin was trying to look innocent.

"You never give them anything back." It wasn't clear whether this was a statement or a question.

"Yes, I've seen you charming the female clients but that's just for the work, isn't it?"

"Well, you know my cond - . . ."

"Yes, your condition, I know. It is a strange one isn't it?"

Martin nodded.

"Tell you what – are you interested in some food?" Susan nodded at the menu Martin was pretending to scrutinise. "I promise I won't do a Maisie on you."

"Yes, why not? Good idea !" He seemed relieved by the idea.

"Not here, in other words?"

"Correct."

"We'll have to try and sneak off with the minimum of fuss," Susan indicated to the gang outside. They could just see one or two of them through the front door and Maisie was peering through the pub window, wondering where they were.

Susan caught Davey's eye and motioned him inside.

"All right, lovebirds?" he laughed amiably as he saw them sat together at the back.

"Shut up, Davey," Susan snapped, equally amiably. "Listen – we're going to slope off out the back."

Davey raised an eyebrow as he raised his glass to his lips – "Oh yeah?"

"I told you, Davey," Susan again, in mock admonition. "Just listen – will you cover for us, mate? When we've gone and if they ask . . ."

"Oh, they'll ask," said Davey nodding his head.

". . . if they ask," Susan continued, "just tell them we got dragged away by some friends of mine. And that we're sorry we didn't have the chance to say goodbye. Will you, Davey? Just cover for us, eh?"

"Yeah, of course," said Davey as he spun round to rejoin the group outside. "Just don't do anything I wouldn't do," his parting quip.

Only Davey knew (and, perhaps, Susan and, perhaps, Martin) the mild reproach and sadness in his taking leave of them. Davey had always rather hoped (somehow he knew, in vain) that Susan might be the one to take the place of his long-lost Julie. But he didn't really begrudge Martin. He had quickly come to like the guy and he viewed them both as his friends. And if he couldn't have Susan, he had the idea that, somehow, she might be the one to 'cure' Martin.   And he laughed to himself at the thought as he strolled back out front, into the warm summer evening sun and Susan and Martin shot out of the side entrance at the rear of the pub onto the street round the corner.

They walked along the streets through Mayfair as the light in the air turned to a warm bronze and the babble from the groups spilled onto the pavements grew louder and more shrill as the evening took its toll. The street lights started to flicker on as the sky darkened imperceptibly but more perceptible was the feeling that always comes with the approach of night in the centre of a city, the feeling of excitement with the knowledge that night's dominion is at hand and that everything changes accordingly. It's the same place but a different world with different people – the dark world inhabited by the night people.

They slipped into a couple of bars and pubs along the way:-

– Julianna's on Beak Street; with an iridescent white bar counter echoed in the table tops spun across the room; discs of glowing light floating in the gloom, offset with splashes of blue glassed cocktails, amber beers, green wine bottles, and thick red candle sticks with a yellow iris of flame settled within them.

– The Assumption in Maiden Lane; a one-room cellar bar with room for no more than 30 people maximum, run by an ageing drag queen called Annie who appeared to know Susan well.

In fact, Susan was by now taking the lead and seemed to be pulling Martin along a nostalgic trail of favoured watering holes from "when I was a student." She was telling Martin her life story along the way and getting more light-headed with each passing era and each chinking glass housing a different drink in each bar. Martin, of course, wasn't drinking – just a coke or an orange juice each time – and so couldn't be swimming in the same mood river that was dragging Susan along but he did appear to be engaged with her company and seemed content to let her do most of the talking.

In fact, anyone present who was rather more objective might have deduced that Martin was artfully keeping any curiosity on Susan's part strictly at arm's length whilst teasing the most intimate secrets out of her. But she loved it. He seemed to understand exactly how she felt – at particular junctures, he would interject the most felicitous comment which instantly told you that he had, indeed, grasped – and empathised with – the exact essence of what her thoughts and feelings were.

They were by now in Belugo, a popular, classy Italian restaurant sat on the southern edge of the river with a fully glazed frontage leading out to a wide wooden balcony, so that you could gaze out on the spectacular vista, either in the warmth of the restaurant or in the fresh breeze rolling over the water. Belugo was a well-run business owned by a canny operator, Carlo Demello, who had built it up over the years to the point where it was by now an institution for the metropolitan elite of politicians, business leaders, media folk and super-artists. The restaurant reflected its owner: an attractive combination of worldly sophistication and earthy humanity.

Like Carlo, its urbane profile was undercut by a concern for simple, straightforward values that banished any lingering suspicion of pretentiousness. Its solid dark wood, country-style tables were the height of fashion but they would still have been there regardless, reminding Carlo – as they did – of the furniture in the kitchens and dining rooms of his mother and aunts and grandmother in Calabria. Carlo was the original country boy who had outgrown – but not stopped loving – the country and found a place in the city where his talent for hospitality, friendship and discretion could blossom.

Carlo was unmarried and – according to the titillated gossip among his loyal patrons – gay; not that that made any difference as homosexuals of both sexes were an integral and accepted part of the mob that crowded around the banks of this river and Carlo's lofty hauteur made it clear that it was none of your business anyway. The wealthy and famous clientele who flocked to Belugo for some reason felt it perfectly natural to unburden upon Carlo their most sensitive (and, sometimes, scandalous and career-threatening) secrets but got little back in the way of Carlo's biography.

When Susan had suggested they go to Belugo, Martin had expressed surprise as he knew this was a famous eatery and appeared a little taken aback at the idea that this was an establishment that they could just waltz into, without booking, on a Friday night but Susan had simply said, "Oh don't worry; Carlo loves my father. It'll be fine." Martin was beginning to comprehend the reach of Susan's family connections. He also realised, quite quickly, that Susan was a particular favourite of Carlo's when they were spotted at the door by the man himself, who immediately bade the doorman to bring them to him at the bar.

"Come here, daughter, and give the old man a kiss," he implored, with outstretched arms.

"Hi, Dad," Susan kissed him on the cheek as they locked in an embrace that appeared to Martin genuinely warm, not just the usual professional bonhomie.

"You've been neglecting us," he admonished her with mock offence.

"Sorry, Carlo – been working a lot."

"Ah, good girl – you keep it up. You gotta work hard, just like your other dad. He's so proud of you."

"Is he?" Susan seemed genuinely surprised. "He doesn't show it."

"Of course he is," Carlo appeared taken aback and even horrified at the thought that Susan didn't know what her father thought of her. "He's a very busy man and he gets very distracted and he's very naughty with those he loves and I know what he feels. He tells me, and I know how proud he is of you."

Carlo was an impressive-looking character in his own right, with an upright bearing, jet-black hair, swept back with no grey showing (or being allowed to show); tall and slim with a presence that was authoritative but not standoffish.

Martin was observing this exchange, noting the familiarity with which Carlo spoke of Jimmy Sachs when he himself was suddenly fixed with the Italian's gaze.

"And you don't even introduce me to your friend." Carlo was looking straight into Martin's eyes and appeared genuinely absorbed. Again, not just the professional blandishments.

"Oh yes, sorry – this is Martin. Martin Dash from work," Susan spluttered, appearing momentarily flustered.

"Martin Dash !" Carlo was obviously delighted by the accord between Martin's name and appearance. "Yes . . ."

And then – a little more respectfully – Carlo extended his hand and nodded his head slightly forward, whilst dropping his eyes. "I'm very pleased to meet you, Mr. Dash. Any friend of the beautiful Miss Sachs is a friend of mine."

They laughed at this and Martin smiled, "You too, Signor Demello," as they shook hands.

"Please: Carlo, please. The Sachs are my family. And I think you would be a welcome addition to the family. Eh, daughter?" Carlo grinned mischievously at Susan.

"Enough, Carlo, enough !" Susan shrieked, laughing but also blushing. "Can you squeeze us in?"

"Oh, I don't know," Carlo sighed, pretending to look at the book.

The place was heaving but in a moment they were seated at one of the best tables against the glass wall facing directly onto the river, now black with a thin ribbon of multi-coloured lights twinkling on the opposite bank.

As he sat, Martin spotted face after face in the Friday night Belugo crowd – you couldn't help but look (although a disinterested observer might also notice that a number of this high-end clientele, male and female, also gave Martin a second look; Susan, although not disinterested, also noticed this and a small shiver of joy wriggled through her frame).

Amidst this social scanning, their eyes fell upon each other and Martin smiled, "This is a bit more rarefied than I'm used to," and – unconsciously – he looked at the menu.

"Yes, it is a bit pricey," said Susan, "but don't worry, Dad keeps a tab here, or something anyhow. Carlo has never let me pay. So we can have what we want !"

"Oh no, I should pay."

"Why?"

A pregnant pause. And Martin mock-surrendered "Oh, go on then . . ."

Susan laughed and patted his hand, "Thank you !"

9

"So, how about your family? Parents? Brothers? Sisters?" Susan had decided it was time to start pumping Martin for information instead of dominating the conversation with the saga of her illustrious father, his triumphs, misdeeds and scandals. They had just been served coffee – after a long, leisurely dinner that Martin suspected had been personally overseen by Carlo – and Susan had given him the full story, most of which had been played out in the full glare of the media (of which he was already aware) but some of which could never have seen the light of day.

Susan had been putting it away steadily all evening while Martin had not shown the slightest temptation to break his long abstinence, much to her disappointment (but what did she expect?). She had become progressively more indiscrete with each glass and had given him at least two stories which, if publicised and verified (perhaps not even verified . . .), would have meant the end of Jimmy Sachs' career (and the final end this time, not all those ends from which he had miraculously resurrected before).

Martin, however, was proving a harder nut to crack, as usual.

"So you were born where?"

"Birmingham."

"You haven't got a Brummie accent. In fact, you haven't got any accent."

"Well, I was born there but we moved around a lot."

Bit of a silence.

"Like where?"

"Oh, all over – Bristol, Uttoxeter, Leicester, Lewes."

Susan was eyeing him suspiciously. Martin was appearing nonchalant.

"How come?"

"Because of the work, sort of – my dad was a teacher and he just kept getting jobs in different places. So we'd move again. But I think he was just a bit restless anyway. He preferred to keep moving."

"What about your mum?"

"Oh, she just followed; just went along with it – she was a nurse so she could always get work wherever we were."

"And where are they now?"

"They're both dead."

Another bit of a silence.

"Both of them?   Oh, I'm . . . I'm sorry but they can't have been very old?"

"They died in a car crash when I was 18."

"Oh, how awful for you. You must have been devastated." Then she realised what she'd said. Martin was just looking at her.

"Did you . . ?"

"Have the illness then? Yes – I've always had it."

You could almost see the questions formulating in Susan's puzzled face.

"I know this sounds like a rather crass question but . . ."

"How did I feel? . . . like always. I never feel anything."

This hit Susan like a slap across the face with a cold, wet, bulky, dead haddock and, after a little while, she realised her mouth was gaping (she promptly shut it).

"Martin, I . . . I don't know what to say. You must be the strangest person I've ever met. You walk around, meet people, get on with them; people like you … and yet, underneath … Your parents die and you can't feel a thing? I feel so sorry for you and I just can't get my head round it … How can you feel absolutely nothing?"

"I know, I can't really explain it. Because I've never known any different. I don't *know* what it is to have feelings, like you do … like everyone else does. I've no idea what that must be like."

Martin sipped from his orange juice.

"Well, what do the doctors say? Because it can go away, can't it? And there are drugs?"

Martin smiled, "You've been researching?"

Susan shuffled and blushed slightly, realising she'd been caught out, but then gathered herself and came back, slightly indignant.

"Well, yes I have, actually, but why not? I was interested – I'd never heard of such a thing before. It just seemed so strange to me. So I just looked it up."

"To check I wasn't making it up .. ?"

"Don't be silly."

Martin simply took another sip and cast his gaze around the restaurant. But without really looking.

Susan was not giving up – "But it can be cured, can't it?"

"There are some people who have episodes and then go back to normality and there are some who respond to treatment. They tried various drugs on me but they didn't seem to make much difference. And my dad stopped it as he said the drugs would make me ill and I was fine as I was. And eventually I think I just dropped off the doctors' radar and I've never really tried again. I'm fine."

He could see Susan's sceptical look.

"Honestly. I am."

The drink had been working its magic on Susan for a while now and she was becoming transfixed by Martin. He was dressed in a blue suit, bright white shirt, crimson tie, immaculate as ever – his blue eyes that looked like jewels, his bright blond hair, his beautiful face – like a girl. She was feeling deep stirrings that were only strengthened by the idea that this gorgeous creature before her might actually be unattainable.

'Is he a virgin?' The thought suddenly popped up in her mind and there must have been some manifestation in her face, a shift of intensity that Martin saw because he pointedly looked at his watch and swigged down the last of his juice.

"Well, that was great food but I reckon it's probably time to hit the trail."

Susan seemed to come round as if out of a dream; swayed in her seat ever so imperceptibly; and looked at her own watch. It was only 11 o'clock. But she acquiesced and, as she looked across the restaurant, she saw Carlo approaching them, with perfect timing to ensure that their departure from his restaurant without having to pay a sou was orchestrated as charmingly as possible.

As they bundled into the taxi outside, the driver asked: "Where to?" and Susan came straight back with: "Bayswater; Queens Gardens, please" – the flat, owned by her parents, that she formerly shared with her elder sister, Maria, but now on-and-off with her friend Charlotte.

She looked meaningfully at Martin. Who said to the driver: "And then Angel, please."

Susan furrowed her brow and whispered: "Why don't you come to mine?"

"Oh, thanks – but I'd better get back to mine. I've got a bunch of stuff I need to do for Barry Rogers in the morning so I reckon I'll need to get my head down."

Susan looked crestfallen and cross at the same time but then a thought came into her head: "Well, you could give it to him in person tomorrow night, if you like."

Martin knitted his brow, puzzled.

"Mum and Dad are throwing a party at the house. Why don't you come with me? All the players will be there . . . and Barry and Joan," she said with a wink. "It'll be a laugh – you'll enjoy it," and then, pulling herself up, ". . . well, you know . . ."

Martin smiled, "It's OK; yes, I'll come – that'll be great. Thank you for asking me. Are you sure they won't mind?"

"God, no – they'd love to meet you. I've been going on about you for weeks." She was throwing caution to the wind now.

"So, Bayswater then Angel?" called the driver from the front, tired of waiting for a decision. Susan laughed, "Yes, Bayswater then Angel," and gave Martin a hug.

10

Martin Dash gazed out of the taxi's rear window as it wound its way along the broad streets of leafy Hampstead Garden suburbs. He had ordered the cab to go from his flat in The Angel at 6:00 in order to arrive at the Sachs' home at the time appointed by Susan – 6.30. Susan had phoned him that day to fill him in on the party and give some directions. She had explained that his invitation was rather last minute because she had not intended to go – her parents, being promiscuously sociable, held such do's fairly regularly and it was generally left to Susan whether she came to them or not.

They were fully aware of her distaste for the political characters who made up the bulk of their social circle but were generally relaxed at this as they also knew she was too well-mannered to cause embarrassment if she did turn up and would usually restrict herself to the odd caustic remark that was expertly balanced between a level of venom that could be shocking if you considered it for any length of time and the kind of roughhouse ribbing that could easily be explained away (if the target got shirty) as what you were brought up to deal with in the 'sophisticated' milieu they inhabited.

In any event, everyone agreed that – amongst the other blessings bestowed upon her – Susan had definitely inherited the whiplash tongue her father had deployed to devastating effect on many occasions, to the delight of all who witnessed it (often including the supposed comrades of the unfortunate recipient). This was one of the reasons he was such a popular figure (for a politician) – he was just so damnably entertaining (as Boris Johnson himself had put it).

So, the Sachs' summer party was a well-established feature of the social round of the London political scene. In fact, not just political as Jimmy and Rosa had both come out of cultured backgrounds and carried the same sense of engagement with the wider world throughout their lives and careers. Rosa had maintained her profile in the arts (initially as a successful opera singer and, latterly, with select trusteeships) in tandem with the career of politician's wife and was equally at ease with a visiting South American novelist as with the hard-nosed political bruisers who routinely came round to empty the drinks cabinet.

Martin knew that Hampstead was, of course, a 'nice' place generally – its heady combination of a patronising liberal / bohemian heritage mixed with a serious accumulation of proper money and desirable properties made it a haven for wealthy establishment types and generational trustafarians, whose preference was to wrap themselves in the comforting security blanket of complacent superiority rather than to slum it among the vulgar Russian arrivistes of Chelsea Harbour; but, as the taxi passed by the perfect customers sashaying through the perfect shops of the perfect High Street, humming in the golden sunshine of the early evening, and wound its way up the hill, past the open human wildlife reserve of The Heath, towards the Sachs' residence, Martin realised that there were some parts of it that were even nicer than the others.

The houses got bigger, the lawns got bigger and the walls in front of them got bigger. And, suddenly, as they rounded a curve in the road, a crush of cars and people hove into view. In front of the Sachs' house. It was a commotion of swanky Mercs, Beemers, Rollers, chauffeurs, guests, celebrities, photographers and even a couple of camera crews with bouffanted society journos beaming their pieces to camera.

"I think this might be it," deadpanned Martin's taxi driver, sardonically.

"Yes, I reckon I might as well get out here, thanks." Martin paid the man, who then started to reverse back down the street with a cheery "Have a good time – don't do anything I wouldn't do !" living up to the cheeky chappy taxi driver persona with grim determination.

Martin's local taxi firm had an unusual policy of only buying (second-hand) Mercedes for its fleet so, when his car had pulled up, there was nothing to remark; it blended in. However, one of the celebrity photographers stalking the beat (an old hand with an encyclopaedic knowledge of the delineations of every noteworthy face, its back story and newsworthiness) spotted this striking young man – with his quiff dazzling in the sun and his profile a direct echo straight back to the 1980s of Duran Duran and Princess Diana – and realised that he didn't know him. Battle-hardened professionalism sprung his camera automatically up to his eye and this, in turn, was a Pavlovian call to his fellow hyenas packed about him, their nostrils twitching for the scent of something interesting, something saleable.

Something about the scene piqued their interest. This brooding young unknown, with the film star looks but without the face recognition, was now hesitantly approaching; he clearly wasn't one of them, appeared completely out of his comfort zone, and yet was walking straight towards the entrance gates – Susan had instructed him to simply go to the gates and give his name.

As he approached, Martin started to notice a number of faces he had seen previously only on the television – politicians, actors, sports stars, artists – but his own presence seemed, for some reason, to be attracting as much attention from the press pack as any of the rest. It was simply one of those funny moments when a reaction happens to occur in a number of people simultaneously and entirely fortuitously and, accordingly, creates something of a feedback loop in the crowd mentality that is as odd as it is sudden. The reaction was to the fact that Martin simply looked *so* fine as he approached them and that they, the crème-de-la-crème of name checkers, had absolutely no idea who he was. It was a sudden – and, therefore, tantalising – mystery and, accordingly, he was questioned as he pushed towards the big iron gates in the front wall of the property.

"Good evening, Sir – are you a friend of the family?"

"Could we get a name, please?"

"Do you work for Mr. Sachs?"

Martin was unsure and totally unprepared for this. All he could think of was: "I'm Martin Dash, I'm a friend of Susan."

"Martin *Dash*?" They all mouthed the question, some audibly, all puzzled. Then their finely-honed calibrators clicked into gear: "With *Susan* – ah, very good !"

"Do you mind if we ask if you're an item, Sir?" Many of these guys had already got Susan on their radar as a potentially newsworthy source; they had spotted early on that she had an independent streak and that her father-like tongue would probably spit out something usable in due course. So to be suddenly presented with this enigmatic character whose first words linked himself to Susan was enough to get their collective antennae twitching.

Martin sensed this and thought to correct them: "I . . . err . . . I work with Susan."

The man on the gate had caught all this and swung it open to let the prey push through – to the loudly rancorous disappointment of the pack.

Martin stood with other guests at the front of a deep forecourt flanked on each side by a lawn and a crushed pebble pathway leading to the glossy black double door of the very large frontage to the very impressive neo-Georgian residence that was home to Jimmy and Rosa Sachs (and their two daughters when they occasionally fell out with the boyfriend / husband and needed to fly back to the nest).

Martin realised that Susan had been there at the door waiting for him and was now skipping towards him, beaming, with her hands held out. With a mischievous glance at the photographers, she grabbed his shoulders and planted a kiss smack on his cheek. The paparazzi had got their prompt and clicked together in perfect synchronicity.

If you look at that picture now it has a haunted quality. Susan and Martin look like screen idols, dressed beautifully, stood in front of the big house, the sunlight twinkling in their eyes and the water spraying from the little fountain to the side.

Susan is smiling but something in Martin's expression tells you that all is not quite right and – just then – Susan seems to have noticed this, even as the joy of the moment is coursing through her.

Susan felt the need to apologise.

"Sorry, I didn't really warn you about this. Dad's been in the news a fair bit since he got back into the Cabinet and this one's a bit busy."

Jimmy Sachs was currently back on a roll since his return to the Blair Cabinet just two months ago. However, this was simply the latest development in a career punctuated by considerable ups and downs since he had gained his first seat at the 1979 election at the tender age of 28.

In fact, that seat – the safe Labour seat of Islington North – had pretty much been gifted to him by James Callaghan, no doubt in recognition of the hard work he had put in for the party for most of his 20s but also by way of acknowledgement of the way in which he had burnished the already potent family brand that had previously been established by his father, Walter Sachs, who had served with distinction in both the Wilson and Callaghan governments prior to his untimely death from a wholly unexpected heart attack in 1986.

Walter Sachs had been that rare thing – a politician of the utmost integrity and rectitude. As a young boy, Walter and his German Jewish family had been saved from the menacing clutches of Hitler's Nazis by the welcoming arms of London's East End just before the start of the Second World War and had dedicated the rest of his life to showing his gratitude with tireless public service to the people who had taken him in. To that end, his considerable gift for organisation, insight and oratory had been given over to the duties of councillor, MP and, ultimately, Secretary of State for Health, Defence and then Home Secretary.

Michael Foot, no less, called Walter a "socialist saint" in the address at his funeral.

This was the standard that his first son, James (always 'Jimmy'), was required to live up to. And, largely, he did if the record was to be measured in terms of service, appointments, offices; the only question with Jimmy being: 'was he a socialist..?' with his card-carrying detractors pointing to:-

(a) his and Neil Kinnock's brutal fight with the Militant Tendency in the 80s that ultimately led to his vacation of the Islington seat (and the apparent end of his parliamentary career);

(b) his support of Tony Blair in the bid to revise clause IV of the Party's constitution that was rewarded by Blair with the candidacy of the Hampstead seat in 1997 (won); and

(c) (most damagingly . . .) his unapologetic taste for the 'good' things in life ('wine, women and song' he, only half-jokingly, listed as his favourite things on Desert Island Discs).

In his defence, his supporters would instantly point to (and many of his detractors would have to begrudgingly accept):-

(d) his unending and blistering excoriation of Margaret Thatcher for the entire 11 years of her reign (and afterwards);

(e) the undoubted intelligence and acuity that he brought to bear upon all of the roles that had been assigned to him (and the unalloyed successes that resulted); and

(f) the endless entertainment and sheer excitement that attended his every move, whether it be his Pavlovian ensnarements by nightclub escorts; pub brawls with enemies, comrades or mere passers-by; or the kneejerk backchat to his ostensible superiors – he didn't actually allow many of these; in fact, really only the PM (who, in the case of Blair, had an enduring affection for Jimmy, regardless of the insults and indiscretions flung in his face) and the Queen (who – he avowed expressly – should be removed, at the first chance, along with the whole panoply of the constitutional monarchy, despite the warm personal friendship the two actually enjoyed).

No, there was no real doubt where his heart lay, ultimately; the issue (unlike the way that people seriously questioned Tony Blair's fundamental motivations) was the other Jimmy Sachs; the one that popped up with mechanical regularity to undermine months or years of prior good work; the one who had been caught, literally, with his trousers down with a room maid in Aberdeen (earning him the everlasting admiration of the Scots male and concurrent exile from both the Cabinet and his wife's household ... to which he had only just returned); who expended as much ardour on his rows with the extreme left of the Labour church as he did on his war of attrition with the right wing Tory enemy; and whose brand of socialism, appeared – disconcertingly – to embrace, wholeheartedly, the imperatives of the entrepreneurial business classes and which repeatedly led him into the welcoming and manipulative arms of 'friends' by whom you would probably not wish to be judged – people like Barry and Joan Rogers, who now appeared, suddenly, at Martin's elbow, as if from nowhere.

"Dashing by name, dashing by nature," Barry leered at the young couple, obviously over-excited by his access to the whole wealth / power / glamour combo.

"Oh, hi Barry" said Martin, momentarily startled. "Joan," he also nodded to the perennially grave Ms. Rogers, who was unashamedly eyeing over, first Susan, and then Martin, with a clinical and not wholly friendly air.

"Good evening Martin ... and Susan," she batted her eyelids, slowly, at both in turn, with an ever so slight turn at the corners of her mouth which might have been a smile but, equally, might not.

"What's my favourite lawyer – Christ, listen to me; how can you favour a lawyer?!" he cackled, delighted at his own 'witticism', believing he was perfectly at liberty to insult fellow guests – even the host's daughter – because he paid them. "What's my favourite lawyer doing here then? Have you smuggled him in, Susan?!" More cackling.

Wearing a smile born more of forced toleration than genuine goodwill, Susan retorted: "I asked Martin to come so I'd have someone sane to keep me company !" with an accompanying dry laugh that was pitched to only just give them the comfort that that was a joke, not a barbed attack.

Barry laughed, both nervously and, again, leeringly, looking sideways at Martin with the thought obvious on his face of the incongruity of the concepts of sanity and Martin Dash. Joan, tall, pale, forbidding, with her black straight hair and black straight clothes simply continued eyeing the two up and down, contemplating what, it was impossible to tell.

"I'll give your mum and dad credit, Susan – they do know how to throw a party. Bloody hell, look there's Elton John. And his, err..." – more leering – "his *friend*; Whatsisname?... Furnished?"

"David Furnish – shut up Barry and stop being so vulgar," Joan now hissed and they all looked at her slightly surprised. This was the first sentence she'd uttered. "Don't go pointing at people. We're not greenhorns, you know."

"All right, all right," Barry seemed slightly annoyed, "I was only pointing out that Jimmy and Rosa can pull in the A-list when they want to. See, look – there's Samuel Jackson !"

"I think that's Laurence Fishburne actually, Barry," said Martin, as tactfully as he could manage. Both Joan and Susan rolled their eyes, Susan looking away.

"Whatever," snorted Barry, slugging back the remains of his second glass of champagne.

The front garden and the entrance into the home was now teeming with 'personalities' right from A list to Z – one thing you had to give Jimmy and Rosa: they were supremely democratic when it came to their friends and house guests; their loyalties lay at least as much with old friends from their youth – Rosa's colleagues from way back at the start of her singing career and Jimmy's comrades from his early communist associations – as they did with the 'celebrities' they'd collected more recently (and even they were an eclectic mix – you were at least as likely to run into a Krankie at one of these parties as you were Simon Rattle).

"I'm going to take Martin in," said Susan, thinking to exit Barry's orbit. "He's not met Mum and Dad yet."

"Aha !" shouted Barry, gleefully. "Going to meet the folks, eh Martin? Must be serious !"

Barry The Cringeworthy.

"We'll see you in a bit then. We'll circulate, shall we Darling?" said Barry, offering his arm to Joan, who took it, abstractedly. "But I want to have a little word later, if you don't mind, Martin . . . about . . ." Barry, nodding and winking at Martin.

"Oh . . . oh, yes – of course," said Martin, as Susan edged him away.

"What was that about?" she quizzed Martin as they entered into the shade of the hall of the front of the house.

"Oh, just work stuff," then, remembering that Susan was work too, "the Crack Harbour funding."

Susan looked concerned and pondered what to say but ultimately contented herself, simply, with: "Just watch those pair. I wouldn't trust Barry as far as I could throw him. Mum's always telling my dad to stay clear of him."

"Why? Your dad isn't much involved with the Rogers is he?"

Susan gave him a look – "I wish that were the case . . ."

Once in through the front door, guests were confronted by a spacious hall, with cream tiling on the floor; ruby-red crushed velvet curtains framing tall mullioned windows; a wide first floor balcony overlooking the scene with a black painted staircase arcing down from either side; pretty chandeliers of glass droplets; and a vaulted ceiling with classical frescoes hand-painted on its panels. This was an impressive residence and standing together in the middle of the hall were its impressive proprietors. They both spotted Susan at the same time, both instantly broke into broad grins, clocked Martin, and beckoned them over.

"Susan, darling," cried her mother, "come and give your mother a kiss."

Rosa Sachs, née Beneditti, was an opera singer who had performed around the world – often, though not always, in the lead – and built up a solid reputation among the cognoscenti. Her parents were – like Jimmy's – 1930s émigrés but from Italian fascism rather than German Nazism; her father – a successful businessman with many international connections – had decided that a London base was preferable to the Rome he left behind under the ministry of what he called 'teste di cazzo del Duce' ('Il Duce's dickheads'). The subsequent years proved his derision correct in his own mind and his children were born, and grew up, calling London home.

Rosa was slightly on the short side of medium height, dark, striking, and her looks and haunting voice had won her many admirers, both opera-loving and otherwise. But there was something about the young Jimmy Sachs that she found compelling. Coming from a family with a constitutional hatred of right-wingers of all complexions, she instantly chimed with Jimmy's socialist belligerence; and his protean passions and no-nonsense style were, if the truth be told, a straightforward echo of her beloved father.

Add to that the glamour and excitement of a life in the glare of front-line politics (only marginally less raucous and deadly than the world of professional opera) and the proposition was pretty much irresistible to Rosa. In due course – and, certainly, once their two girls had arrived – she had decided that the supreme effort and slog required to maintain an elite singer's career were not worth the trouble and definitely not compared with the comfortable life of a high-ranking politician's wife in cosmopolitan London, with all the attendant conveniences.

No, Rosa Sachs had, for many years now, reserved all her energies for the several roles – mother, philanthropist, patron – that together made her the prima donna of the political and social set of which her husband's family and friends were such an important part. And if that demanded a grim nonchalance in the face of her husband's childish indiscretions, then so be it – she was the child of Italians by whom anything other than a cold-eyed acceptance of the realities of human weakness was itself considered pathetically infantile.

Jimmy and Rosa had, of course, seen it all and had 100,000 faces thrust in front of them by way of introduction over the years, so their professional poise wouldn't miss a beat if you presented Lucifer himself to them – they'd simply proffer a hand and a smile whilst instantly appraising the subject from top to toe anyway. But something about the vision of Martin Dash appearing before them did make them stop, if only for a moment. Perhaps it was that this person was not only unnervingly beautiful and strange but *with their daughter.*

Susan noticed this and was suddenly embarrassed by the fact that her parents were actually staring at Martin, with their mouths open. Martin was simply staring back at them. So she broke the spell with: "Mum, Dad – this is Martin; Martin Dash. I told you – who works with me."

These words make Rosa's head tilt towards the direction of the speaker but her eyes remained fixed on Martin until she also suddenly realised she was staring and snapped to.

Also slightly embarrassed. And nudged Jimmy, who was a little slower to come to.

Poise regained, hand and smile proffered.

"Hello, Martin – I'm so pleased to meet you. Susan has told me so much about you."

Martin was all polish. He took Rosa's hand, flashed her the 100 watt smile (producing in Rosa the same reaction as it first had in Susan), and bowed slightly.

Just for a moment, Susan thought he was actually going to kiss her outstretched hand and click his heels! Rosa beamed back.

Then Martin turned his attention to Jimmy, stood more upright, held out his hand and intoned: "Sir, it's an honour to meet you . . ." and, with a nod back to Rosa, ". . . both of you."

Jimmy was tickled by the touch of the old world that Martin had somehow managed to bring to the occasion and, laughing, responded in kind –

". . . And an honour to meet you too, Mr. Dash."

Martin took his cue and laughed too, as they all did.

"But please call me Jimmy; only the Speaker and the Revenue call me 'Sir'!"

There were a number of people standing around the hosts and a gentle chortling rippled around the group at Jimmy's witticism. This prompted Martin to look round at his fellow guests and he realised that one of those joining in the fun, standing right next to him, was Jude Law, the film actor, whose ravishing features and stellar celebrity conferred on the select parties a satisfying glow of A-list endorsement.

And now people suddenly noticed the miraculous serendipity of he and Martin standing together. It was one of those occasions when everyone present realised that the same thought was suddenly occurring to them all simultaneously and a breeze of magic hazed between them, like a guttering candle, flickering a shimmering light upon the scene.

Jude Law had long since been accepted as the gold standard of male sex appeal and was accustomed to always being top dog in the looks class of any social gathering. But he was now stood next to a creature whose allure was at least his match and, as they stood eyeing each other, they looked like brothers. From an alien civilisation of idealised mannequins. Like Sweden, say.

One of the wandering celebrity photographers allowed in the home spotted the moment and snapped, which broke the spell and prompted a low murmur of '*Aaahh*' from the assembled, like a group of old ladies circling a new born baby, realising immediately that they'd been there when a photo like that (which would undoubtedly appear somewhere in the media tomorrow and recurrently thereafter) was taken.

"Separated at birth?!" cried Jimmy, sparking another burst of laughter. He was on good form tonight. And a fourth Martini.

"Martin, this is Jude Law, who – I imagine – you might have seen in the odd B-movie here and there."

"Fuck off, Jimmy," Jude shot back, good-naturedly.

Jimmy carried on, heedless of the profanity, "Jude is helping Rosa with her UNICEF project." (One of Rosa's charitable works, corralling celebrities and politicians to raise money for Afghan children and their mothers, her husband having prepared the ground, as it were.)

"And Jude, this is Martin Dash, who works at Stone Rose with Susan."

"Pleased to meet you, Martin," said Jude, genially pumping Martin's hand. "Jimmy says we look alike – what do you think?"

"Well, I don't know about that," replied Martin, "but if so, maybe we could swap, like Dickie Greenleaf, and I'll have your life."

Jude's eyebrows shot up, "So that would make you Tom Ripley – but that's the role I always wanted!" He was delighted at this little joke. And Martin looked rather pleased with himself, mused Susan, rather disconcerted by this apparent playfulness on Martin's part. It was most odd. Meanwhile she could see her father was furrowing his brow, obviously having been left behind.

"The Talented Mr. Ripley, Dad," she explained. "Where Tom Ripley swaps places with his rich friend, Dickie Greenleaf – Jude played Greenleaf in the film."

"Not so much swaps as kills!" Jude exclaimed, with mock accusation at Martin.

"Ah, yes, I remember," said Jimmy, turning to look again at Martin. "He's a psychopath who assumes a new identity."

"Fuck..." thought Susan, suddenly feeling warm in her cheeks. She had told her mother about Martin's condition but had she told her father in turn? This was getting fucking weird. She looked at Martin and he looked entirely unruffled and she recalled it was he who had made the joke in the first place, laughing. Yes, he was unruffled but at the same time he now appeared to be entirely detached from the proceedings, his gaze focussed on something that was miles away, out of this room, out of this house.

"But don't worry – he gets away with it, doesn't he, Martin?" said Jude, bringing the joke to a satisfactory conclusion and, indeed, this triggered peels of relieved laughter. But Susan had felt quite odd about the exchange, even paranoid about what her parents (and Jude Law?!) thought about Martin. Proper paranoid. And disconcerted.

As a senior member of the British Government, Jimmy Sachs had an actual bodyguard on hand at all times (from the Specialist Protection branch of the Met) and, just at this moment, Susan thought she saw this gentleman – a hitherto anonymous figure stood just behind Jimmy – look Martin up and down, his interest in the young interloper perhaps alerted for the first time? Christ ! She *was* getting paranoid, she decided, and resolved to move Martin out of the house, and into the garden at the back.

"I'm going to show Martin around, Dad – Mum. Please excuse us."

"Certainly, my dear – have a good time, you two," Jimmy raised his glass genially.

As they eased past the group, Susan swore she saw the bodyguard's eyes following Martin. But she was being paranoid, wasn't she?!

"This is an amazing place isn't it?" said Martin, abstractedly, as they moved down the hall towards the back of the building. "And a hell of a party. Your dad really is the big cheese, isn't he?"

"If you say so."

"Yes, I do – look at the people who are here. This is proper A-list territory."

"Well, it might get a bit A+ soon."

"Why? What do you mean?"

"Oh, nothing," Susan smiled enigmatically as they walked, squinting against the sun, into the expansive rear gardens. "A surprise. Possibly."

"Well, look who *is* here" said Martin, gazing around the crowd. "Jack Straw ... Vanessa Redgrave ... Alex Ferguson ..."

"... and Jude Law," interjected Susan. "So what was all that Tom Ripley business about?"

"How do you mean?"

"Oh, you must remember: the psychopath pretending to be someone he isn't. There was you and Jude Law competing for the role, my dad making insinuations. It was all a bit odd – you seemed to be going along with it somehow ..."

Martin scrutinized her but, as usual, with no visible clue as to whether he might be annoyed, glad, indifferent ...

"Susan, you really do need to rein in the paranoia, you know; after all, it's supposed to be me who has the mental illness."

"Supposed to, Martin? – supposed to?" Susan didn't know why she was choosing this time and this place to be having a go at Martin but something about the exchange inside had set her wheels rolling.

There was an uneasy silence between them which Martin broke – "You think I'm a fake, Susan?"

Susan looked into his eyes and was tempted to say 'yes' just to watch his reaction – to see if she could get a reaction – but, while she couldn't say she could see actual hurt in his eyes, she thought she could see there a weariness borne of not being believed or understood many times over and found herself being afraid that she could see him mentally moving her onto the list of people he could no longer trust – the list of suspicious people. And she didn't want that.

"No, no – I don't, Martin," she moved closer to him and took his arm in her hand, earnestly. "No, you need to know – I'm your friend."

He could see her genuine anguish and smiled, "Sorry. I didn't mean that."

Susan was relieved and they both lightened up. As Susan was leading Martin towards the back of the gardens, the gentle babble of the party's chatter swelled suddenly to an all-out hubbub which seemed to emanate from the forecourt on the other side of the building.

"Ah!" cried Susan. "The surprise! Come on," and she grabbed Martin's hand and led him back into the hall they had not long left. As they entered, it became clear that the noise had come from the press pack milling at the gates; the party guests themselves were trying to be more cool but there was no doubting a heightened sense of excitement amongst them as, just striding into the hall, Martin saw, was the Prime Minister, Tony Blair himself, flanked by two bodyguards like Jimmy's (one).

Susan shot a mischievous sideways glance at Martin, smirking, which Martin had to acknowledge.

"OK, A+," he smiled.

Here he was, in the flesh – the great political ogre of the age; the man who had sent British troops into more wars than any other prime minister in history; who cosied up to the big beasts in Washington and Jerusalem; who – in the opinion of many of Jimmy's friends and colleagues – had long since sold out the proud and principled traditions of the Labour movement. And yet Jimmy stood by him; Jimmy – whose family name was a byword for the eternal struggle against the imperial and corporate depredations.

No, whilst accepting unreservedly that Blair was not perfect (indeed, few of Blair's trusted circle had challenged him quite so much), Jimmy pointed to the minimum wage, gay rights, the Northern Ireland peace, and the redistributive record for which he was never properly credited. Jimmy said that you had to be realistic, pragmatic; that Tony Blair had won three general elections in a row; that he was the best weapon the Labour movement had for keeping the Tories out. And it was that sort of pragmatism that had kept Jimmy in the game of front line politics for 30 years now.

No, Tony Blair saw a kindred spirit in Jimmy, someone he could trust not to stab him in the back when the going got tough, and, indeed, someone he could trust to deliver. Thus, the warm embrace between the two men now; thus, a serving British Prime Minister makes time in his schedule to pop into his old friend's party for a few drinks in the first place; thus, Jimmy's latest rebirth, phoenix-like, into the Cabinet, after the debacle of 2004, when Blair had been forced to let his trusted ally return to the back benches following the revelation of Jimmy's involvement with the Sunny Glades development. Some had presumed that would be the last time they saw Jimmy Sachs in front-line politics; others knew better the regenerative powers of the 'Hampstead Hound', (a moniker bestowed by appreciative colleagues in a conscious twinning with the only other Labour member who was considered to match Sachs for fire and brimstone and wit: 'The Beast of Bolsover' – Dennis Skinner).

There was no great crush around Blair; all the guests considered themselves important and, again, were playing it cool. So Susan had no difficulty in marching Martin straight into the circle surrounding her father and the Prime Minister, who were chatting amiably, swapping notes on the holidays they'd both recently taken. She managed to catch her father's eye at an appropriate point and Jimmy got the message straight away.

"Oh Tony, you know Susan, of course, but here's her friend, Martin, as well – Martin Dash, who works with her." This last qualification – made, it seemed to Susan, with every mention of his name – was by now beginning to grate with her but she held out her hand and smiled sweetly anyway (and actually bowed, imperceptibly).

"Prime Minister."

"Good evening, my dear – lovely to see you again. Thank goodness you've taken after your divine mother in looks rather than this old croc," and he kissed her on both cheeks in the continental fashion.

"And . . ." he turned to scrutinise the vision stood next to her ". . . I'm sorry . . ?"

"Martin, Sir – Martin Dash," his hand reaching out to shake the great statesman's.

"Well, hello Martin – charmed, I'm sure."

"We reckon she's landed herself quite a catch, Tony – we've been debating who's the better looking between Martin and young Mr. Law here . . ." (Jimmy had downed two more Martinis by now and was loosening his tongue) ". . . What do you reckon?"

Jude Law blushed and Susan spun on Jimmy, furiously, "Father, don't be so rude – you'll embarrass Martin." But Martin wasn't embarrassed (Tony Blair – the ultimate operator – noticed that, as he had the young man's striking countenance in the first place); he just stared at the Prime Minister with that far-off look that no-one had yet fathomed. And the security men – including Jimmy's from earlier – noticed that. And Susan noticed that too. Paranoid again.

"Jimmy, you old rogue. I'm not here five minutes, haven't even had a drink yet, and you've already got me judging a beauty contest of young Adonises. And," pointing to the photographers on hand, "with the wolves waiting and slavering in the wings." Effortlessly, Blair had broken the ice, and continued: "I'm sure there's a whole lot more to you than good looks if you get to work with the redoubtable Susan – a chip off the old block, that one – and this time I'm referring to her father."

Susan blushed again but Jimmy beamed with pride – he loved both of his daughters dearly but had always felt that, if at all, it would one day be Susan that carried on the Sachs mantle of campaigning public services, despite her protestations to the contrary.

And now he waded in: "Oh yes, there is; there's a whole lot more to Martin . . . as I understand," Jimmy looking from Susan to Martin, praying for leave to continue.

Susan glared at her father.

"Oh?" said the Prime Minister, his interest piqued.

Martin simply smiled with the slightest nod to Jimmy, which he took as the green light to press on.

"Well, I hope you don't mind, Martin, but Susan tells me that it's something you wish to be open about; perhaps to make people aware of the condition and help other sufferers?"

"Yes, it's fine."

Blair was definitely interested now – "What's that then?"

"Well, as Susan's described it to me – and I hope I have this right, Martin, so please correct me if I don't – Martin bravely carries on his life and a successful career whilst suffering from a condition that means he feels nothing. Is that right Martin? Do I have that right? Andonia is it?"

"No, anhedonia," corrected the Prime Minister, "It's anhedonia, Jimmy. I know of it." All heads swivelled to Blair.

"I do sympathise, Martin. I knew someone – years ago – who suffered from the very same thing." He was scrutinising Martin closely now. "No desire – for pleasure, for money, for anything, and no sadness or upset either.

It's most . . . interesting. But a strange thing to have to live with. I do sympathise."

"What became of your friend, Sir?" asked Martin, intensely, and Susan thought she'd not seen him as engaged with anything before.

"Oh, he . . . he learned to live with it. In fact, he became very successful. In many ways he had the advantage over other people, he wasn't held back by . . . well, feelings and anxiety; he simply took decisions and did things . . . logically and rationally, without impediment."

All in the group were now staring at Blair, who was looking wistful.

"But he had no feelings for anyone? No . . . love?" asked Susan.

Blair looked around the group and seemed to correct himself somehow: "Well, yes; that's the tragedy of it, the flip side . . . you don't have the downside of life – the upset, the sadness – but you don't have the upside either."

He looked again at Martin and then, realising he was describing something that was probably very personal for the man in front of him: "Well, at least that's how I understood it."

"Yes, that's it," said Martin, flatly.

"Who was this, Tony? I've never heard you mention him before?" asked Jimmy, who had known Blair as well as anyone for 30 years now.

"Oh, someone from years ago – you don't know him, Jimmy. I ought not to say who it is, actually," and then back to the younger man: "But I believe that it can be cured, Martin?"

"That's what I've been told."

"But . . . not yet, eh?"

Martin shook his head.

"Well, I hope you do work your way through it. You're to be commended for not letting it stop you from getting on with your life and making friends."

He glanced at Susan (blushing) and back again, "I admire you."

"Well . . . thank you."

"Martin, you're now supposed to say: 'And I admire you too'" chipped in Jimmy, joking again; everyone laughed again and so did Martin. But he didn't say it.

Blair turned to Rosa, "And how's the lady unluckiest in love that I know?"

"How so?" said Rosa, taken aback.

"So beautiful, so talented, and yet ends up stuck with this old bugger !!"

Cue more merriment and the premium grade craic continued on with Blair and Sachs trading affectionate punches to the delight of all. For most of the assembled, their usual view of these two political heavyweights was on the television, robot-like, doling out bland platitudes, so to see them now, relaxed, boozing and joking was a real eye-opener and, truth to tell, not something that they were afforded too often – at least in the case of Blair. The Prime Minister was coming under particular pressure at the moment as people worried about the sustainability of the long economic boom the country had enjoyed up to present and questions were beginning to be asked – most dangerously, by some cabinet colleagues – as to whether the curtain would also be coming down on the reign of a man who had now been in the job nearly 10 years and was perhaps beginning to look like damaged goods.

So it rather looked like he was taking the opportunity of his friend's summer party – with no other functions to attend afterwards – to wind down a little.

In fact, the whole shindig was going swimmingly. Even though there were a few handpicked photographers allowed in, the party had a relaxed, informal feel with many of the fêted celebrities present allowing themselves to be off guard and, with the champagne flowing freely, they were getting louder and more playful. In all of this they took their cue from Jimmy and Rosa – Jimmy, in particular, was known for his no-holds-barred personality and penchant for a good time. He was not going to allow any party of his to be inhibited by the Presbyterian killjoys from the celebrity fanzines (or 'shit paper', as Jimmy liked to call them), perpetually lying in wait, and the great and the good now thronging in his hall, kitchen, sitting room and the green, red and gold of his garden seemed to appreciate this too. It felt like an exclusive gathering to which only the cool dudes had been invited, without – for once – the attendant drag of the bores they were usually obliged to humour.

Susan was, despite herself, having a good time and Martin looked like he was too. She generally avoided these affairs, decrying the awfulness of the political types usually gathered around her father but, happily, there were few of them here and this was a trend that appeared to have been established for this mid-summer party of Jimmy's in recent years: a largely politics-free oasis in the otherwise sodden social calendar. Perhaps in recognition of Rosa's oft-cited argument that he needed a break from the back-stabbing, intriguing and pressure that otherwise attended his every waking hour. An exception had been made for Blair, of course, and perhaps this was why he also appeared to appreciate the chance to let his hair down and turn off the approved script for a while. Why, he might even get the guitar out later !

In due course, Susan had found herself in the kitchen, mixing another drink and chatting to her aunt, Jimmy's younger sister, Audrey. She had decided to let Martin explore the party on his own for a little while (sending him on his way with a little quip that had delighted her as soon as it entered her head, on the subject of their encounter with the PM: "The Great Communicator meets The Great Non-Communicator !") and she was now catching up with family and friends whilst trying to set her stamp on the music being played on Jimmy's impressive sound system (for these sorts of parties he didn't hold with the usual tasteful quartet in the corner, so you might just as well be confronted – on entering the place – with 'Sympathy for the Devil' being blasted from every strategically placed speaker).

As Susan was moving through the kitchen towards the patio doors leading onto the garden to look for Martin again, she heard his voice just around the corner, outside – talking to Barry Rogers – and something made her pull up short to ponder the spines of some books on the shelf just by the doors, so that she didn't look as though she was ear-wigging.

"The £15 million will come through next week and the other £5 million probably the week after," Barry was explaining to Martin.

"And we do the property transfer when?" asked Martin. They were talking about the Crack Harbour development.

"Only when the second lot arrives," Barry, emphatically.

"OK, so where's it coming from?"

"Ad Jalal – the investors I've been telling you about."

"Who's acting for them?"

"Nobody, you'll just get the money direct from them."

A moment's hesitation from Martin, "What about their due diligence? Who's going to do that for them?"

"No need. They trust me. I've told them what a good lawyer you are ! We've done a proper job, haven't we?"

"I suppose so. But we'll need to do the usual anti-money laundering checks on them if we're dealing with them direct."

This time a moment's hesitation from Barry, then: "Nah, no need – Gerry knows them. Have a word with him if you're unsure."

Martin simply concurred, "OK."

Susan desperately wanted to jump in to ask 'Oh really, Barry? So Gerry *knows them* does he? What's that mean? We act for them too? We're acting for both sides on this? You and some dodgy outfit from God knows where? £20 million sloshing through our account?! Jesus Christ, Barry, do you think we're stupid or what?'

But she knew she couldn't. She'd already learnt enough in her time at Stone Rose to know that you do not front up to clients like that – valuable clients, as Barry undoubtedly (irritatingly) was. But by the same token you don't expose yourself and the blue-chip business that's been built up over decades (two centuries, in fact) by playing the patsy to a fast-and-loose merchant like Barry Rogers. So any concerns get dealt with quietly, among the partners.

She could have a word with Gerry. However, it wasn't her matter – Susan had been assisting Martin on a number of projects but not this one. Had Gerry kept her off this one because of her father's – what: acquaintanceship? friendship? – with the Rogers? Involuntarily, she shuddered inwardly.

Also, she was suspicious of Barry's relationship with Gerry, who seemed to do whatever Barry told him. Did Barry have something on Gerry?

Did Barry have something on her father? A horrifying thought.

Some other rather unpleasant speculations on Barry were drifting cheerfully through her mind when her reverie was interrupted by a tap on her shoulder and a "Hi, Susan !" It was only her cousin, Trudy, but Susan jumped and promptly spilled her drink down the front of her dress, which caused her to let out a shriek.

Which drew attention.

Barry's and Martin's faces appeared from around the patio door jamb in a way that only added to the comedy.

But Barry was perhaps less than comic: "Oh, hello Susan. We didn't know you were there . . ."

Susan gathered herself but was clearly somewhat flustered – "I was just bringing out drinks but it looks like I'll have to go back for more now" – and turned on her heels back from whence she came.

Barry turned to Martin and grinned.

Martin smiled back.

11

Barry was musing on this little incident a week later, as he paced back and forth in front of his dark oak fireplace, cigar in hand, holding forth on a range of issues that appeared to be diverse but were – each in turn – soon reduced to the common theme of the superiority of Barry's view of them: the level of influence and power wielded by Susan's father and the high degree of reliance placed by him upon Barry's own sage counsel; the state of British commerce and how Barry would fix it come the day that he was given the brief by a discerning Prime Minister of the future (probably not Jimmy . . .); etc; etc.

The rhetoric was accorded the full degree of gravity that Barry considered it was due, despite the audience on this occasion, regrettably, being limited to just Martin and Joan; the former called to the Hadley Wood mansion for Saturday dinner, the latter constrained to suffer this sort of thing more as a matter of course.

Barry had decided that it was high time that Martin be admitted to the inner sanctum of 'Rogers Towers', the mock-Gothic pile that he and Joan shared on the top of a hill girded with spruce pine and a patchy brick security wall broken in its whole circumference by just one iron gate at the front and a locked door at the back. (Barry was uncommonly fixated with security, which merely confirmed, for many, the suspicion that the company he kept was as much to be feared as cherished.)

He had issued the summons to Martin, furtively, during a lull in proceedings at the Sachs party and it was evident – somehow – that the invitation did not extend to Susan. Martin was becoming increasingly valuable to Barry's operations and Barry, in turn, was becoming increasingly intimate with Martin. For her part, Joan seemed largely content, this evening, to lounge tastefully on her Arab divan and appraise the young tyro beadily as she belted brandy after wine after gin down her maw.

For Barry, the house was one of the central planks of his prospectus to the world – along with the yacht in Antigua, the chalet in Vail and the Porsche on the drive; proof – to those who would doubt – that this was a man to be taken seriously, not for a ride. It had been built in 1965 for Giles Premander, the acclaimed film director who – along with Hitchcock – had done so much to hold up Britain's end in the overpowering Hollywood of the post-war years. Its steeply-pitched roofs, pointed arches and oriel windows bore witness to the deep impressions made upon him (consciously or otherwise) by the homes of the stars he befriended on Mulholland Drive and Bel Air Road in those heady days.

Barry had initially been dubious about buying the property, essentially because it seemed to him so unusual – rather less like the status symbols of other people in the area (by which he took his measure) and rather more like something he remembered from the Addams Family movies. But, when Joan explained that this was exactly the Spanish-style gothic favoured by the likes of Howard Hughes and Orson Welles back in the day, he was sold – although there always remained in the back of his mind the nagging suspicion that he had, in fact, allowed his vixen of a sister to trick him into buying something that would ultimately be revealed as an elaborate joke . . . played at his own expense. But that might, of course, be equally attributable to the old friend who always walked hand in hand with this new master of the house – Brother Paranoia.

For Joan, however, this place clearly suited her gloomy temperament perfectly, and, in her own mind, she was immediately installed as the tragic mistress, somewhere between the tortured sister Madeline in the House of Usher and the insane Rebecca de Winter, cruelly destroying her husband's beloved Manderley.

As he spoke, Barry might have felt the presence of the figures in the huge picture that hung over the fireplace behind him and dominated the area all around. This was the – now (in)famous – image that had originally been created more than 20 years previously, when the Rogers siblings (only ever the two of them) had been rather more outgoing and high-spirited than latterly. They had run with a fairly hectic crowd that swept incessantly across national and continental borders in an increasingly desperate attempt to maintain the initial rush of euphoria from when they had first discovered high-octane partying in their youth. It was a privileged slice of society that took the dissipation of family wealth only marginally less seriously than the parents took its preservation and Barry and Joan duly burned through a good portion of the funds built up by their stockbroker father over many years of diligent graft and careful husbandry.

Thus it came to pass, one evening, that the two of them blew into a fetish-themed party at a friend's large townhouse in Paris, 1983, clad in matching black leather outfits that exposed more flesh than they covered, accessorised with dog collars, leads and whips. At the end of a bumpy and grinding night of pouting, frisking and squealing, the pair were caught in a series of photographs that included the truly arresting image of Barry on his hands and knees, wild-eyed, sweating, snarling at the camera and straining at the leash being pulled hard on his neck by the statuesque figure of his sister towering above and behind him, legs wide apart in fishnets, nipple piercings, a biker's cap and swirling a black strap high in the air as an apparent prelude to delivering a sound thrashing to the exposed buttocks of the brother beneath her. A bizarre husky sled, pulled not by a noble canine but a coke-addled fiend taken a wrong turn somewhere on the frozen tundra.

This was the image that now hung above the sober Victorian fireplace and totally transfixed one's gaze from the moment one entered the room. When Barry first saw the photographs (some weeks after the Paris party and when he'd forgotten they'd even been taken) he was unsure of his reaction – deep down he couldn't deny a certain thrill of titillation at such a thing (with himself at its centre !) but, at the same time, he wasn't so naïve that he'd fail to recognise the possible damage that such images could do to his reputation in the serious commercial world he was just then beginning to probe.

It was only when his mentor at the time (a well-established developer helping Barry out) jokingly suggested it should be framed to intimidate his guests, that Barry started to wonder about the picture's potential for knocking people off their balance and promoting in them a healthy wonderment as to the kind of man they were dealing with. He realised that such a bold statement – along with other little plays he was also wheeling out – could contribute to the creation of a useful mythic aura about the person of Barry Rogers, the feared market raider who made his own rules. This all appealed to Barry's rampant ego.

And thus it was that he had the image blown up to fill a frame that moved with the siblings from house to house, its notoriety happily feeding their own, until it now took pride of place at the top of the hill, lording it over the sceptical neighbours in this splendid Enfield manor. Whenever the subject of the picture was brought up, Joan would simply smirk inscrutably, glad that the picture at least admitted an element of ambiguity into the question of who was the true master of this confused household.

She was not looking at it now but across at the winsome features of their young guest. Martin was sat back from the hearth, on the left, gazing up at the preening speaker, either rapt in attention or miles away – it was difficult to tell.

"He's spoilt that girl, I'm telling you now." Barry was extemporising on the subject of the younger Sachs daughter. Joan groaned and took another gulp of her brandy.

"No, no, Joan – I've told you: she's simply spoilt." Barry stabbed the cigar in his right hand in the direction of his sister. Joan simply rolled her eyes as if to say, 'Here we go again'.

"She's always had anything she wanted. Anything. And she goes around with her nose stuck in the air as though she's better than anyone else. Not grateful at all. Turns down every marriage proposal that comes her way, like none of them are good enough."

"Including Bertie," drawled Joan, sardonically.

"Yes, including Bertie," Barry spat back, emphatically.

"And what's wrong with Bertie?! Father's a multi-millionaire. Good family. Gone to the best schools. A smashing lad."

"And look what she did to him," Joan could be heard to mutter under her breath, if your hearing was good enough. Martin turned his head to look at her just as Barry intoned: "And look what she did to him." Martin's and Joan's eyes met.

It was 10 o'clock now and the room was only dimly lit by candelabras on the walls and pedestal tables holding *actual candles* (another Joan touch). The reflection of one of the flames could be seen flickering in each of Joan's dark irises.

"Poor Bertie," Barry was pressing on – oblivious – with the story of Susan Sachs' humiliation of Bertie Sanchez; a story that clearly still rankled with Barry, representing – as it had – a serious setback in the grand plan for his personal entrenchment in the upper echelons of London society.

Bertie Sanchez was the only child of Daniel and Abril, who – having cashed in massive landholdings in their native Argentina to migrate to these shores – had spent the last 15 years buying their way into the connections and affections that bound together the moneyed classes of their adopted country. Barry had, somehow, got his claws into the pair when they were still finding their feet and managed to cling on – tenaciously – ever since, despite the warnings given them from many, more reputable, quarters as to the fitness of the Rogers' provenance.

Straight after the completion of his degree, Bertie was brought into 'Uncle' Barry's firm for some expert tuition in how to invest/spend other people's money (including Daniel's) and, in time, Barry rather came to view young Bertie as the son he'd never had. Of course, Barry's friendship with the Rt. Hon. James Sachs had played its part in maintaining his grip on the Sanchez imagination and, when Bertie and Susan began spending time together, he immediately spotted a stupendous opportunity to cement his own position as the vital link between the two grand families.

All had gone perfectly well right up to the point where Bertie, rather boldly (and rather disastrously, in fact), chose to pop the question to Susan without warning in front of a roomful of friends and family one fateful Christmas Eve. Susan – not unnaturally – was struck rigid by the suddenness and horror of the situation; slapped down the plaintive Bertie with a look that shrivelled his nerve; and stormed out, leaving the assembled throng aghast but warm with the glow of schadenfreude and a terrific story to tell.

That episode was nearly enough to sever the ties that bound Jimmy and Barry; but only nearly, as they both, ultimately, knew the value that the other brought to their 'arrangements'. Nevertheless, Barry never quite forgave Susan for the humiliation and the mere mention of her name in his presence invariably triggered an observable narrowing of the eyes.

"I know you're friendly with her, Martin," he droned on, "but I'm telling you now: be very wary of that young lady. And I don't care if she's Jimmy's daughter or not. She's still a little bitch".

"Barry !" Joan barked at her brother with unmistakeable outrage.

Barry had managed to get himself rather worked up and now, realising he may have overstepped the mark, put his hands up with a (slightly grudging) 'Sorry . . .' to Joan and, then, Martin. Joan glanced across to see Martin receive the apology without any sign of intent appearing in his demeanour, whether to be gracious or to glower. And she wondered.

"Martin can come and keep me company while I have a smoke," Joan announced and promptly swung her elegant legs down from the divan to stand upright, brandy glass still clamped in hand. She looked the full Vampira tonight, complete with the figure-hugging black velvet dress, heavy kohl makeup and the trademark fringe that suggested both innocence and villainy. This prompted more narrowing of Barry's beady eyes but she glided across to Martin, nevertheless – hand outstretched and determined to grab some time alone with the boy, regardless of her brother's feelings. Like a gentleman, Martin got to his feet to take

Joan's hand, nodded to the sullen-faced Barry and trotted after the mistress.

Out of the room they walked through a short corridor that opened into what appeared to be a large conservatory. Martin looked up to see the night sky through the glass ceiling above them, the silhouetted tendrils of unidentifiable vegetation reaching up, imploringly, to the moonlit panes. They might have been triffids for all Martin knew. They looked like triffids.

The air in the glasshouse was noticeably more humid, clearly to suit the displaced fauna planted within it. They hadn't taken many steps along the stone path that cut through the jungle before Martin could feel the sweat rise out of his skin and trickle down the back of his neck. Joan momentarily looked back to check that he was still following her lead in the gloom and, just for a second, the iridescent moonlight that flashed across her showed the wet beads that were forming on her white cheek too.

Soon enough they reached the other end and Joan eased Martin through a high glass door onto a crunchy pebble path at the edge of the garden outside. Even though it was, in fact, a warm summer evening the contrast of the fresh air from the wet warmth they had just left made it feel cooler and a slight breeze accentuated the effect.

The path led round to the back of the house, which looked out over the garden to the city below and Joan sat them both on a curved wooden bench positioned to make the most of the view. The moon was bright tonight, rendering the scene ethereal and rare, the silver rays catching the edges of walls and the canopies of trees so that they glistened like snow. Even the centre of the metropolis, though a good distance away, could be glimpsed faintly as a filmy presence brooding on the edge of the horizon.

Joan said nothing as she lit a Dunhill pulled from the red pack in her clutch and remained silent as she blew the wafts of smoke heavenward.

Finally, she said what was on her mind – "He likes you . . . you know that?" Joan looked slyly at Martin from the corner of her eye to gauge the younger man's reaction. There was none but, after a moment, he turned to look at her with an odd look that didn't seem entirely friendly.

"How do you mean, Joan?" He was staring straight into the older woman's eyes and she detected a hardness in his gaze that she hadn't expected and made her wince inwardly.

"You know . . ." Another drag on her fag as she searched for the right words.

"Well . . . you're a nice boy, aren't you, Martin?" The words hung in the air.

Martin smiled. "You're nice too, Joan."

She thought she saw his shoulders relax.

"And so is Barry."

Joan blew more smoke out in front of her and narrowed her eyes to try and see through the cloud.

"Sometimes he is."

Martin raised his eyebrows and, with a somewhat laconic expression: "Not always .. ?"

Joan turned down the corners of her mouth and returned the sarcasm with a stare – "I don't suppose any of us could be nice all the time, could we?"

She thought she saw a chuckle sparked, then smothered.

After a further pause, she continued.

"My brother – for whatever reason – needs to be on top, Martin. To dominate."

Martin said nothing.

"Sat in this place, he thinks he's Citizen Kane," she laughed, drily, "and dreams of Xanadu."

"So, there's a Rosebud?"

Joan seemed miles away before she replied, "You fucking betcha."

She waited for a supplemental question but none came.

"Look, Martin – I know that everyone views me and Barry as odd. That a brother and sister could live together – stay together – as we have but I don't give a fuck, OK? No-one knows what is what in other people's lives and the truth isn't always so clear. You know what I mean?"

Joan seemed to want an answer to this and Martin replied straight off: "Yes, I do, Joan."

"I've had a strange life and I rather think you have too," Joan's gaze ran over Martin's lovely face as she spoke. "You know it's not easy when you're trapped; properly trapped. When you know there's no escape."

Joan stubbed the cigarette butt on a stone flag, turned to face Martin again, close, and he could discern the slightest signs of tremor under the skin around her eyes and mouth.

"I want to tell you that you don't want to pass up all the chances you get, Martin. There may come a day when you wish you had another. Take it from someone who knows."

She didn't cry but bit her lip and a single tear snaked down her smiling face. She let her head drop onto Martin's shoulder and he put his arm around her, to comfort her. She felt slight, bony. Like a child.

"You know, not a lot of people realise that Barry and I are, actually, twins."

12.

Martin Dash is sitting on the standard issue executive chair in his office on the sixth floor of Stone Rose's building. It's black faux leather upholstery and chrome tubing and it tips back, encouraging you to swivel around and gaze through the window behind you at the city outside – as Martin is doing now.

He looks as though he's contemplating something. 'Or is he just gazing vacantly?' thought Susan as she, in turn, gazed across at Martin. She was standing at the printer in the central area of the floor, amongst the secretaries, waiting for a contract to spew out to take to discuss with Martin. 'But, if he is thinking, what is he thinking about?'

Maybe the new development he was doing with Barry. Since the successful conclusion of the Crack Harbour deal a year ago Barry had gone from strength to strength, apparently bucking the wider property market that was now showing distinct signs of a major slowdown, if not slump. Property traders were now looking to sell their assets and Barry was only too happy to oblige in buying them.

Bad news had been filtering across from the US for several months now. New Century Financial, which specialised in sub-prime mortgages, had filed for Chapter 11 Bankruptcy in April; last month (July) investment bank Bear Stearns had told investors they would get little, if any, of the money invested in two of its hedge funds after rival banks refused to help bail them out; and, on this side of the Atlantic, French bank BNP Paribas had, just yesterday, issued the news that money could not be withdrawn from two of its own funds because it couldn't value the assets in them, owing to 'a complete evaporation of liquidity in the market' – a clear sign that the contagion of credit crunch was now beginning to sweep across the whole world's financial markets.

In this event, asset values were dropping – like a stone – and the billion dollar question, as always, was how low would they go? The counter–cyclical kings of such a situation would always be those who were not highly indebted, i.e. cash rich, and therefore in a position to buy the assets everyone else was unloading at historically low prices. The trick was to know when the floor had been reached, when there would be no further falls.

Many were intoning dreadful warnings that values could ultimately halve. The markets were nowhere near that yet, but if that was believed to be an accurate prediction of what was to come, the smart move was to hold tight and wait before buying, to get the assets at an even cheaper price in due course. But Barry was buying now, which meant either that he knew something the doom-mongers didn't (that the prices would not fall much further) or that he had sufficient funds to not have to care, so that, even if values fell further, he could afford to wait while the properties he was buying now bounced back in value in due course, as history told they always did.

But where was his money coming from? This was a question that exercised some in the higher echelons of the Stone Rose partnership. But others were happy to simply bank the stupendous fees being generated and rely on Gerry Bild's firm assurances that all was above board and that Barry and Joan Rogers' success was simply the result of bold tactics, shrewd negotiation and clinical planning.

Maybe Martin was thinking about his imminent promotion to partner. For Martin also was riding high on the back of Barry's prodigious deal-making. Martin had been at Stone Rose for just over a year now and had not let the grass grow under his feet. His astonishing work rate (he seemed to do nothing but work), clinical mind, and charming persona kept him much in demand. Other partners had tried to get him involved with their clients – believing he was absolutely the right man to nurse their projects – and he did undertake a range of work for various banks, investors and developers across the firm but the majority of his time was taken up with Grudge Holdings and the rest of Barry and Joan's expanding empire.

Gerry Bild had been the partner designated to care for this particular client for many years – and all agreed that he'd done an exceptional job (although eyebrows were sometimes raised at the extent to which Gerry appeared willing to do Barry's bidding) – but Martin seemed to have taken the job to another level entirely. Barry appeared to have reached a point where he relied on Martin's expertise and opinion above all others, including Joan. It seemed that Barry had become enthralled at the idea of having such an unusual counsellor at his side; the sheer out-there combination of Martin's drop-dead looks, weapons-grade efficiency, and exotic illness appealed to the fetishistic Barry enormously. In his childlike outlook, it felt like he was now living in some sort of twisted Bond film, with burgeoning success and a beautiful Oddjob at his side, cutting down his enemies for him.

In turn, Martin seemed to exercise increasing influence over Barry and, to some, it appeared that it was he who was guiding (almost goading...) Barry into ever bolder deals. In an audacious move in the spring, Martin had connived to bring Barry together with one of the firm's other stellar movers-and-shakers (the London Head of Crédit Banque de Paris) over a golfing weekend in Portugal to put together a mammoth deal for the sale to Grudge of a portfolio of assets that really announced this brash upstart company to the wider investment community as – potentially – a proper, mainstream player.

All of this was making Martin something of a hero at Stone Rose. In the last 14 months, he had billed close to one million pounds in fees on the Grudge account and other jobs – much to the delight of the partners who would be sharing those fees. So there were some who were saying that it was only fair that his efforts should be recognised, that he should be allowed the due rewards, and (perhaps more pertinently) that he should be made to feel wanted enough to ignore the blandishments of rival firms eager to poach such a talent for themselves.

Thus, a recent vote on partnership promotions was almost unanimous for Martin.

Almost, but not completely, unanimous. For there were still those for whom there would always be something not quite right about Martin. Andrew Weiss, the head of the firm's litigation practice, had said, right from the outset (and had stuck with this refrain), that if it seems too good to be true, then it *is* too good to be true. The idea of a commercial lawyer who literally had no feelings, no emotions to distract him from the ruthless pursuit of his quarry (like a robot, almost) was simply taking the stereotype that bit too far in his incredulous opinion and, although there were some who said that this was a bit rich coming from a litigator and wondered whether such a pious view might not derive from the rather less worthy source of professional envy, Weiss remained the focal point around which coalesced the curmudgeonly rump of Dash-sceptics in the firm and this included those who found Martin – frankly – creepy.

For some, the more they thought about what his condition actually meant, the more uneasy they became when they realised that, when he laughed, he was faking it; when he expressed concern, he must be faking that; and when he was chatting amiably to them, he can't have been the slightest bit interested in them. These views, where they did exist, tended to reside more amongst those not managing the firm – the secretaries, support staff and junior lawyers – where the distraction of his money-earning potential didn't tend to skew their viewpoint; and, for those who subscribed to them, the very fact of Martin's being became more – not less – offensive, the longer he was with them. A number of them had rather expected him to 'get better' somehow – or perhaps that they would at least get used to him – but he remained the same, always, which tended to puncture the argument of the minority within the minority (who suggested that he was actually a double-fake, that he had no such illness) as the feeling generally was that it wouldn't be possible to keep up such a façade indefinitely and, in any event, why on earth would anyone do that?

Vanessa Carr was one of the few who couldn't quite make her mind up. From the outset, she had – in her habitual manner – not been inclined to simply take the thing at face value and something was telling her that there was probably more to the phenomenon than met the eye.

But the Weiss contingent were in the small minority and Martin's promotion, due to take effect on the 1st of next month, September, was waved through by the overwhelming majority, the prevailing view being: 'What's not to like about a young man who dedicates his life to his work, is sober, un-entangled and earns monstrous fees for the partnership? Trebles all round, for goodness sake !'

Or maybe Martin was thinking about Susan? Not very likely, she thought, disconsolately . . . but, then again, who knew?

She had spent a lot of time with Martin during his first year at Stone Rose, mostly at the office, but with the occasional foray into the recreational. The problem, as she had slowly learned, was that Martin genuinely appeared to have no interest whatsoever in (a) music, (b) films, (c) dancing, (d) romance, (e) sex, or (f) any merriment of any kind.

She knew that she had, of course, been told this at the outset but, like some of the others, she had – against all reason – felt that he would somehow get better. Or, again vaguely, that she would somehow get used to it. But no, he remained the same baffling enigma now that he was 14 months ago. She found that, when they were alone (i.e. when she had contrived for them to be alone), the conversation trailed off to nothing quite quickly but that he could keep it up almost indefinitely when he had to (e.g. with clients that had to be charmed or at office functions he couldn't avoid) and the awareness of how little it was done when there was not the need made her realise how much of an effort that was.

Thus, he would watch the television, or listen to the radio, but only really the news or documentaries or the like, all of which appeared solely a means to ensure that he was kept up with events, government policies and social trends that he might need to be aware of in his work, or in discussions with clients. That much and only that much – if the conversation strayed into films that people had watched or music that they liked, he was all at sea and would generally resort at that point to simply nodding and smiling, like a tourist not conversant with the lingo.

But he didn't seem to mind having her around. She would occasionally invite herself over to his flat of an evening – they would eat a meal; watch something on the TV; and she might mooch about reading a magazine while Martin did bits of housework – basically saying nothing.

And she had become quite used to this and, indeed, still came round for more. For, as she watched him cooking a bolognese, ordering his laundry, catching up on some work, the questions kept coming and she would, in fact, raise them with him quite openly: why wasn't he seeking treatment? (A: he'd tried it but there had been no effect and, anyway, he'd always been like this, it was normal to him, so why would he want to change?); why, if he had no desire, did he appear to be ambitious given that he was so successful at work? (A: he'd just turned out to be good at what he did and simply went with the flow); and so on and so forth. She could not square the thing in her mind. There was a nagging voice telling her there was more to be found and that he was worth it.

Of course, it was the ultimate in playing hard to get and, if it was a ploy, it was working a treat on Susan. Despite the obvious shortcomings in conversation, in passion, in *fun*, she found that she was drawn to him. And, of course, he was gorgeous and she was the envy of every woman in the room if they thought he was with her. And, after all, he didn't behave like an arsehole and talk crap like the vast majority of men she routinely encountered.

And didn't two-time her.

Not that there was anything to be duplicitous about. She had twice tried to lunge Martin over the course of the year. Once, by way of the mandatory Christmas Party toe-curler, when her alcohol intake accidentally prejudiced her ability to accurately judge the maximum intake level for retaining her – normally sound – judgement (perhaps this was another feature of her father's personality she had inherited?). In a rush of gay abandon, she had flung her arms around his neck when they had gone up to her office to find her keys and planted a vodka-tinged smacker on his bashful lips.

This elicited no response whatsoever – maybe he had spotted the signs of danger ahead and was ready for the lunge as his only reaction was to take her by the shoulders, smile and say (somewhat patronisingly, she thought): "I think we're all rather tired and ready for home, aren't we?" which had provoked her into a foul-mouthed tirade which, whilst satisfying at the time, never failed subsequently to trigger a warmness in her cheeks whenever the thought of it popped up in her mind: "I'm not fucking tired ! The only thing I'm fucking tired of is fucking you; well not fucking you, actually" – meaningful look, still no response, carry on – "Not fucking getting anything back from fucking you; who the fuck are you anyway?! Who the fuck am I, while we're at it?! I'm fucking . . ." At this point she tripped over her waste basket and slid gracefully onto a pile of files, her further considered observations upon the state of the relationship trailing off somewhat.

The second occasion had been a rather more considered affair at his flat one evening when she convinced herself that she was actually making some headway in trying to reach the personality hiding in Martin Dash.

She was cautiously interrogating him about his childhood and, for some reason that evening, he appeared to be rather more engaged than usual and had offered up a couple of remarks that hinted at a real relationship with his mother, at least.

"So, did you not feel anything for your mother?"

Just for a moment, he seemed to stop, to check himself, and Susan thought she saw a shadow pass in his eyes, that caught his attention.

"Martin, I'm not sure if I'm doing right but I want to help you. Something tells me that you won't always be the same as you are now; that there are feelings in there, waiting to be released, and I'd love to be there when it happens. Because . . . because, I do love you, Martin."

She was by now standing right in front of him and still watching those blue eyes, looking for signs. She brought her arms up around his back and gently placed her lips on his. She thought she could feel his hands rising to her hips, see his eyes flick to lock onto her eyes, his head incline forward and his mouth slide against hers. She felt herself wavering on the edge of a black chasm, suddenly nothing solid under her feet, as if in a dream.

And then realising that Martin was not moving.

She had closed her eyes but now opened them again to find that Martin's eyes were now cast down and she felt him move imperceptibly backwards. Whatever had happened had now past and Martin was back to his usual self, albeit a little sheepish perhaps, which Susan found interesting – but only in hindsight, for now she was crushed and felt like crying.

'Disappointed' didn't even come close to describing her state. 'Why?' she thought. 'Why does this have to happen to me?' Martin was actually the nicest, kindest, most beautiful man she had ever met and had all the apparent attributes to be The One. Susan had had plenty of offers – a stylish, attractive, smart young woman with some serious family connections: you can bet she'd had some offers. But she had always rebelled against the too obvious ploy of marrying the well-heeled investment banker, or one of the thrusting political tyros who courted her father, or even the famous actor who had actually *proposed* to her at one of the Hampstead parties.

Maybe she had been watching too much Bette Davis – as the irrational, obsessed tragedienne – but she was holding out for something she wasn't even sure existed, to the increasing concern of her mother, who had now sunk to trapping Susan in social set-ups with *her* idea of eligible types.

And she was holding out for what? For a robot who couldn't even bring himself to kiss her? What sort of a bet was that?! Way to go, Susie !!

So she had stomped out, phoned Bertie Sanchez (who was always to hand) and given him a surprise that forced him to re-evaluate his previously cast-iron conviction as to the nullity of a benign deity.

And felt dirty in the morning.

And guilty – which was ridiculous, considering she wasn't even Martin's girlfriend, was she? Well, anyway, she put the episode behind her, gave the glass eye to the increasingly desperate imprecations of the miserable Bertie (who, before long, came back to his original creed – or at least feeling – that, if there was a god, he must be the cock-teasing, spiteful kind of divinity), and resumed her thankless, patient stakeout of the inscrutable Mr. Dash.

"Is this a stakeout, Susan?" Maisie whispered in her ear as she brushed past Susan on her way to Martin's room. Susan jumped and realised that she'd been lost in her reverie, gazing at the back of Martin's head, her document long since printed out and awaiting her attention.

Susan was slightly piqued at having been caught Martin-gazing by Maisie but couldn't suppress a wry smile as Maisie turned to smirk at her before pushing open his door. Although the two of them appeared, on the surface, to be in conflict over Martin's 'affections', it was a phony war as Maisie had long since realised that she was wasting her energies in the pursuit of 'the Monk' (as she had taken to calling him, behind his back) even if Susan didn't have the good sense to admit defeat and an easy accommodation had been reached: Maisie, as Martin's secretary and the class Tart with A Heart, would be permitted to flirt with and tease Martin so long as it was understood that Susan, his ablest team member and all round Good Egg, had the prior, exclusive rights should the miracle of Martin's emancipation ever come to pass.

Susan liked Maisie, and even admired the ruthless way she manipulated her hapless beaux for her own single-minded ends. And she had a neat line in pricking Mr. Dash's bubble, which was always entertaining to behold.

As she brought the contract into his room, Susan found Martin trying to defend himself against Maisie's barbed comments regarding his new circumstances – Martin's upcoming promotion had already been announced and he was, this weekend, due to move into a swanky new flat in Kensington. It really did appear that he was on the up.

"I suppose you'll be wanting a new secretary once you're a partner, Mr. Dash; one that's more serious ... and efficient." She sighed as she piled files back into a cabinet.

"Why would I want to lose you, M?" Martin intoned with a smile but not looking up and carrying on with his work as though he knew his part well in this well-trodden pantomime.

"Exactly. Why would you do that when I'm out there covering your back all the hours God sends; making you tea; seeing to your every need," she fixed him with a stare. Susan couldn't help but laugh – Maisie had a fine line in arch ribaldry.

"Go on Maisie, give it to him. Show no mercy !"

"Don't worry, I won't."

"Good grief, what have I done to deserve this?" protested Martin, now looking up and slatting his pen down in mock anger.

"Oh, I don't know – getting above yourself; buying swanky new apartments; treating your secretary like a rubbing rag," Maisie listed off his sins.

"I'm not getting above myself and I'm not buying the apartment, just renting it," he protested.

She waited. "But the secretary mistreatment – you admit that?!"

"Is the new place sorted yet then?" enquired Susan.

"Yes, I'm getting the keys tomorrow, so I reckon I'll do the move then."

"What, just like that? No van or anything?" quizzed Maisie.

"You're joking, M," said Susan. "Everything he's got will go in the back of his car, won't it, Martin?"

Martin just shrugged his shoulders.

"You travel light, don't you, Darling?" Susan ruffled his hair indulgently. It was so soft. Maisie looked on.

"Well, do you need a hand? I could come and help you?" Susan offered.

Martin sat up and thought. "Well, yes, that would be useful actually. Thanks."

"*Useful* . . ." Maisie shook her head in despair.

"I've got to meet the agent at the apartment at 10:00 tomorrow morning, sign some papers; he's going to give me the keys; then I'd planned on getting the Tube back up to mine, fill the car and drive it back down."

"OK, I'll meet you at the apartment then. What's the address?"

"Fatima Mansions on Valhalla Avenue, Flat 3."

13.

It had been raining earlier but those heavy, black clouds had exited the stage now to be replaced with smaller, fluffier, whiter cousins, drifting along in clumps rather than gangs, so the sun was now coming out periodically to blaze away and shrink the damp circles on the pavement below. Susan was looking down onto the street through the window of Martin's new flat. She felt excited for him. The place was lovely, with big rooms, pale wood floors, all modern furniture provided – everything new – and, as Martin stood behind her with the agent at the breakfast bar, signing papers, taking the keys, shaking hands, she let herself imagine for a moment that they were a normal couple, starting out on a new adventure, getting their first place together, planning for the future. As she turned back from the window, he glanced up and they both smiled, the agent smiled – another satisfied customer, another commission cheque in the bank – and took his leave.

"What do you think?" asked Martin, when the agent had left.

"It's lovely" she said, swivelling her gaze around the room. "How did you find it? Must be expensive."

"No, it's not too bad – you'd be surprised. The rents on these sorts of places are coming down now."

"Yes, everything's coming down, isn't it – what do you think's going to happen?"

"Who knows."

"Well, you can't be blasé about it Martin, we could end up out of our jobs. Well, some of us – I imagine the partners will look after each other" – a sly little dig, which Martin laughed off.

"No, but seriously, do you think it'll be as bad as they're saying?"

"Oh, it'll go down. Then back up again. Then back down – that's how it works. You've just got to keep ducking and diving."

"Is that what you do? – duck and dive?" Susan was in a teasing mood, but playful.

"Yeah, float like a butterfly."

"And sting like a bee . . ."

"Right, that's it – enough badinage," he laughed. "Let's go and get my stuff."

"The closest Tube is High Street Ken isn't it?"

"Yeah, we can change at Monument to get on the Northern Line up to Angel."

14

As they sat on the bench on the eastbound platform at High Street Kensington Underground Station, they chatted while they waited for their next train. Martin was telling Susan of Barry's antics in a recent meeting with the planners on his new development in Richmond and, once again, Susan marvelled at how well Martin dealt with his condition, really. The more she had looked into it online, the more she had noticed that Martin was an unusual case study.

The condition was usually described as a clinical symptom in depression with most sufferers having an incredibly flat mood and major difficulties with motivation and yet here was Martin blossoming in a great job, finding his way in the big city, collecting the keys to a fine new apartment

'And chatting happily to his beautiful girlfriend,' a mischievous little voice piped up in her head, which made her smirk to herself.

"What are you smiling at?" Martin had noticed and interrupted his story.

"Oh nothing – carry on."

"OK, well . . ." Martin carried on and Susan glanced around the scene as she listened.

The sun was really out now with a vengeance declared against the black rain that had been sent scurrying to the hills in defeat. This part of the station was overground and its customers were now being warmed by the bright radiance of the morning rays.

Susan preferred these parts of the Tube to the dark caves of the rest of the network. Many of the overground stations were built over a hundred years before and the original styling was often still intact so that, as Susan sat looking up towards the ticket office and exit – watching the travellers scurrying through the ticket hall and the flower seller standing with his red carnations, pink chrysanthemums, and yellow and white daffodils against the ochre bricks of the station wall – she could trace the black ironwork of the railing panels ascending up the steps; the shaped curlicues decorating the canopy edges overhanging the platforms; and the bright red and green painted doors and windows of the ticket office and toilets. The scene might have been transplanted from a hundred years before at the inception of the mighty network that now criss-crossed the sprawling metropolis, with travellers in bowler hats and tight buttoned-up suits, swaying pleated skirts and jaunty bonnets.

Then Susan became aware that Martin had stopped talking very suddenly and, now looking at his face, she saw something she had never seen in Martin during the whole 14 months she had known him: an emotion. And the emotion was fear, pure and simple.

He had stopped talking, mid-sentence, and his entire frame had frozen rigid. Plain to see in his features and demeanour was a frantic battle for supremacy between hyper-alert animal instinct and terrorised blind panic. But it was his eyes that told you what was going on. They had clearly locked onto something that had shocked him to the core and was now absolutely monopolising his attention and holding him like a starship tractor beam pulsing fear data into him and drawing the life force back out of him.

Susan swung her head to follow the line of his sight and immediately she saw that it was fixed on a man sat on a platform bench directly opposite them, on the other side of the tracks. This man was staring directly at Martin with a look that could equally be for an enemy as for a friend.

He appeared to be a similar age to Martin, with curly sandy hair; freckles carried over from his youth; eyes that simultaneously threatened and implored and a mouth that looked lively but was now very still. He looked to be a good height and naturally slim but was by now clearly working on the beginning of a paunch that was only going one way. His outfit comprised a rather loud brown and green check sports jacket, tangerine shirt, dark blue chinos and camel loafers.

In short: 'Dodgy', thought Susan.

From the look of horror on Martin's face, you would have imagined that we were looking upon a cat with a bird pinned under its claws but there wasn't that degree of dominance in the gaze that was cast upon Martin – he was staring without inhibition but also without a fixity of purpose. In short, Martin could have been afraid as much of what the guy represented as of who he was.

But it was the fact that Martin appeared afraid at all that was unnerving Susan rather than the threat that 'Dodgy' might actually represent.

"Martin, what is it?" she asked. He didn't appear to hear her.

"Who is that man?" she hissed, trying not to motion in his direction.

Her words now pulled Martin's face round to look at her and, as he did so, a realisation broke his trance that Susan had seen him in that state and was now questioning him. He had trouble both sides. Susan watched this pass across his features and now their eyes locked. That decadent face never looked so beautiful as it did now, thought Susan.

He knew what she was asking him.

But he couldn't answer.

He dropped his eyes and then his head lowered and she knew that something had happened.

Martin angled his face back to look across to the opposite platform again to see that the onlooker had swivelled his gaze to Susan and a none-too-innocent smirk now played around his mouth, which Susan caught too.

The two men then did something so totally in unison, it might have been choreographed. Further down each platform (to Martin's right and the onlooker's left) a wide flight of steps led from each platform up to the gantry concourse that ran at right angles to, and overlooked, the tracks below. These provided the access between the platforms and the ticket hall and station exit beyond and, therefore, the means of access to get from one platform to another. The two men looked simultaneously to the set of steps from their own platform and, again simultaneously, back to each other.

"I've got to go," croaked Martin in a voice that, again, seemed changed to Susan. Just as Martin grabbed his bag and stood up from his bench, she saw the same motion on the opposite platform and both men started for their steps in an increasingly hurried fashion.

Susan's head involuntarily jerked backwards and she mouthed a 'What?!' without actually saying it. As she had a grandstand view of the two men running up their respective set of steps, a certain inertia disinclined her to follow on, at least immediately. She had perhaps imagined that, from her vantage point, she would have the best view of the two of them meeting but hadn't accounted for the fact that the parapet of the gantry directly above the train tracks between the two platforms was actually rather high – no doubt to frustrate the foolhardy and the depressed alike – so that, from where her bench was located (not far from the steps), she couldn't actually see up and over it to where the two men would have met after they had scaled their respective steps. If they had, in fact, met ... what if one had chased the other out through the exit (and, if so, who would have been doing the running away .. ?)

So she lost them – at least she lost sight of them – but she was able to *hear* one thing: just a second after they both turned out of view at the top of the steps she heard Martin's voice – again, strangely animated – shout "Michael !"

She realised all of a sudden that she ought to get up to that concourse and so grabbed her bag and set off. This was the third person the other travellers had seen jump from a seat and career up the steps in dramatic fashion and so, given the less-than-gratifying experience of some underground users reported by the slavering media over the years (preyed upon by terrorism, fire and faulty switchwork), a number were now looking nervously around and up and down like meerkats at a speedway, wondering whether they should be doing the same.

At the top of the steps she looked this way and that but there was no sign of either man. Out through the barrier onto the bustling street ... but they had gone.

Her bearings were lost but a feeling was acquired of things now never being the same again.

15

But, come the Monday morning, it was just the same again, or at least appeared to be so. She had tried to catch up with Martin over the weekend but to no avail. Straight away after the Tube station incident, she had tried his mobile but it went straight to voicemail. So she tried completing the journey they'd been on when they were so dramatically separated, back onto the Tube up to the Angel and stood ringing the bell on the door of his house.

This was a Georgian townhouse split into three flats – basement, ground floor and upper – with a common hallway behind the street door to the entrances to all three and Martin occupied the middle of these, with a lounge window that looked out onto the street but also had net curtains to frustrate those outside who wished to have sight of those inside.

So she rang the bells for the other two flats. No answer from upstairs but a Dalek voice answered the basement bell with a curt "Hello?" It was Sean, one half of a gay couple that Susan had met once or twice when passing in and out of Martin's flat. She apologised profusely and explained that she was concerned about their upstairs neighbour but she realised fairly quickly that she would be getting no help from that quarter: hardened city-dwellers like Sean and Ray knew better than to open the door to the first person ringing the bell after a domestic row.

On the Sunday, having – again – got no response on the phone, she had gone back to the Kensington apartment but, once more, no-one was home.

So, come the Monday morning, she was all fired up and ready to give it to Martin with both barrels. How dare he abandon her like that? Why didn't he answer her calls? Who the hell was that guy?

But she was temporarily denied. When she arrived at the office, Martin was already in a meeting 'upstairs' that lasted through till 11 o'clock, by which time she'd been required to go to the City to see a new client Vanessa had pushed her way. And when she returned late in the afternoon, Martin had apparently gone off somewhere with Gerry and was not expected back.

Finally, she got a text from Martin later that evening: "Sorry about the weekend, Susan. I'm still with Gerry at the moment and out in the morning but let's go for lunch and I'll explain?"

Susan texted back: "You'd better !"

16

The next day, Martin and Susan sat together at a table near the back of The Range, a bistro recently opened around the corner from the office, with pink flamingos painted on jungle green walls, serving light bites to the stressed execs of the surrounding reserve.

Susan was looking for clues on her immutable quarry, signs that the Tube incident might have left its mark on the smooth sheen of the Dash countenance. The passage of a day at work had served to calm her somewhat – if she'd have got hold of Martin during the Monday, there would have been more of the bad cop to his grilling than the slightly more forgiving interrogator that now sat before him. Now, her injured pride at being cast aside in such a manner had begun to give way to an overwhelming curiosity to find out (a) who it was that had spooked him and (b) how come he could feel so spooked anyway?

She scrutinised him. On the face of it, things appeared as normal with Martin – he had been his usual gentlemanly self when they met at the restaurant, kissed her on the cheek and squeezed her hand – but she sensed that, underneath the façade, something had changed in him and she was trying to calculate the best strategy for teasing the truth out of him.

Interestingly, he was also not wearing his work suit: still smart – russet brown jacket, cream shirt, pale blue jeans and pebble-grain leather Derby shoes – but more the outfit of a successful Hollywood film producer than a top-draw City lawyer. But she decided to get to that later. First there was the immediate business.

"So who – or what – is Michael?" Straight in, feet first.

Martin looked momentarily startled.

"I heard you shout his name."

Susan could see him casting his mind back to the Tube station. To re-check his story. And then –

"Michael Green."

"Michael Green?"

"Michael Green."

"And who is Michael Green?"

"He's someone I knew from years ago."

"A friend?"

An involuntary laugh escaped from him. Again, very un-Martin-like. Then he deadpanned: "No, not a friend; more of a . . . stalker really."

"A stalker?!" Susan was wide-eyed. "He stalked you?"

"Yes, I got a court order against him eventually."

"Wha . . . where was this?"

"In Lewes, a couple of years after my parents died."

"Oh Martin, you poor thing," Susan thought of him all alone at 18, having his parents die on him and then having to go through that; her heart melted and she reached over to take his hand. Martin smiled a wan smile.

"But stalking? Why?" and then she started to think of what he was talking about. "You mean he . . ?"

"He was after me, basically. He was a bit of a thug – worse than that, in fact; came from a real criminal family, they were well known in the area. And it turned out he was a homosexual and he propositioned me."

Susan was agog but managed to say: "And you turned him down?"

"Yes . . ." Martin gave her a quizzical look which made Susan realise what she'd asked. But she just shrugged.

123

He returned to the story: "Anyway, that's when the trouble started. He didn't take kindly to it. Started coming round my house at nights, harassing me, chucking bricks through the windows. Said he was going to kill me. Burn the house down."

"Unbelievable !"

"Well, the police did get involved eventually. Warned him off and arrested him a couple of times and, finally, I got the court order which is basically indefinite and says he must never be within 500 metres of me."

"Is that why he ran when he saw you?"

Martin huffed, "I'm not sure he's that bothered about it – he breached it once or twice before, nearly went to jail. And I'm not sure he was running to get away at the Tube."

"You mean he was coming to get you?" Susan was horrified at the thought. And then she puzzled a bit more – "Well, what were you doing, Martin? Running away? Because I heard you shout after him."

"I don't quite know what I was doing. I think partly I was trying to get him away from you . . . to protect you."

Martin was now looking straight at Susan but, not for the first time, she was left wondering what the hell was going on behind those eyes.

"Martin, I saw your face when you first spotted that guy and you looked . . . terrified. I've never seen you display such . . . emotion before." The word was loaded.

"Just because I am how I am, doesn't mean I can't be concerned about things. To be motivated to act !"

"Really?"

"Yes . . . it's more of a . . . heightened concern really."

"For me?"

"Well, yes, you're my...friend." He was now even beginning to appear somewhat indignant – this was getting interesting.

"So, what happened when you got to the top of those steps?"

"He'd moved quicker than me and was disappearing out of the exit when I saw him."

"And you were calling after him. What were you going to say to him?"

"I don't know. I think both of us may have changed our minds half way up the steps – he was coming after me and then decided to run and I was running away and then decided to go after him."

"Well, how did it end up in Lewes – I mean, did he stop the harassment or what?"

"I left. I had nothing keeping me there really and I was always looking round every corner to see if Michael was there. It was intolerable. I left."

"But now he's here. Did you know he's in London?"

"I had no idea, no. That's why I looked so . . . surprised when I saw him."

"I'll bet."

Susan surveyed this strange person before her and considered the 'facts'. He looks like a latter day James Dean but prettier. He has an illness than deprives him of the fundamental traits that make a human, apparently. He takes on the sharpest, roughest commercial lawyers in the capital and runs rings round them. He comes with no family or back story whatsoever, except bullshit. And now he produces some evil sex predator who can make him sprint out of a crowded Tube station just by looking at him, or the other way round . . .

Martin must have been reading Susan's mind.

"It all sounds a bit mad doesn't it?" was all he could say, with another wan smile.

"Martin, it sounds tragic . . . if only it were true ! I've never heard anything like it – not, in fact, since the last bloody line you spun me," she could suddenly feel that the brakes had come off and the train was starting to pick up speed rolling down the hill.

"Mate, I've stuck by you over these last few months when the knives have come out for you." That made him sit up and take notice.

"Ah, yes – you didn't know that, did you? I know it's mostly professional envy but the fact is you have riled quite a few of them over at Stone Rose and they're saying it's not right and there's something creepy about you but, oh no, faithful little girl scout Susan defends you to the hilt. Even though I then get ridiculed along with you. 'Oh no,' I say, 'You don't know what he's been through.' But neither do I ! Because you don't tell me anything, do you, Martin? I've told you everything about me; I've given myself up to you; and I know you've got this . . . illness . . . but you could at least tell me a bit more. I know you're keeping something from me. Don't ask me how but I know you are."

By now she was pretty much shouting and, as she paused for breath, she realised that no-one else in the restaurant was talking and everyone else was either looking directly at their table or, at least, listening in, surreptitiously. As soon as they realised that she had realised, they all jumped back into what they'd been doing before Susan's histrionics had overborne them.

All the time Martin's eyes had been fixed on the condiments that sat on the table, like a battle line between them. And as she looked at him again, through the fading smoke of that fiery exchange, she thought she saw definite signs of anguish. Not that she was cheered by this. Oh no, for that would be mean. But still, there seemed to be a hint of misery in that otherwise impassive demeanour that suggested that he might be feeling an emotion. And that would be progress, wouldn't it?

And then he said: "You don't understand Susan – Michael Broad is a dangerous, evil man," and, at this, he was staring at her, a picture of misery, his eyes edged with red and she thought he was going to cry.

"I thought you said his name was Green?"

The conversation stopped.

And then he came round – "What?"

"His name – you said he was called Michael Green."

This threw him but he recovered.

"Michael Green. Yes it's Michael Green".

"So who is Michael Broad?"

"Nobody, that was just a slip," and he suddenly seemed back to himself. He picked up his napkin, flicked it open, placed it on his lap and cast a determinedly casual look about the restaurant.

Susan sighed, "OK, Martin. Have it your way. But just be aware – now I *know* there's something going on with you and if you think you can't trust me with it, you're wrong. But you'll find all that out in due course. I'll give you time."

And with that she smiled, flicked open her napkin and cast a determined casual look about the restaurant. Martin could only stare in wonderment and an involuntary smile snuck along his lips.

"So what's with the mufti?" she asked breezily.

"What?"

"You're in mufti: non-uniform," and nodded at his shirt.

"Oh, yes. Sorry. I've been over at Barry's."

"Oh?" Susan raised her eyebrows.

"Yes, a few . . . things to discuss . . . about Crack Harbour."

"Oh, really?" Susan waited for some further information to be offered up but just got "Hmm . . ." as Martin scanned the restaurant, again.

"I thought that was all done and dusted, re-financing completed. Wasn't it?"

"Yes – yes, it was but there's a few loose ends to tie up, you know."

"That require you to go over to Barry's house of a morning. In disguise?"

Martin was actually looking sheepish now. Out of his comfort zone. Again.

"Well . . ."

"Oh, fucking hell Martin; I'm getting a bit tired of this – and this is work. I'm not the fucking enemy you know – we're actually on the same side on this !"

Their fellow diners were, again, cocking an ear, gleefully – a double show !

Martin brought his head forward closer to hers and spoke more quietly: "I'm actually thinking more of your father, Susan."

Now it was Susan's turn to be taken aback.

"What?"

But Martin didn't get the chance to explain.

"Mr. Dash? Martin Dash?" came an authoritative voice behind Susan. She spun her head round to see three men stood in an arc behind her. Two of them wore suits, very like the men back at the office, but the other was a uniformed police officer and he took a step towards Martin.

Susan felt disorientated, as though she'd slipped into some sort of bizarre dream sequence. She spun back round to face Martin, who had simply raised his eyes to look at the suit immediately behind Susan, evidently the one who had spoken the question.

"Yes."

Susan back to looking behind her – she was now in danger of inflicting irreparable damage to her neck. This man – tallish, 40s, with thinning black hair, combed back, a strong smell of a particular aftershave and (she noticed) short black hairs along the top of his hands and fingers – had now fished into his jacket breast pocket and produced a black card holder that he flicked open to reveal a picture of himself and an official crest.

"Detective Fallon, Mr. Dash, from the Serious Organised Crime Agency. I'm sorry to be interrupting your lunch" – he looked down at Susan and back again at Martin – "but we've been trying to get hold of you and this is the first time we've spotted you. We need you to come with us, please."

Martin appeared momentarily to be looking for an escape route but the uniform and the other plain clothes were standing either side of the table. Those who had been earwigging Martin and Susan's earlier row quickly concluded that they had never before been treated to such entertaining fellow diners.

"Martin, what the hell is this?" Susan demanded.

Martin looked as if he knew, shook his head and shut his eyes to indicate that she should enquire no further.

"I don't think Mr. Dash would like us to elaborate . . . here." Detective Fallon looked around the restaurant as he said this.

Martin began to stand and simply said (remarkably calmly, as Susan later recalled): "OK, let's go."

"Well, I'll come with you," Susan made to get up but Martin made with his hand to tell her to sit down.

"No, no – I'll get in touch. Don't worry."

"That's right, Miss – you'll not be needed, thank you." Detective Fallon couldn't help but sound condescending so, inevitably, he got a glare from Susan, which made him involuntarily shrug in apology.

As Martin walked away from the table with the officers, he looked into Susan's eyes and smiled and she suddenly felt that was the first natural look he had given her, that the wee person inside that strange carapace had just appeared at the window of his eyes and waved: 'Hello.'

As Martin was led out of the restaurant (and she saw for the first time that there had been a car waiting for them outside) Susan stood open-mouthed by their former table. She couldn't quite believe this – in the space of four days, Martin had gone from Mr. No-Personality to gangland fugitive cum racketeer with barely a pause for breath. Susan, being the girl she was, had to admit that she felt a distinct frisson of excitement but then her mind was suddenly cast back to what Martin had said – he was thinking of *her father* . . .

Shit. Her father was Secretary of State and her so-called boyfriend had just been arrested in a public venue, frequented by the sort of people who probably knew who she was. As this thought occurred to her, she looked around to see that a number of the diners were now tapping on their mobiles and she could have sworn that one was surreptitiously videoing the scene.

Double shit.

But her father had something to do with this, anyway? She grabbed her coat, suddenly thought of the bill, realised they'd not actually got round to ordering anything and looked at the waiter who, however, put his hands up in front of him and shook his head, indulgently, as if to say: 'God no, you've nothing to pay – you've been worth it !'

Something told her to go to the office first.

On the walk back to Stone Rose, Susan began to think about what to do. She realised that it might not actually be the best idea to walk into their employers to advise that Martin had just been arrested – and by SOCA, who were all about serious financial impropriety. It had been lurking in the back of her mind and she'd probably not really wanted to look at it but now she had to bring herself to rest on the thought: Barry Rogers. Barry fucking Rogers. It bloody well would be, wouldn't it?

And one ugly thought sparked another – that was the link with her father. She'd never really known exactly what Jimmy's dealings with Barry entailed; she only knew, instinctively, that they wouldn't have been a good idea. And she'd tried to tell her father this a couple of times but he pretty much did as he wanted to, didn't he? And, while she knew he loved her dearly, she also knew that she wasn't going to succeed in persuading him out of misadventures when many others – rather more senior than she – had failed on numerous occasions. With this thought in mind, she was even less sure that it was the right thing to start interrogating Gerry Bild as to whether one of their clients had just landed Martin in chokey. She decided to simply go back to work, play it by ear at first and wait to see what she might glean.

She didn't have to wait long as, five minutes after she had plonked herself down at the desk in her room and commenced to stare glumly at her computer screen, Gerry appeared at the door, red faced and looking distinctly out of sorts. In fact, his appearance suggested he was about to burst into tears. He shut the door behind him and she noticed that many of the staff outside were looking through the glass partitioning into her room, rapt in attention.

The thought occurred to her that the police may have been here first. And someone had told them where they were. Her eyes fell on Maisie – *her* secretary. Who had booked the table for her. And who now flipped sheepishly back to her filing when their eyes met.

"Have you seen Martin, Susan?" Gerry blurted out. He didn't seem very composed.

"Err . . . yes, why?" Play it by ear.

Gerry stood for a moment, apparently unsure of what to say next. His fingers were limbering up as though they were about to have a crack at Chopin's second sonata.

Finally, he spluttered: "The police have been here for him."

OK, forget playing it by ear.

"They've just arrested him at the restaurant, Gerry."

Gerry's face went from red to white in an instant and it seemed that, suddenly, his bones must have turned to string, as he slumped into the chair by the door, rested his head on one hand and shut his eyes.

"Oh, God."

And then: "Did they say why?"

"No, I don't know why. Do you, Gerry?"

Gerry opened his eyes and realised that Susan was scrutinising him. Something of the seasoned commercial lawyer came back to him and she could see him thinking now.

"They're raising some questions about the Crack Harbour development."

"Barry Rogers?"

Gerry looked at her again, uneasily "Hmm . . ."

"What questions?"

"I . . . I don't know exactly . . . that's . . . what I wanted to ask . . . Martin."

Susan thought about this.

"Why? – what does Martin know that you don't?"

No answer.

"Gerry?"

A moment or two passed. Gerry seemed to be steeling himself. "Well . . . I don't know . . . that's why I wanted to talk . . . to Martin."

"But you must know something of what's going on – Barry's your client, after all."

Gerry gave out a short, desperate laugh at this as he stood up and started shuffling against the filing cabinets. "Well, he's . . . he's rather more Martin's . . . *client* . . . nowadays. Isn't he?" A weak smile.

Susan could feel the brakes coming off again and fought to retain her composure but the sight of Gerry Bild in front of her fidgeting and squirming up against her filing cabinets, avoiding eye contact and clearly scrabbling for a way to save his own miserable freckled skin was just about beyond what she could bear.

She'd never had any real problems with Gerry and, to be fair, he'd always given her credit for work that she'd done but she'd always known, deep down, that he was ultimately the same as the rest of his ilk – basically interested only in number one, heedless of the collateral waste that fell by the wayside: spouses, children, subordinates and now Martin – her Martin – was to be cast onto the sacrificial bonfire.

Well, not if she could help it, he wasn't.

"Martin's not going to be hung out to dry on this – whatever it is – is he, Gerry?"

134

Absolute silence in the room. And what they didn't know – hadn't noticed, really – was that, outside of the room also, all conversation had stopped as everyone was straining to divine exactly what was going on.

"I don't know what you mean, Susan." Gerry was trying his best to look indignant but it came out rather more at the pompous end of the scale.

"I think you do, Gerry . . ." She stood up, wheels screaming down the track now, wind whistling through her hair. "You know who my father is." (Good God ! She never thought she'd hear herself saying that !) "I'm my father's daughter and I will not stand by and watch my friend being sacrificed for the likes of Barry Rogers . . . and you !"

Suddenly Gerry was steely now. And cold. And he looked her straight in the eye when he said: "Yes, well I think you'd better have a word with your father before you go and do anything rash . . . for your Mr. Dash."

18

That was twice her father had been brought up. She had to speak to him, so she excused herself from the office and, out on the street, phoned the private number that Jimmy had given to both of his daughters for when they needed to get him urgently.

As she stood on the pavement in the bright afternoon sun, waiting while the call rang, she looked every inch the professional young modern woman in her smart pencil skirt suit, black high heels and the large Jackie Onassis sunglasses she had slipped on. She could have been the typical high-flying young executive, beloved of glossy TV adverts across the western world, unburdened by the old traditional obligations of marriage and childbirth, confidently making a deal, toughing it out with the boys (being harder than the boys in fact).

But she felt vulnerable now. As the child of an eminent politician, she had become accustomed to the idea of actions having consequences, of being under scrutiny, and being judged – in fact her father's robust attitude to adverse publicity generally had endowed all the family with a degree of nonchalance in matters of scandal and hype. However, Susan found herself disorientated in these circumstances – true, she'd never before been that close to an actual arrest by the Serious Organised Crime Agency and this felt like the sort of scandal that could bring down the final curtain on Jimmy's tumultuous career, but she rather felt that her heightened anxiety was probably more closely associated with the Martin factor.

Her dad would survive (naturally) and she didn't give a shit what happened to Barry – but she feared for Martin.

"Hello, Darling," her father's voice came through on the phone.

"Dad, can I see you?"

"Of course – when?"

"As soon as possible – now really."

"Well . . . sure. But what's up?"

"Not sure I should say on the phone."

Some hesitation on the other end.

"Well, this line's safe – just give me the gist."

"It's Martin. And Barry Rogers."

Bigger hesitation.

"Listen, I was about to finish up here shortly anyway. I'll give you an address – meet me there in about half an hour."

Address, what address?

"Address? What address?"

"It's a spare flat, not far from where you are. One of the perks of the job, you know."

Susan could hear the smirk in his voice.

"Bloody hell, Dad."

"What?" All innocence.

"Give me the address then."

"23 Benbow Square. It's just round the corner from Marble Arch Tube. A black cab will find it. Just ring the bell and I'll be there as long as you arrive after, say, 2:30?"

"OK, see you there."

19

As the cab swung into the aforementioned Benbow Square, Susan realised she passed the top of it every day of the week as she walked from the Tube station to work. She'd never seen her father in the vicinity. Never knew he'd been there. Doing God-knows-what. What was it anyway? Some sort of knocking shop? Perhaps he had never been there before. Perhaps he'd got scores of such addresses dotted all around London to nip in and out of as the need took him.

Jesus! Was she losing it? Was she starting to imagine nonsense?

She wondered about what her father did. What he had done. She had always been naturally curious and quizzed him whenever she judged the time was right (usually after he'd downed a few whiskies) and he did tell her things – probably a few things he oughtn't to have told her – but she didn't assume that she'd ever got the whole story. Jimmy always liked to see Susan as his ally, his political heir even, and – for all her loathing of the vast majority of his supposed comrades – she, in turn, did often wonder whether she would actually be better suited to the vigorous world her father inhabited than the arid landscape of commercial law that she saw before her.

But, equally, she had no illusions about how rough it could get. The US / UK invasion of Iraq four years previously had aroused disgust and damnation in many quarters, not least in the Sachs family, with Susan and Maria particularly critical of their father's support for Blair's war (Rosa had played the supportive wife rather more, maintaining the line that they should trust that their father knew what he was doing). Susan had not held back from expressing her anger at the whole affair but she was also confused because she knew that, ordinarily, every fibre of Jimmy's being would rebel against such an impertinent adventure, led by the Americans too ! Indeed, many on the left of the Party had looked to Jimmy to take this one opportunity to fulfil his widely-perceived role at the heart of the government, as the conscience of an otherwise heartless regime and, thus, there was widespread dismay and disappointment when Jimmy, after some apparent prevarication, finally voiced full support for the action in a BBC TV interview.

It had to be said that he didn't look entirely comfortable doing it but he still did it and, subsequently, always maintained his support – even when no weapons of mass destruction were found in the newly 'liberated' Iraq, nor evidence of any links to Al-Qaeda. Then, one night – when she had come across her father in his library, morosely, but determinedly, working his way through a bottle of Chivas Regal – he had furnished the only near-credible explanation she had heard for the UK's supine obeisance to Bush's command, muttering darkly about people not realising the degree to which this country was harnessed – with the Americans – to the international bankers' yoke, that the UK was going to war because those who were "*really in charge*" had decided that such was needed and that the country would ultimately pay a heavy price if it had the temerity to disobey a command given such a high designation – code red, in effect.

Susan recalled how shocked she had been at this statement. Shocked because this was one of the country's most senior ministers of the day basically telling her, frankly, that the public statements on the war's rationale were all lies; that the country was, in fact, doing what it was told by an *extra-governmental* force, more powerful than itself; and shocked because this was her father – who she (and most others) had always assumed could not be bullied by anyone into doing what he thought was wrong – meekly submitting to the gang of financiers that (in private, at least) he had always condemned.

He had said that he had not realised, until recently, what these people could do to a country if they thought it needed bringing into line and she thought she had never seen him so depressed. And it had depressed her too. Badly.

The next day – when he was sober – he had phoned her and told her to forget what he had said, that he had been drunk, and not to repeat it.

That was about the time she had decided to go and work at Stone Rose.

And now she found herself sat in the sitting room of a plush flat in Mayfair with her father in the armchair opposite; he with a glass of whisky in hand, smiling indulgently; she with no drink, tense, scrutinising him.

He himself had let her in when she rang the doorbell and that, in itself, was unusual or, rather, the fact that he appeared to be alone. For many years he had almost always been shadowed by at least one faceless attendant – be it bodyguard, PA, driver, whatever – but here he was, by himself, just like a normal private citizen. Most odd.

The walls of the room were covered in what she assumed must be paper but the surface was a soft textured pale green – like velvet – and, with the dark wood cornicing, striped blue and grey carpet, oak Georgian furniture and old fabric lightshades, the whole effect was surprisingly cosy – soothing, even. A grandfather clock with a sunny smiling face ticked discreetly and the only other sound was the muffled whoosh of the odd passing car in the street outside to remind you that you were, in fact, in the middle of the bustling metropolis.

"OK, tell all," said Jimmy, sitting back in his armchair. He seemed relaxed but Susan knew that her father was a sufficiently hardened pro to be able to appear unconcerned even when he most definitely was. And, again, he had come rushing over to meet her as soon as she had called. And come alone. But then, she was his daughter and she'd obviously sounded upset.

Anyway, she came back: "I was going to say the same thing to you, Dad . . ."

At first Jimmy said nothing. This was a funny moment for them both. The nature of Jimmy's career and position meant that he constantly had to be careful about what he said to anyone but, at the same time, he had always tried to be honest with his wife and children so that, if he was unable to tell them things, he would simply tell them that that was the case rather than spinning them the sort of bullshit he was obliged to feed the rest of the world. And Rosa and the girls had come to understand that this was the best way for them to all rub along with it and to trust Jimmy to share with them what he could and only keep back that which could not safely be repeated to anyone.

Thus, even if they disagreed on things, Susan had always felt that she could trust her father to at least be honest with her, even if he was being utterly wrong-headed, in her eyes anyway. But there was now an external agency involved of a sort that had never been a factor before . . . something that, for the first time, raised the possibility of divided loyalties in a way that had not hitherto seemed possible.

And its name was Martin Dash.

Could his daughter really not be trusted to not use information to help Martin if it meant hurting Jimmy? Would her father really try to dupe her if he thought that necessary to protect himself?

Susan thought she saw some sign of resolution in Jimmy and he sat more upright and started the conversation off proper.

"You said it was about Martin and Barry Rogers?"

"Martin's been arrested, Dad."

Jimmy didn't appear to be shocked, or even surprised, at this news.

"You knew?"

Just a moment's hesitation . . . "Yes, I knew."

"How?"

Another moment – "Joan Rogers told me."

"When?"

A pattern was setting in now of quick fire questions from Susan and a rather slower response in each of Jimmy's answers.

"This morning."

Susan thought for a moment. "But that was before he was arrested. How did she know?" Susan felt a certain warmth at the back of her ears.

"They lifted Barry this morning – at their home. Asked them if they knew where Martin was as well; they were having some difficulty locating him – apparently he's not been seen in his flat for a while."

Susan realised he was referring to the Angel flat but she was focussing instead on Sister Rogers: "So, what? – she *phoned* you?"

"No, no – I met her."

"Where?"

Another hesitation. "Well . . . here, actually."

The heat in Susan's ears seemed to be developing into a kind of anger.

"Joan Rogers . . . came here?"

No matter how much of a pro he was, Susan thought she saw him turn, ever so slightly, in his seat.

"Yes . . . It wasn't something to discuss over the phone . . . you know . . ."

"First time?"

"What?"

"She's been here?"

He didn't just move then, but flinch.

And then he seemed to gather himself.

"No, it's not. But that's got nothing to do with anything. Joan is a friend – as is Barry – I see the pair of them. On and off. Regularly."

Some silence between them, briefly. Both Susan and Maria had, for some years now, got used to the idea that their father hadn't necessarily always been absolutely faithful to their mother (and, in fact, there was some suspicion that Rosa had, at some point, given up worrying about it and decided that what was good for the goose was good for the gander; maybe more than once). They had, perhaps without a conscious decision, ultimately come to the view that they were the sort of sophisticated family that didn't really make a fuss about such things. But, even so, Susan had to acknowledge that the thought of her father 'betraying' her mother with Joan-fucking-Rogers did raise her hackles somewhat. And in this very place, where she was now sitting with him !

The room seemed suddenly less congenial. Perhaps they had romped around naked in this very room ! On the bloody seat she was now sitting on !!

Susan nearly leapt straight out of the chair at the thought. But she was going off track and Jimmy brought her back anyway –

"Joan told me that there's a joint investigation by SOCA and the Financial Conduct Authority into the Crack Harbour development and that they're picking a number of people up as well as Barry and Martin – she's only avoided arrest because they appear to think she's little more than a sleeping partner in the whole venture."

"Oh really? Not because she's done some deal with them?"

Jimmy's chin bumped up and his brows furrowed, as though this possibility had not occurred to him before.

"But why is this happening, Dad? And what's it got to do with you?"

More fidgeting from Jimmy; he breathed out heavily and continued: "It's a joint investigation because there are allegations of money laundering *and* sanctions busting."

Susan stared at Jimmy.

"Some of the investors are possibly less than kosher . . . It's possible that money has come out of Syria in exchange for military hardware, through criminal enterprises in London and into Crack Harbour, to come out clean at the other end. Many millions – and, possibly, other Grudge developments as well. That's the allegation, at least."

"And why does your name crop up, Dad? Both Gerry Bild and Martin mentioned you today."

Jimmy gave a start – "To the police?!" His face was changing colour.

"No, to me."

"Jesus Christ, they should keep their fucking mouths shut. If they know what's good for them."

It was Susan's turn to start. Again, she was not innocent in the ways of the world but it was a shock to sit and listen to her father talking like some two-bit gangster.

"What do you mean?"

Jimmy looked at Susan, checked himself, and talked more measuredly. "Only that they're dealing – *apparently* – with Arab gangsters, for God's sake, and if they're perceived at all as being unable to hold their tongues then these are the sort of chaps who'd be inclined to take matters into their own hands." This last part seemed to be delivered with something of a sarcastic edge.

The thought sprang up in Susan's mind that she'd possibly never seen her father look less appealing than he did right now.

And the whole situation was starting to appear, if possible, even worse than she'd thought.

"But why are you mentioned?"

Jimmy looked almost sheepish now.

"I'm another investor – I've got shares in the damn thing."

"Bloody hell, Dad," Susan moaned. "You were warned about Barry before – you only just got out of the last bloody job."

"That was all a misunderstanding – nothing came of it and you know it. And Barry seemed to be moving on. Making a more mainstream company. Respected. And doing it properly. He bloody assured me that this was risk–free. We're on the biggest sustained boom since the war and everyone's making. He was talking about a big return for me . . . for us . . . for you." He looked imploringly at Susan, saw no help, and slammed his palm on the arm rest as he jumped to his feet in anger and started pacing across the carpet, stopping only at the drinks cabinet.

"Fucking Barry," he shouted. "I fucking told him it'd better be right and he swore it was. Instead of which he's taking money from those fucking Arab friends of his. And where's it coming from?! Bloody Syria !! They're only on the 'Axis of Evil' that idiot Bush goes on about – the worst of the worst !"

"But why did he come to you? It's not like we're rolling in spare millions to invest and he's got all the investment from those guys hasn't he? And why, for heaven's sake, did you go for it?"

"It wasn't my money he was after, particularly; you're right – they've got quite a bit more than us."

And now Jimmy looked rather beyond sheepish – "I've been able to help in other ways."

"Oh God, do tell." Could it get any worse?

"You know ... with the planning. And all that. You've got no idea, Susan; you've no idea how much it all costs. That house in Hampstead. The villa. Your schooling. All the rest of it – you don't think that's all paid for on an MP's salary do you? Or even a Minister's. I have to earn, Darling, and property investment is a perfectly legitimate concern."

Susan was speechless. She did wonder sometimes if her father had a death wish. His whole career comprised extended periods of good, solid work when his natural talents came to the fore and he made serious progress – only to be punctuated (with monotonous regularity) by insane blow-ups, entirely self-inflicted, that might even seem to have been *designed* to undo all the good work, so that he then had to start all over again.

But even he was only ever going to have so many chances and he'd surely used up all his lives. A scandal like this, now, could finish Jimmy for good.

"And what did you do on the planning, Dad?" Susan was beginning to sound as exasperated as she felt.

"Well, in reality, it didn't take all that much, actually. To be honest, it could easily be passed off as normal lobbying if it came to it. I just had a word with Johnny Adams, who heads up the local Planning Committee. Loyal party man is Johnny . . . and he owed me a favour . . ."

"And this is normal lobbying that's been disclosed?"

"Well, no. That is a problem, I suppose. But nothing that can't be got round. Anyway, Johnny will keep his mouth shut. Everyone just needs to keep their mouths shut." Jimmy looked at Susan pointedly and he saw Susan wince in turn, at which he moved to embrace her.

"No, no – you know what I mean Darling. Everyone simply needs to be sensible, stay calm, and we'll all get through this . . . including your Martin."

But Susan pulled away and was having none of it – "But why is Martin being dragged into it? He's not being set up as the fall guy is he?" She was indignant.

"No, of course not, but the point is that Martin has apparently signed all this off . . . for the banks, you know? As a solicitor he was trusted – they probably couldn't have done it without him. He's agreed to skip the usual checks, allegedly, which is what has got it through."

"Or Gerry Bild has told him to."

"Well, I don't know whether your Martin is so much the innocent, you know, Darling. Joan reckons he's actually suggested to Barry the complete refinancing of the project that's just gone though. Worked it all out to pull the full value of the thing through again – had never occurred to Barry."

"What?!" Susan was incredulous.

Jimmy put his hands up defensively – "I don't know. All I can tell you is what Joan's told me, Darling. And to be honest, I reckon Joan would just as soon see Barry go away as Martin."

Again, he looked at Susan rather archly but then decided to move the conversation on before Susan started processing that comment.

"But, you're right – they're not Martin's shareholders; it's not Martin's development; he's only the lawyer. Barry's the key man in all this. If anyone's taking the drop, it's him. And he'll fucking deserve it, quite frankly." He smiled at Susan – "Pardon my French."

She let him put his arm around her this time – "But Barry's one of your oldest friends, isn't he, Dad?"

"Was, my dear. Was."

20

The next two days meant simple frustration for Susan. After leaving her father, she had returned to the office to see Gerry Bild again; to ask if he knew where Martin was being held; when (if?) he would be released; would he be coming back to work . . . all that. Gerry really didn't have much information to impart to Susan in response and she realised that, even if he did, he probably wouldn't pass it to her anyway – she and Stone Rose weren't necessarily on the same side anymore. As if to echo that thought, Gerry told her that she should take a couple of days off ("more, if you would like . . . given the circumstances"); that Martin would undoubtedly be realised on bail by then; that the police had told him that Stone Rose would be advised when Martin was being released; and that he would, of course, let her know as soon as he heard anything.

Somehow, Susan hadn't felt massively comforted by any of that but she knew, for something like this, that the police would undoubtedly be holding Martin for a couple of days, at least, and that he wouldn't exactly be receiving visitors during that time.

Apparently he had been set up with a top-line defence lawyer but Gerry had indicated that this hadn't been arranged through Stone Rose and at this stage he didn't know who it was – it must have been something organised by Martin himself or by someone on his behalf.

Susan wondered at this.

She realised there was little point in trying to quiz Gerry about what had been going on with Barry Rogers and that, if she had declined Gerry's offer to take time away from the office, the offer would likely morph into something more forceful.

Thus she trudged back to her flat, took a long hot bath and slumped on the sofa to try and digest what the hell had happened in the last four hours. Her father had suggested that she might like to stay with he and Rosa for a while but, at least for the time being, she was content to be alone in her own place, not least so she could think in peace.

In fact, the last four days had been bizarre to say the least. All that business with Michael Green, or Michael Broad, or whoever he was, and then this. Was it coincidence that the two incidents had happened within days of each other? She had a lot of questions for Martin when she next got a hold of him and that man would feature.

She scanned the internet and TV news channels but there was nothing that evening about the earlier arrests. But there was the next day. By lunchtime on the Wednesday, reports started appearing that the prominent London developer, Barry Rogers, had been arrested – with others – in connection with sanctions busting vis-à-vis Syria and money laundering in relation to his Crack Harbour development. The reports simply said "with others" so there was no mention of Martin by name (or image) as yet. Nor did her father really feature – although one or two reports provided some background to the effect that Mr. Rogers was close with the Labour Party and Mr. Jimmy Sachs in particular; there was so far no hint of an actual involvement by said Member in the story as such – maybe Jimmy would get away with it and Barry take the fall .. ?

Thus, when she woke on the Thursday and there were no further developments reported, Susan began to feel some stirrings of optimism. Martin's name did now appear in some of the reports (along with a number of others, including a London accountant and a Syrian businessman) but only as an afterthought in a story which was essentially about the terrible property developer, whose reputation seemed to be getting more villainous with each successive report.

Perhaps her father was right and Martin might be viewed simply as a dupe of the manipulative Mr. Rogers and actually escape serious censure completely? OK, he might get struck off as a solicitor but, quite frankly, Susan was beginning to care less and less about the legal profession herself all of a sudden and radical plans were beginning to form hazily in her mind, involving she and Martin striking out in some new venture. She felt sure that she had been on the verge of a breakthrough with Martin in The Range before they had been so rudely interrupted by the police and now felt confident that whatever blocks were stuck in Martin's psyche would ultimately have to give way to the irresistible force of her rational ardour.

She phoned Gerry Bild, who advised that he expected Martin to be released that day but that he couldn't provide much more information as he hadn't been in touch directly with Martin at all given that Martin was now being guided by the legal team that had taken him on shortly after the arrest; yes, he now knew who they were (Sparkes Mael, led by Bob Latchford) but didn't know how they'd come to be hired by Martin. Susan got the distinct impression that there was, by now, in effect, an unbridgeable distance that had been put between Martin and Messrs. Stone Rose. Again, this was, no longer, something that particularly surprised or bothered her. But Sparkes Mael – how had they been brought in? By whom? She decided to wait for the call that would, of course, come from Martin as soon as he was freed.

She bustled about the flat, tidying away clothes and books, washing cups, vacuuming the large patterned rugs on the pale wood floors and dusting the bookshelves, coffee table and chairs dotted about the large airy living room as if in preparation for the little prince's homecoming. Outside, the sun was shining strong and her mind was cast back to the visit she and Martin had paid together to his new flat in Kensington only five days ago and it suddenly struck her how alike that flat was to this.

Which of the two would they give up? she wondered – she was, by now, getting totally ahead of herself.

Then it occurred to her to fill in the time with a bit of detective work. She had wondered whether she might be able to hunt down Mr. Michael Green / Broad as she just knew, somehow, that he held the key to a greater understanding of Martin, who he was, and where he had come from.

Accordingly, she plonked herself on a stool at the red and white breakfast bar and set to giving Google a real test. She decided to try 'Michael Broad' first – she'd got the distinct impression from the conversation with Martin that this was his real name, rather than the 'Michael Green' that Martin had first used. She wasn't really sure how to start, how to proceed. All she could do really was to go with what Martin had told her, which could well have been lies but 'Michael Broad, Lewes' was it.

Nothing that looked particularly relevant came up. She tried entering search words that might reflect the police case that Martin referred to.

Nothing.

She tried widening the geographical area. Various 'Michael Broad' references appeared but nothing that suggested a link to Martin – an electrical goods retailer in Willesden; a lottery winner in Bournemouth last week; a guy who'd lost his sister in a fire in Cornwall 10 years before; an academic paper for The Medical Society in Birmingham. There were either no photographs or photos that bore no resemblance to the Michael she had seen.

OK, try Michael Green, London and – bingo ! – there he was on the first page. An article from The Evening Standard from 2005, headline: '*Move Over Paul Raymond – The New King of Smut has arrived !*' and, under an immediately recognisable photo of the man himself, a strap line that read: '*Businessman Michael Green moves into Raymond's territory with new Burlesque concept.*'

Burlesque.

Burlesque?

What *was* burlesque?

Susan had a vague idea of the term from the back of her mind that suggested seedy clubs; Liza Minelli in Cabaret; and, above all, *strippers*. As was her custom, Susan immediately went to Wikipedia for enlightenment:

'*Burlesque is a literary, dramatic or musical work intended to cause laughter by caricaturing the manner or spirit of serious works, or by ludicrous treatment of their subjects. The word derives from the Italian 'burlisco' which, in turn, is derived from the Italian 'burla' – a joke, ridicule or mockery.*'

'Interesting,' thought Susan and returned to the news story:

'*Does Paul Raymond finally have serious competition for the King of Soho title? Probably not – at least, yet – given that the aged entrepreneur's empire took 50 years to build up to the megalithic billion pound enterprise that now comprises prime real estate, publishing and financial assets to make him one of the country's richest men.*

However, there is a young pretender coming up in his wake who cites the great man as a major influence and wants to emulate his unique route to success. He is called Michael Green and, while that name probably won't mean anything to most of us, it has been creating a stir in the world of finance – Green's Mu Productions appeared to have come out of nowhere five years ago but made an immediate impact in the City with its buccaneering style of venture capital investment and Green's own unconventional personal image.

The company has made a string of lightning raids on singular but substantial businesses across a range of sectors (including manufacturing, renewable energy, media) that amazed investors with the shrewdness of their operation, whilst leaving some commentators concerned at the obscurity of the funding. Add to that Michael Green's cryptic utterances and his eccentric appearance (he generally stands before board meetings and press briefings alike looking like a cross between a new age traveller and a Dickensian villain) and you have a story fizzing with intrigue and interest.

Well, now young Mr. Green (still only 28) has decided that he wants to contribute to the capital's cultural experience with the opening of his new club right next to the famous Windmill Theatre in Soho (once owned by the Raymond Organisation – a point, no doubt, not lost on him).

The club is to be called 'The Black and Blue Dahlia' and Mr. Green's aim is for it to help revitalise an art that seemed to have lost its credibility and appeal many years ago – Burlesque. He addresses its slightly shabby, nay seedy, reputation (that perhaps aided its demise) thus: "Burlesque is a medium that has been sorely neglected over the years but deserves greater attention. Yes, it's bawdy and rude but so is life and our wonderful performers will give the punters something that's wild but life-affirming".'

The article went on to fill out the salacious details of burlesque acts both from the past – such as Minsky's and Tempest Storm – and the so-called neo-burlesque movement of recent years – like The World Famous *BOB* and Julie Atlas Muz – that made its claim as much to high-concept performance art as the time-honoured business of peeling one's clothes off in front of strangers. There wasn't much more on Michael Green but she found additional material on other sites, including more than one article that openly questioned what – or who – was funding the vertiginous rise of this hitherto unknown enfant terrible and an array of frankly contradictory quotes that seemed to suggest someone hell-bent on making mischief or suffering from an acute personality disorder.

That thought made Susan pause. How on earth did Martin know this guy and what was the true nature of their relationship?

She had, by now, dismissed Martin's story of homosexual passion on the Jurassic Coast as just that – a story, to put her off the trail.

The afternoon was passing by and she'd still heard nothing from Martin.

She phoned the office to speak to Gerry: "Gerry, it's Susan. Have you heard anything of Martin? He must be due to be bailed soon but I've had no news."

"They're out, Susan – both of them. Bailed this morning," Gerry replied, slightly hesitantly.

Susan was stunned. He hadn't phoned her.

"He hasn't phoned me."

Gerry, more hesitantly still: "Well, give him a call on his mobile. You'll get him now, I'm sure. He's probably been a bit disorientated."

"OK, I'll do that. Thanks Gerry."

"No problem, Susan. Don't worry, it'll all work out. Look after yourself, kiddo." Gerry suddenly seemed strangely warm and friendly. Susan was rather bewildered. All she could manage was "OK, bye" and they then both did that thing where callers repeat 'bye' to each other, ever more quickly, quietly and distantly as though neither of them wants to guillotine the call but both are being dragged away against their will.

But Martin didn't answer his mobile – straight to voicemail. And she left a message that was heartfelt in its concern for Martin's wellbeing but also began, halfway through, to acquire an edge of irritation at his apparent failure to call her the very moment he was released from custody. She did wonder, with a gnawing regret, whether the final "Call me !" wasn't perhaps a little too autocratic in the circumstances.

But still, she was beginning to feel more than a little frustrated at her ostensible demotion in the pecking order of Those Who Need to Know in Martin's life – apparently below Gerry Bild ! And she suddenly felt the need to do something proactive, beyond sitting at home, meekly, like the good wife; putting her life on hold and waiting for however long it took for her convict boyfriend to return to the homestead, tarnished but heroic.

Fuck that. She was going out.

To 'The Black and Blue Dahlia'.

21

Come 9:00 p.m. Susan was sat at a table near the stage of the burlesque club with Carol Gee, sucking lustily on Singapore Slings with a carefree abandon that might subsequently – with hindsight – have been viewed as somewhat negligent. Or entirely appropriate, depending on your viewpoint.

Carol, frankly, hadn't been Susan's first choice as partner for her gumshoe'd night out but, basically, answered the call when others further up the rankings had let her down and so deserved her chance, decided Susan, haughtily.

Clearly, she couldn't embark on such a mission alone and needed a girlfriend who could carry off the proposition of two apparently respectable young ladies venturing into a strip – sorry, burlesque – club without manly escorts and provide a bit of backup should the occasion call for it. Susan wasn't entirely sure that Carol matched these prerequisites exactly but, then again, she had always felt somehow that beneath the quiet, diligent surface of her colleague, there might be something a bit more earthy flowing and she reckoned that now was as good a time as any to find out.

In any event, she hadn't much choice; her first call would obviously have been to Charlotte – her best friend, sometime flatmate, and co-defendant in many a scrape, going years back – and Charlotte would have loved this but, sadly, was currently holidaying with her family in the south of France.

Several more of her sure-fire go-to girls proved not so sure-fire, citing the short notice of the call, the fact that it was a school night, and the general lack of appeal in going to see 'ageing failed dancers' peel off their clothes in the company of 'sweaty, beery perverts' (as Lauren Masters had deemed it). Susan tried to assure them that it was a rather more cultural affair than that but they seemed unconvinced. She was most disappointed in her gang but, then again, wondered how receptive she would have been to such an invitation had she not been caught up in the thing in the way she was now.

She had considered Maria but decided that she didn't actually want any family eyes looking on at this; she had nearly called Maisie but something told her that might just be too combustible an ingredient; and, finally, she had even thought of the hapless Bertie Sanchez but realised that would really over-complicate things and, anyway, she wasn't sure even Bertie would tolerate (or deserve ...) further ill-treatment after their last dalliance.

So Carol it was. Susan glanced across at her companion, who shot a look back and smiled. Susan smiled back.

Carol basically looked as if she had stepped straight out of one of Doris Day's films from the 1950s, playing the star's nerdy younger sister; the wallflower sitting on the sidelines at the High School Prom. With the cream-coloured Alice band on her light brown hair, thin yellow cardigan, pleated A-line skirt and low-heeled pumps she looked every inch the Head Girl. The big round glasses just topped it off.

She even still lived with her parents and Susan felt sorry for Carol as they always seemed to be warding off suitable suitors whereas Susan often thought she detected in her an ardent – if repressed – interest in the opposite sex. Susan had noticed that Carol nearly always had a bonkbuster on the go – 'Dangerous Kiss' by Jackie Collins or 'Riders' by Jill Cooper – and she would eagerly join any discussion on the merits of Colin Firth's Mr. D'Arcy with a wide-eyed intensity that could be a little unnerving.

Perhaps this was what had inspired Susan to phone Carol when she was desperately running out of options but, anyway, Susan did like Carol – she would often come out with hysterical lines that Susan wasn't entirely convinced Carol had understood herself, which made her even funnier. And she was eternally kind in her dealings with everyone, which was a refreshing change from most of the pitiless denizens of Stone Rose.

The two girls picked up again where they had left off – scanning the room, not wanting to miss anything.

For there was plenty to see – both on the stage and amongst the audience, picked out from the shadows randomly by the swooping lights from the lamps turning and spinning in the gantry up in the ceiling.

It was not a big club, holding about 300 people, and it was full tonight – Susan had been lucky to get two of the last tickets available when she phoned the box office earlier in the day.

It was decked out in a modern style with little in the way of decoration. The walls were painted black, the same as the stage, which thrust out at a low height into the audience, which was, therefore, ranged on three sides of it. The whole idea was, basically, black and chrome, so that the bar – which ran along the back wall opposite and facing the stage – was all chrome tubes around a shiny black counter and silvery mirrors running along behind the bartenders.

Otherwise there was simply a shimmering silver curtain at the back of the stage, through which the performers made their entrance, and the obligatory disco ball – a big one – suspended above the front of the stage, turning and firing out its lasers of light.

They had only just arrived at the club, having spent a couple of hours in the bars around Soho first by way of a warm-up. Evidently they had just missed an act as the stage hands were clearing away the detritus: various lurid-coloured items of women's underwear, feather boas, and what looked to Susan suspiciously like dildos – several large ones – again of lurid colours. There was also a reddish liquid splashed about the stage, which was now being cleared and dried up. Susan thought that must have been a hell of warm up act – the crowd was still buzzing and there was a crackling atmosphere in the room.

The audience was an unholy mix of young professionals, out for some deviant kicks to leaven their otherwise dully shiny careers – sorry, lives; bohemian types with long ringlet hair and multi-coloured waistcoats; leather and denim-clad bikers trying to out-mean each other; genuine freaks of all shapes and sizes (the noisiest group); and a general morass of hard-core, seasoned Soho dwellers identifiable from their black clothes, white pallor and studied nonchalance.

The one thing common to all was that they were, to a man / woman / in-between, heavily drunk.

Everyone was nominally at one of the small circular tables that arced in rows around the stage and terraced back towards the bar and side walls, the last two rows being at slightly higher elevations. But the tables weren't holding them as many were up on their feet, moving from table to table, or simply meandering about the place, entirely without purpose.

There was a heavy disco track bumping away in the background and some were swaying along; others were simply hollering and screaming randomly; and amorous couples were pawing at each other, obviously over-stimulated by what they had already seen. The whole scene pulsed with a throw-caution-to-the-wind, end-of-the-century, wild abandonment that was itself intoxicating. The numerous drinks already downed by

Susan and Carol were, in any event, doing their remorseless damage but the two adventurers were also being carried along by this heady atmosphere.

They looked at each other again and simultaneously burst out laughing together.

"Wow, what a place !" shouted Susan above the din.

"It's awesome !" shouted Carol, happily.

They clinked their glasses together and took another ill-judged glug.

Their table was a couple of rows back from the front of the stage, not centre but more towards the wall on their right as they faced the stage. As Susan's eyes tracked along the row of tables up against the wall, she noticed that there was a larger table at the end nearest the stage that was empty (in fact, it must have been the only empty table in the place) but it was roped off with the red tasselled rope beloved of egotistical club owners the world over.

She presumed, matter-of-factly, that this must be Michael Green's table but he didn't appear to be in the house this evening. Through the alcoholic haze, the common sense voice told her it was obviously naïve to assume that she only had to turn up at one of his many business ventures and expect him to be sat waiting for her. But still, she was disappointed.

However, that disappointment didn't have time to linger for, at that moment, the swell of noise suddenly increased to a roar of approbation and she spun her head towards the stage just in time to see the entrance of a sparkling, throbbing vision in a full-length red sequined fishtail dress, bare shoulders, huge cleavage, full length black satin gloves, big blond hair, stacked black eyelashes and pouting fire engine red lips – a picture of voluptuousness.

This was The World Famous *BOB*.

Susan had done her research on booking the tickets and found that this lady appeared to be a genuine star on the New York neo-burlesque scene, so the club had scored something of a coup in booking her as MC for the evening.

Model thin she was not but she oozed sexuality and confidence and the crowd clearly knew and adored her. A full-on sassy big band jazz number blasted from the house P.A. lead by a filthy trumpet sounding like the clarion call of an advancing army of raving degenerates.

The lady sashayed around the stage, waving regally and blowing kisses to a crowd whooping and hollering like the Messiah had just landed. Susan and Carol looked at each other and just beamed. Wow !

The World Famous *BOB* began to peel off her gloves, to the resounding approval of the mob, her hips swaying as she went. Each glove was tossed aside in turn to reveal a bare pink arm and Susan thought she had never seen anything so directly erotic.

BOB gyrated as her hands went behind her back and Susan realised the dress was going next. Bloody hell, there was no messing around with this woman. With a graceful twirl the dress crumpled in a shimmering heap on the stage and the lady stood in all her glory, legs apart, arms aloft, fists punching the air, glistening red mouth wide open with a joyous scream, liberated, in her head a wild, wild Marilyn Monroe, high on cocaine, performing for the Kennedy brothers and their buddies at a boys-only party in an alpine lodge, miles from prying eyes.

As noted, *BOB* was not what you might call slim, but neither was she fat; she was simply all woman, with a tremendous pair of pendulous breasts packed into a large, red sequinned bra that matched the snakeskin just shed onto the floor and knickers that just held in a round-the-world bottom (from front to back); breasts that were now

162

being flaunted in the face of a lucky punter on a ringside seat, who gasped and grasped as if it were his dying wish.

BOB moved towards a small table that stood just off centre near the front of the stage that Susan hadn't noticed until now. The spotlight followed her and so now lit up the table, which was draped in a gold lamé throw on top of which Susan could see a bottle, a bucket of ice, a silver cocktail mixing cup and an empty martini glass.

Again, this was clearly a crowd that was familiar with the routine as another roar of approval rose up as *BOB* now stood with the table before her, facing her adoring fans. They knew what was coming but Susan had to wonder. She looked again at Carol who, shrieking, pointed at the table and cried: "Watch this !"

'What?! – how does bloody Carol know?' puzzled Susan as she turned back to see *BOB* theatrically holding the mixer high above her head and presenting it to both sides of the stage, as if she was about to perform magic.

Susan's vivid imagination quickly – and shamefully – conjured up all sorts of possibilities before *BOB* deftly opened up a dark crevasse between bra and cleavage with one hand and slipped the cup in with the other. A little shiver and a knowing wink later and the cold vessel was nestling happily in its padded saddle.

Then it was the bottle's turn to be brandished aloft before *BOB* aimed its top above her breasts and began to pour lasciviously into the cup while bending her legs up and down – knees together – in a rhythmic motion. The light began to dawn upon Susan and she burst out laughing with sheer delight.

This experienced pro now had the audience in the palm of her hand and was clearly enjoying the fun at least as much as they. She grabbed a couple of ice cubes from the bucket and plunged them into the cup, causing a cold splash onto the surrounding flesh that made her properly jump and the crowd thrill.

BOB stood over the martini glass, legs apart, and began to bend forward as if to pour but then stopped, stood back up, wagged her finger, shook her head and strutted away from the table, teasing the people and the people loved it.

She did a little wiggle with her hands on her hips and her back to the audience before reeling back round and returning to the table to pick up a last prop that Susan hadn't spotted before – a stainless steel flat handle cocktail ice strainer. *BOB* bit the handle between her teeth and now she was ready to pour. Legs apart once more, the crowd baying, and she jammed her chin in to her collar bone to position the strainer on the top of the cup, inclined forward carefully and the clear liquid fell through the air into the glass directly below.

A shake of her bent frame, boobs swaying, and a last drop was squeezed through the strainer. Back upright, arms in the air triumphantly and the place was going wild. But this was a proper performer – always holding something back.

As they were clapping and cheering, the crowd noticed *BOB*s left hand pull the elastic of her knickers forward and a low moan rumbled down through the rows of tables as her right hand dove into the shadowed gap that had opened up. Susan and Carol were frozen, open-mouthed, until they realised what she was doing. With a flourish, the star plucked three green olives from that warm repository, unceremoniously slung two in the martini with a splash, popped the third in her mouth and masticated wickedly with a homely wink that simply said: "Join me ..."

Pandemonium broke out as she calmly passed the ennobled drink to the first punter who stretched out his hands. It was the same Joe that had unwittingly come into such close proximity to those same olives just two minutes before. Obviously his lucky night. He beamed at his prize, unsure whether to drink it down or take it home to put on the mantelpiece.

Susan and Carol leapt to their feet, cheering wildly along with every last person in the house.

The World Famous *BOB* was not even finished at that but promptly unleashed that magnificent creamy bosom from its glowing red housing, revealing matching red tassels hanging and twitching on her nipples.

Everyone was on their feet by now doing their damnedest – encouraging each other – to collectively punch a hole through the fabric of their normal humdrum reality. In this room.

BOB glided around the stage some more, collecting the payoff for all her hard work and expertise; waving, blowing kisses, spinning the tassels round like X-rated Catherine wheels; and finally took a microphone from a disembodied hand at the side of the stage.

"Thank you. Thank you, my darlings. You're too kind. Please, no," her American accent sprinkling another layer of glamour on the proceedings.

Once the tumult had dissipated sufficiently, she stood centre stage to address her people, apparently heedless of the potential incongruousness of standing casually like that, virtually nude and having just dispensed cocktail comestibles in such a lewd and despicable manner (as the Christian Mothers of America had once described her act).

"It's so good to be back among my English friends again," then she hesitated, apparently genuinely caught in two minds for a moment, "or is it British?" She looked to the side of the stage for help, her palms uplifted, shoulders shrugging: "What?"; got no help and turned her best, big, genuine showbiz smile on to the audience: "Well, whatever – you all shouldn't be hung up about that shid anyway."

A loud cheer of approval and everyone clapped.

"I can see we've got all sorts in here tonight, anyway" – ostentatiously peering at the crowd. "Yes, I rather do think we've got people from all corners of the planet here in this wonderful city of London" – working the crowd, feeling it up.

"We've got a few who are off the planet too, I believe; yes," pointing, smiling, at a group of long-haired freaks at a table near the front: "Am I right?"

She was now making them laugh as well as holler and whistle.

"We've got them all. Alive or dead. Yes, we've got some of the Undead amongst us; I think they need to take The Cure." This time moving to a group of Goths, all in black, lurking in the corner shadows; representatives of a tribe not habitually known for their carefree sense of humour but, with the spotlight on them and The World Famous *BOB*s milky orbs slapping their cheeks, the unusual sight of happy, childlike grins on their pallid faces was caught, just for a moment.

She playfully ruffled the hairsprayed nest of one of the gang before stepping gingerly back to the stage on her high heels, intoning on the way: "We love you, yes, we love all of you."

She stood before them centre stage once more. Exposed and unashamed.

"Ladies and gentlemen. If all this is about anything it is about one thing. And that is love, people. Love each other. No matter what you look like or where you're from, you are loveable and we all love you."

A wave of contentment washed over the crowd and, suddenly, this appeared to Susan rather like a bizarre evangelical gospel meeting with *BOB* as their Billy Graham. 'Christ, what could my father do with a bit of this?' she thought. And then a faint echo that, unconsciously, she didn't really want to hear: 'What could I do .. ?'

BOB continued: "And now, my friends, here is a special person I know you're going to love – a fellow Yank and a very dear friend of mine; please put your hands together for the very wonderful . . . Candy Stripes." *BOB*s table and garments were scooped up by lightning-quick stage hands, a pounding soul track kicked in and another startling vision of bohemian glamour strode onto the stage.

Susan waved to one of the bunny-clad waitresses for more drinks and the two friends proceeded to laugh and shriek and holler their way through two of the happiest hours they would ever spend.

At 11:00 o'clock they were transfixed by the penultimate act of the night – Stacey Stax in 'Beauty and the Beast'. This was a fairly easy proposition to grasp but its power lay in the intensity of its execution. The performer – a female, Susan was fairly sure (although one or two of the earlier acts had taught her not to assume too much on that point) – was made up brilliantly so that when she faced stage left the audience saw her right side got up as a virginal bride, all in white with a satin bow headband, sheer veil, chiffon dress and lace glove; when she spun around 180°, however, the audience saw her other half as a devil, blood red from tip to toe, complete with a horn protruding from the head, sharpened teeth, pointy ear and a cloven hoof.

The premise was evidently of the repulsive temptations put before the bride by the corrupting fiend and her heroic efforts to resist them. Accordingly, the audience would see him produce a bottle of Jack Daniels and wave it in front of her, then spin around to see her raise her hand to her mouth to stop the vile liquid from entering, then back again to see him take a long slug himself and fling the bottle away in disgust.

He then produced a syringe and leered horribly; spun back around to see the bride waving it away and almost swooning; back again and the devil stabs the needle into his own leg with a roar of ecstasy.

All the time 'Lagartija Nick' is rumbling like thunder out of the speakers.

In due course the devil has become completely unhinged by the enormity of his lust and the stimulants ingested into his body and mind and begins to paw frantically at the increasingly terror-stricken bride. Finally, he tears the dress off in a frenzy so that the bride is stripped to reveal a pale white breast, lace panties and white stockings.

An audible gasp could be heard from the audience at this outrageous violation.

The artiste turns one way and the other so that the crowd sees, at once, the panting devil's left hand move over his victim's pale flesh, over her hard purple nipple and disgustingly down her stomach. Another spin and the bride's wide eyes dart beseechingly and she flings out her hand in a wordless cry for help.

The brute snatches at the elastic of her knickers and snaps them off in one go. Another gasp is wrenched from the audience and they gaze, wide-eyed, in horror as his next move tells them worse is yet to come. Much worse.

The beast has spun back in view and we now see his hand go to his own groin as he grasps his own scarlet leather loincloth and yanks it away to reveal a full, dark penis that he now begins to caress with his eyes screwed shut, moaning.

One or two screams are emitted.

'How the fuck does she do that?' pops into Susan's head as, now, the performer turns slowly to face the crowd head on, so that the two halves can be seen together, a perverted mirror image.

Susan concludes that the penis must be some sort of prosthesis as the woman's vagina can also be seen clearly next to it. And then: 'Oh, my god. No . . .' – more screaming now from around the room as the red fingers crawl across to assault that self-same vagina.

The fact of the performer's face and body being split in half this way somehow contrives to present, utterly realistically, the tormentor and tormented, simultaneously – the bride cries in terror and the devil in lust.

It gets worse as the red hand now grasps the penis and begins to arch it towards the opening next to it and a horrified realisation of what could be happening next sweeps the room.

Susan begins to feel panicky and looks to her friend. Carol appears to be in some sort of trance. There are big droplets of sweat on her top lip. Her cheeks are flushed with a scarlet red that seems to have been scratched in, her Alice band has gone, her wet hair is stuck to her forehead, and her eyes – whilst ostensibly directed at the stage – are actually far away.

In a moment of fate, Susan's gaze slips past Carol to the VIP table that had been empty before. Suddenly everything slows down and she is in a tunnel lit only at the end, where she can see figures moving. There are people at the table now, gyrating and jerking. A splodge of blonde, like a knob of butter dropped in a black frying pan, smears across her vision.

Now the tunnel has lurched forward 90° and she is falling down it, feet first. She can hear the air whistling past her ears, her stomach departs and two giant thumbs press her temples into her head.

It's Martin.

At the table with Michael Green.

And two beautiful young women.

All of them on their feet, dancing and shouting with their shirts and blouses undone, holding onto each other and laughing uproariously.

Martin has a velvet black shirt half on and half off above jet black jeans, swigging from a bottle of Budweiser in his left hand and his right arm over the shoulders of the taller woman – a raven-haired beauty who is now down to her bra and also swigging from a bottle in her right hand. They kiss urgently and passionately and, together, look extraordinary.

Michael Green is (just about) wearing a sparkling violet shirt and has his arms around the proverbial blonde bombshell and his hands hovering over the tiny blue vest that is struggling to contain the pneumatic swaying breasts beneath it.

Martin Dash, that is. The same fucking Martin Dash who for the last 14 months has not touched one drop of alcohol, displayed the passion of anything more than a broken trouser press, or gone within 50 feet of any dance floor.

At least to Susan's knowledge . . .

She could feel the fury rising up in her as she slowly realised she'd been taken for a first class fool.

'He's been leading a double life', she thought, 'but how could he do that?!' She stared at the man she thought she knew (she could feel her teeth grinding) and realised that he seemed completely different. Apart from the fact that he was obviously drunk – very drunk, in fact – his whole demeanour and body shape, his very features, appeared so much more animated. It could have been another man.

Her head was spinning. She couldn't quite believe this was happening and was struggling to get over the shock, although she could also feel a momentum building to get over to that table and vent the rage that was threatening to swamp her.

"Bloody Hell."

It was Carol's voice.

Susan's attention was momentarily diverted back to Carol and she suddenly realised that she had completely missed the denouement of the previous thing that had been gripping her attention only a minute ago.

'What?"

"I said, bloody hell, eh?" repeated Carol, now blowing out her cheeks as though she had just completed the London Marathon. "I can't believe we just saw that...it was...awesome."

Susan was struggling to pay attention but swung her head back to the stage just in time to see the polarised garb of the Dark Lord and his virginal Queen being scooped off the floor by the hard-pressed stage hands. Susan hardly dared to ask what she had missed but Carol had by now recovered herself sufficiently to notice that Susan was distracted by something behind her. So she swung around to see the party in the corner, adjusted her glasses, peered and turned back to her friend.

"Isn't that Martin?" she said, blinking, apprehensive.

"Yes, it fucking is Martin," hissed Susan.

"Oh," said Carol, grimacing and realising that things had taken a bit of a tricky turn, "Oh dear."

"Fucking Martin fucking Dash with a pair of fucking bimbos having the time of his fucking life. The fucking cunt."

"Oh, fucking hell," blurted out Carol and adjusted her glasses again.

"I'm going to bloody see about this", growled Susan, now determined (and fuelled by 27 units of alcohol). She made to get out of her seat.

"Do you really think you should?" said Carol, nervously; placing a hand on Susan's forearm.

Before anything more could be said a deafening banging sound filled the room, as of a hundred mighty hammers crashing against the walls of a grit stone cave, and everywhere was plunged into the most complete blackest darkness.

Despite her bleary state, Susan recognised what the noise was in an instant and the recognition gave her a jolt. It was the introduction to 'Martin', by Soft Cell; an awesome piece of gothic electro dance music that she loved dearly. Since meeting her Martin, she had often smiled wryly to herself at the consonance between the demonic character described in the song and the real-life enigma of her acquaintance.

It was a piece clocking in at over 10 minutes that had been written and performed by the legendary synth pop duo of Marc Almond and Dave Ball and pressed onto a complimentary 12" disc packed in with their 1983 album, 'The Art of Falling Apart', that Susan had acquired – over 10 years later – when she was discovering a whole range of formative influences in her teens.

The song was inspired by the classic cult film of the same name by George A. Romero about an American teenager who may or may not have been an actual vampire but certainly had a taste for blood. And, sure enough, as the mock-horror beginning of the record was disgorged out of the speakers (with a disembodied voice intoning "Martin is talking to you" over a sizzling synthesiser noise), a dazzling spotlight was suddenly flicked on to display the striking vision of a classic Christopher Lee Count Dracula – black cape and all – in a circle of blinding light, crouched back on his haunches; his hands held up before him trying to shield his face; flinching against the onslaught of the brilliant chalk-white column boring relentlessly down upon him, pinning him like a trapped butterfly to the floor of the stage.

His face was white, of course, but it was split by the vile gash of his mouth, like a slice of black melon, studded with piss-yellow shark teeth, that dripped with vivid red blood and snarled and hissed like a cornered puma's. His eyes were nearly as frightening – wide and crazed with black irises and the whites more pink than white; flitting manically from side to side, like a fatally wounded animal shivering in its death throes.

As the heavy dance beat rumbled in, the beast sprang into life and began to scurry to the side of the stage and back again, perhaps becoming bolder; not just seeking to avoid the burning light now but straining to see individual audience members; starting to wonder if he might actually be able to turn the tables and make them feel what it's like to be attacked.

The song's lyrics kicked in with the whip crack of the synth drum beat, sung in Marc Almond's seductive, corrupting contralto.

Susan was open-mouthed at the congruence of all this and swung her head right, from the stage to where the present-day Martin was stationed. There was a bit more light on the audience now and she could see he was stood with Michael and the girls, apparently transfixed, as if the song was calling to him. His expression appeared first confused and then delighted at this paean to his name. It was obvious to Susan that this rendition in his presence was a complete surprise to Martin but the idea of grasping and exalting the moment was clearly now taking hold of him. He began to jig about with the girls, who were now dancing, laughing and mouthing to Martin: "It's you !" and shrieking and throwing their heads back. Susan had never mentioned the song to Martin (she rather liked to keep it to herself as her own private motif) and had no idea whether he knew the song or not but it occurred to her that this whole situation would be rather more unsettling to Martin if this was the first time he'd heard it.

Michael was also grinning, but in a rather less childlike fashion; as much as Martin's surprise seemed obvious to Susan, Michael's artful manipulation of developments appeared equally clear. Michael looked to Susan like nothing so much as a villainous stage Svengali, his grin that of a sinister puppeteer, successfully cajoling his dolls through charming pageants contrived by himself, taking delight in his total control of the affairs of his human subjects.

This was his club, of course – his acts; so what would have been easier than to line up the performance now unfolding before them, right on cue? Michael's attention – and the others' – was snapped back to the stage by a second bolt of light that now hit the stage to introduce to the crowd another figure: what looked like a medieval peasant girl (clothed in a bright white milkmaid's bonnet, fitted lace bodice with a plunging neckline to reveal a heaving cleavage, and voluminous skirts that fell only to the knees), apparently tied to a thick post standing firmly upright and swooning and crying at the sight of the vile creature that is now gazing horribly at her, his tongue rolling over his dry lips and the record's voice, hauntingly wails over and over: "Martin. Martin. Martin."

Susan felt a tug at her arm and turned to see Carol's shining moon face bobbing along to the music, laughing gleefully: "I wonder what's going to happen next?!" They both shrieked and threw their heads back. Not for the first time that evening, Susan congratulated herself on having brought the right person along to enjoy the show with her.

And Carol was right: fairly predictably (but no less thrillingly !), the vampire was soon gliding menacingly towards his powerless prey, who wriggled gamely against her bindings and screamed her best Hammer horror lungfuls. Some of the crowd were noisily booing the stage villain but a disturbingly large proportion were lustily cheering him on . . .

With a quick slashing movement, he had torn the bodice away to reveal where the heaving was emanating from. The girl's full red nipples shuddered in unison with the heart-rending sobs wailing from her quivering lips, her head tilted back to the right to show the full expanse of her milky white neck.

Her supporters in the crowd suddenly seemed to change sides and the whole audience was now literally baying for blood as Marc Almond's voice, eerily in tandem, called: "Kill ! Kill ! Kill !"

It struck Susan how well staged this affair was as she could have sworn she saw the demon's sharp hard fangs pierce slowly into the pale flesh so that dark red blood gushed – not flowed, but gushed – from the girl's neck, ran like a river over her left breast and splashed onto the floor. This was real Grand Guignol stuff – no fucking around – and it got the desired reaction as many genuine screams escaped from those in the crowd who'd really not been ready for that level of horror.

However, the beast's assault served to stop the girl's wailing at least – her head fell back, her eyelids closed as if in a dream, and her body slumped into the arms of her attacker as another impressive piece of stagecraft unfolded. The girl's bindings appeared to have magically dissolved and, as she lay on the left arm of the evil Count, his right arm discretely brought his black cape over the whole of her; dry ice swirled about the stage floor and a nauseous green light now shimmered over the scene as the music pounded away.

Then, with a flourish, the bloodsucker flicked the great cape back and out bounded a total reincarnation of the peasant girl into a fully-fledged vampish Countess in a tight black leather catsuit and heels, her own vivid red cape and black hair framing cruel eyes and a wide-open, red-lipped mouth snarling with the same sharp teeth as her new beau.

The crowd loudly cheered her stunning fall from grace.

The newly betrothed pair stalked the stage, here and there singling out particular individuals or groups for special hissing treatment.

The music had, by now, reached the song's middle section, a rumbling undertow of synth bass and drum denuded of the melody and lyrics, and The World Famous *BOB* took this opportunity to make a return to the stage to join her supernatural co-workers, prompting more raucous cheers.

She had now jettisoned the red two-piece outfit for a long white druid's cloak, with the hood thrown back off her head to show the sparkling white band in her hair to its best effect.

As she sashayed to the centre of the stage, it immediately became clear that this newfound modesty in her choice of attire was purely notional as the movement rhythmically swung open and closed the neck-to-toe fold at the front to show tantalising glimpses of her complete nudity underneath.

She flashed the dazzling Marilyn smile and waved to her fans, eyes twinkling like deep sapphires. She had in her left hand a microphone which she now raised to speak:

"All hail, bloodsuckers !" she cried to the congregation and the delighted roar in response temporarily drowned out the pulsing backbeat. "I think I can safely say that we know what *you* want, you vile degenerates !" – music to the ears of the happy crowd.

"Well, I hope you do love creatures of the night as much as we think you do because … ladies and gentlemen" – showbiz pause – "we have in the house tonight our very own Martin."

Susan froze.

A frisson of excitement rippled through the mob. No-one had expected this and there was a sudden anticipation as to what she might mean.

"Yes, thrill-seekers: an earth-bound angel with baby blond hair and a corrupted mind – let us draw into the fold the divine Martin Dash !"

Susan felt weightless, as if she had awoken in a dream. The whole evening had been a rollercoaster of shock, elation and dread but, suddenly, things seemed to be careering out of control to another frightening level. She spun round, saw Carol's awe-struck face on the way, utterly agog, and there stood Martin, with a new spotlight bathing him in a pool of white light for all the crowd to see.

Again, this new development had clearly taken him off guard as he simply stood stock-still for a moment, blinking in the light, obviously unsure of what was now happening. He turned to Michael, who was simply beside himself with glee, grinning and laughing manically, clapping his hands like a demented child on Christmas morning and nodding vigorously to Martin: "yes ! – Yes ! – YES !"

The two girls were whooping and dancing, with their arms draped over the boy, delighted to be, suddenly, at the centre of attention and determinedly making the most of it. Martin turned to look at the crowd and – Boom ! – there was, once again, one of those moments caught forever in the mind's eye of those who saw the sudden identification of the crowd with the golden sun god that looked down upon them, like a staged Versace fashion set. Martin looked magnificent – the twin veils of shadow hanging from his cheek bones, the full red lips parted in the formation of a sneer or a kiss (it was tantalisingly hard to tell which), the cloud of blond hair now turned stormy and streaked by the heat and sweat of the night's exertions, and everything else below all in black over his tall, lean physique.

The throng surrendered to him in a heartbeat, not knowing who or what Martin Dash was but, somehow, knowing intuitively, in an instant.

The harsh crack of the synth snare kicked in with immaculate timing and Marc Almond's voice swooped in once more crooning, "Maaaaaaartin, Ma-ah-ah-ah-ah-ah-aaartin," in a way that evoked the call to prayer from a lofty minaret in some faraway sheikdom. Martin looked to the stage in an heroic pose to see *BOB* beckoning him to her, siren-like, and calling to him seductively and in tandem with the disembodied chanteur and, indeed, many in the audience: "Martin – Maaartin."

He looked again to Michael who was now holding up his right arm, pointing the way to the stage and nodding once more. Martin's body suddenly snapped into life and he began to gyrate with the pounding music. Something in him had clearly decided to get into it and he was now moving, panther-like, along a raised rail that ran from their table and against the flank wall all the way to the stage, the spotlight tracking him as he went and the mob now almost totally delirious. He was swaying to the beat as he went and clapping his hands at shoulder height like a twisted flamenco dancer, nostrils flaring and head snapped back.

He looked superb. Susan felt a spasm between her legs, like a twitch of electricity, and her knickers were suddenly wet. This was Martin Dash – *her* Martin; former android, now all at once alive, sensationally alive – what might that mean?

As Martin arrived on the stage he was drawn to The World Famous *BOB*, her arms outstretched and open, serving to reveal the full glory of her magnificent naked breasts. Martin dropped slowly onto her left arm and she held him there, surprisingly strong, his face upturned to hers as their lips began to move towards each other as if impelled by some invisible magnet.

The two black-clad fiends started to circle the pair in the middle and, for the first time, Susan noticed that the Count held down low in his right hand, almost as if he was trying to conceal it, a sharp wooden stake, and – with a flush of horror – she saw that the Countess was, similarly, bearing a heavy wooden mallet. Things were getting completely out of kilter now. What the hell was happening? Her vision seemed to be juddering and she felt dizzy and sick. She'd taken numerous drugs at different times when she was younger and this recalled those nights when she'd been out of her mind on ecstasy and cocaine but was starting to come down and feeling ever so paranoid and edgy. Had someone spiked her drink? The whole thing seemed to be getting darker and more menacing. She was struggling to focus and squinted determinedly at the stage. Martin was prolapsed into *BOB*s yielding arms, looking up beautifully into her eyes, mesmerised like a baby in its mother's wrap, totally unaware that the stake was, at that moment, being positioned by the Count with the sharp end touching his left ribcage, the shaft standing jauntily upright. The Countess sidled up next to him, her long bony fingers, with the sharp red nails, nervously gripping and ungripping the handle of the mallet.

Susan couldn't believe what she was seeing. She frantically looked around in panic, desperate for some reassurance but all around her were hideous faces straight out of Goya's nightmarish paintings, leering and shrieking, apparently baying for the blood of her man. A tight ball of pure fear was rising up from the pit of her stomach, through her oesophagus, and another wave of nausea swept over her.

Could no-one else see what was happening? Martin himself appeared totally oblivious. She looked to her side and Carol's eyes met hers and said, silently: "What the fuck?!" Susan's head was now pounding, she could feel the music building to a crescendo but all sound was muffled as if she was under water; her arms and legs were heavy, she couldn't move.

She fixed her gaze back upon the stage just in time to see a grimacing Countess raising the mallet with both of her hands in front of her – up past her waist, past her chest, past her shoulders and, as she brought it high above her head, she turned to look to the table from whence Martin had come, her eyebrows raised as if in a question. The Count and *BOB* both did the same. Susan swivelled fast along their line of sight which ran to the agitated figure of

Michael Green, gripping the rail before his table, leaning forward excitedly, and Susan saw his head dip forward emphatically: "YES !!"

"NO !!" she heard the scream somewhere close to her but couldn't pinpoint where exactly. But all was total confusion now. Shapes grew before her, changed instantly in line and colour, dark and light. She didn't know where she was but felt things against her, sometimes soft, sometimes hard, sometimes sharp. She felt centres of pain arise – on her forearm, in the centre of her knee, her cheek.

It was as though she was in a washing machine going through a colour cycle on acid. Then she felt weightless again but, worse, she was actually flying now. And all the time there was a high-pitched scream of "No ! NO ! NO !!" piercing through the druggy miasma, echoing between her ears.

Then an almighty bang, a flash of bright white light, and the last image her eyes recorded before she lost consciousness was the face of Martin Dash looking down at her with a strange, confused look on his face, as though he had put his money in the chocolate bar machine and a firm, pungent turd had dropped into the tray.

22

When Susan had telephoned to ask if she wanted to go out, Carol had been rather taken by surprise. Sure, she knew Susan well enough at work and they'd done some socialising together but always as part of a wider group – this was the first time she'd suggested just the two of them go out.

However, Carol wasn't daft and had worked out that Susan's regular options – the great Charlotte, for example – had probably not come through so that she was, in reality, the rescue pick. But she just mentally shrugged and gladly accepted; to Carol it was perfectly understandable that, with her famous parents, striking good looks, and the rest, Susan would move in more rarefied circles and, in any event, Susan had never been anything less than friendly and kind to Carol. So why shouldn't she grab the odd crumb when it fell from the table?

Carol's life so far – with her parents, schooling, church and work – spoke of nothing so much as conformity and docility and, yes, that was the dominant tendency in Carol's psyche but it wasn't the only one because, now and then, a mischievous imp would seize her imagination and lead her to wonder what it might be like to not conform, to cross her parents, to *deviate* . . ?

And, wow, was she glad she'd done so tonight ! Little had she known what the night had in store for them when Susan's call had ended and she had scuttled upstairs to run a bath. They had got blind drunk, witnessed the wildest show she had ever seen or even heard of and were now in the Devil's lair . . . doing drugs ! Yes, angelic little Carol – cherub of Southfields Methodist Church – was now sat at midnight in the apartment above The Black and Blue

Dahlia that belonged to its lizard king impresario, Michael Green, who was, at this moment, sunk into a red leather armchair to her right, drawing heavily on a fat joint fashioned by himself.

In fact, Carol had taken her lead from The World Famous *BOB* (sat opposite Carol !) in politely declining Michael's offer to indulge, when he had finished rolling it.

"No, thank you, Michael – you know I don't. I have enough excitement in my life," was *BOB*s pithy demurral.

Carol had merely chirruped, "No thanks," at the same time thinking: 'I don't have enough excitement in my life.'

She had, in fact, tried marijuana when she was younger – at a college party – but had ended up being violently sick, driving the porcelain bus with her head down the toilet; an embarrassing episode she'd sworn never to repeat.

Her friend Duncan – the party host – had given her the joint; had told her the mistake had been to try it after drinking a whole load of alcohol; and that she should try it again when sober. And she had been tempted by Michael's offer, feeling that she would appear rather gauche by declining in this company (and worrying that she might be needlessly denying herself some genuine fun, yet again) but then she remembered that she'd drunk rather a lot of alcohol this time too and she didn't want to disgrace herself and spoil the moment she was in.

So she had been mightily relieved at *BOB*s refusal; and slightly surprised, having rather assumed – once she had seen the stuff come out – that it would be seen as a de rigueur badge of sophistication for all to take a tug in such worldly company.

No, she wanted to drink all this in and remember as much as possible. And who knew where it might lead? But even if it led nowhere – and she continued merrily through her predetermined roles of worker / wife / mother / housewife / pensioner / widow / patient / deceased – she would always be able to look back, smiling, at times like this when she had briefly cut loose and lived a little.

This was the living room of the apartment, which had a bathroom over to her right side (she knew because she had been in there not 10 minutes ago splashing water on Susan's bewildered face); a kitchen behind her right shoulder (she knew because she'd grabbed a glass of water for Susan from there not five minutes ago), and a bedroom or bedrooms behind her left shoulder (she didn't know but reasoned that must be where that passage door led).

To her left side – behind the slumped form of Susan – was a window onto the street and, although it was clearly well glazed (you couldn't really hear much more than a muffled echo of the Soho symphony being played outside – shouts, car horns, dance music, clacking shoes, tuneless singing and slamming doors), you could still watch the myriad colours that bounced up from the shop fascias, bar lights, street signs and traffic below.

The room enclosed a mishmash of conflicting effects. It had clearly started out as a coordinated design, with charcoal grey walls, a steel blue fitted carpet and shiny black painted doors, but now plonked within it was an assortment of furniture, equipment, books, paintings and curios that was suggestive of an owner who was more swayed by influences bearing upon him in the moment than an overarching drive to create a planned scheme of harmony.

Thus, the garish red armchairs in which the four of them now faced each other; the coffee table between them hewn from a big old tree, sanded and varnished; the Chinese lantern dangling from the ceiling above; the Victorian gilt mirror on the wall behind *BOB*; and so on and so forth.

Having said all that, the one impression Carol immediately obtained was the slightly unsettling thought that this was the sort of room that might be used for shooting porn films (she was not so closeted that she hadn't acquainted herself with the captivating spectacles that Google now made so readily available to all) but this might, of course, have been sparked by the heightened state of her senses at the time; the night they'd had; and their host's distinctive aura.

BOB was playing mum and had offered to make them all tea. The only one to decline was Michael, obviously determined that the night's revelries were not yet to draw to a domestic tea-coloured close and, instead, pouring himself a liberal dose of Jack Daniel's Tennessee whiskey. The teas set down before the assembled ladies, *BOB* now turned to Susan and asked: "Are you sure you're all right, darling?"

Susan interrupted her intense scrutiny of Michael to smile wanly at *BOB* and croak: "Yes, thank you . . . *BOB*?"

"Yeah, *BOB*s the only name I need, honey."

Susan's gaze swivelled back to resume her baleful campaign of staring at the man opposite.

Her body and soul had taken quite a pasting on the way up from her chair to the stage just half an hour ago and the audible crack of her head on the floor when she'd aquaplaned across a pool of (fake) blood had proved to be the final straw for her flagging consciousness. So it was only now that she was beginning to comprehend what had actually happened in that tumultuous climax to the show's final act, with the aid of Carol's description of the excitement that attended her incursion onto that hallowed square of performance space.

The story went that, upon seeing the hammer raised above Martin's prone body, Susan had leapt to her feet, screaming "No, no !" at a horrible volume; upset their table (drinks and all); begun weaving through the thickets of other people's tables, upsetting them (drinks and all) along the way, slashing at them like some jungle explorer; and advanced menacingly to the foreground in a ziz-zag pattern, like a wrecking ball Pac-Man in a glitch-ridden video game.

This had evidently caused pandemonium in the audience and a shocked halt by the performers, who naturally assumed that they were about to be attacked. And, indeed, they were subjected to an attack of sorts, with Susan flailing indiscriminately once she had reached the group and sobbing hysterically at the startled Martin who seemed to have snapped out of some dreamlike state, only to be confronted by a confusing nightmare.

The Countess' rash decision to try and resist Susan's grab for the hammer only served to push her assailant into another gear and was quickly reversed by a dash for the back of the stage, only to be pursued by the gatecrasher, who appeared to have decided to now go for the befanged thespian. It was at this point that the blood-streaked stage floor came to their collective rescue and Susan's mad adventure came to an abrupt end.

At this the music stopped, the house lights were thrown on and the entire club seemed frozen just for a moment, as if caught in a particularly gruesome Bruegel, their eyes blinking in the unwelcome light that now shone on their individual nefarious activities. It made quite a biblical scene, a disturbed Adoration of the Magi: Martin – with his golden hair shining like the halo of the baby Christ, his eyes wide at the forceful agency of the moment – lay between *BOB* and the Count (as Mary and Joseph), dread etched on their faces at the threat that had visited their domestic arrangement; all of them looking across to where the fallen angel lay – blooded, body mangled and wracked by the torments of sin that had laid her so low, and stood over by the hammer-wielding, redemptive Gabriel only partly covered by a black velvet cloak ...

In the right wing, a chorus of the heavenly saints looked on, appalled, and among the heaving throng in the foreground was a cornucopia of delightful tableaux to pick out and linger over at leisure if only there was the time – tangled limbs, faces stuck together, wine, undress, horror.

Eventually, Michael had gathered himself, hurried onto the stage and taken charge. Despite the general consensus that an ambulance should be called for the stricken clubber, he insisted that she would be fine and all she needed was a rest and a hot toddy in his apartment. Still unconvinced, the Count was, nevertheless, persuaded to wrestle Susan up into his arms and carry her where Michael led to the side door and up the stairs to the first floor.

And she had indeed started to come round even as she was being carried upstairs. She must still have been fairly groggy as the impression that she was being carried away by the very vampire from whom she had just tried to save Martin didn't seem to perturb her massively and, in fact, merely produced a wry, enigmatic smile. Once she'd had a few minutes in the chair she'd been deposited in, she gained a rather more accurate appreciation of her true circumstances beyond her apparent liberation from the earthly chains of mortality by a swarthy bloodsucker.

And she stared at Michael. And stared and stared. To say that she had gained a rather poor first impression of Michael Green was something of an understatement. This was the man whose mere presence had apparently terrified her beau into fleeing a packed Tube station in broad daylight; who Martin had called 'evil', but who, nevertheless, appeared to have been the first person he had turned to upon release from the cells *in preference to her*; and who seemed happy and able to procure *tarts* for Martin at a moment's notice, again *in preference to her*.

And neither did he seem to be busting a gut to make amends now. He had sauntered into the bedroom to change his sweat-soaked shirt to a green polo-necked top, and then set to building his spliff with an unconcerned air. His head still showed signs of the sweat that had screwed his ginger hair into darker, more defined curls – as if wrapped around the curlers old ladies used, heedless of the invention of curling tongs – but it was drying now, back to its softer, lighter undulations. His face had been made paler – and marked with pink blotches on the cheekbones – by the drama and exertions of the last half an hour but he had the smug, self-satisfied air of one who knows his job has been well done.

BOB had decided to delay the ritual shedding of all the accoutrements of her stage persona in the dressing room downstairs in favour of sitting up here with the two girls for a while to ensure their wellbeing; along with the Count, she had questioned whether they shouldn't have had Susan checked out at the hospital after a bang on the head like that and was now keeping a watchful eye on the girl for any signs of a problem. Thus, she had – for now – contented herself with a full-length pink towelling dressing gown; her big blonde wig thrown off to reveal straight corn-coloured hair flattened to her scalp; a hand-held mirror; and make-up remover that she was now daubing down her cheeks and across her forehead, nose and chin.

Carol wondered how well Michael and *BOB* knew each other – when they had got up to the flat and brought Susan round, *BOB* had nagged Michael to try and find the girls a change of clothes from somewhere in a way that suggested they'd known each other for years but, nevertheless, Carol was fairly sure that they weren't a couple.

As it happened, both girls were adamant that they didn't want to change clothes and, given that *BOB* had said they would get them a taxi once she was sure Susan was OK, they didn't expect to be staying long. Thus, the two girls sat, still venting wisps of steam from the heat and sweat of the club floor, with Susan in a particularly dishevelled state – her hair like a banshee's; one sleeve of her blouse torn; and much of her black skirt still smeared in the blood that had been her undoing on the stage and which was now being deposited liberally on Michael's upholstery. Not that he seemed to bother. Perhaps it wouldn't show so badly on the red leather, thought Carol, abstractedly sipping her tea.

An awkward silence had descended upon the motley quartet at the point when Susan's companions could no longer convincingly feign disregard of her obviously hostile appraisal of their host. Finally, it was broken by Michael after another long exhalation of smoke aimed up at the lantern . . .

"Looks to me as though you might have some questions, Miss Susan," he drawled, smirking and looking her straight in the eye now. His speech was gruff but had good intonation and there was the hint of a West Country burr.

*BOB*s head jerked up to look at Michael.

"Do you know this girl, Michael?" It was only then that it occurred to Susan (and Carol) that *BOB* might have no idea of the background to all this.

"Certainly," Michael inclined his head to *BOB* while still smiling / smirking at Susan, "although we've never been formally introduced . . . *BOB*, may I introduce you to Miss Susan Sachs, youngest daughter of the Right Honourable James Michael Sachs, Secretary of State for Transport and one of the senior members of the Government of this fine country."

BOB turned her gaze to Susan, looking more, not less, concerned now. Not fazed though. And, having apparently thought about it for a moment, gave Susan her friendliest smile, dipped her head and said: "Well, I'm pleased to meet you, Susan, even if it is in rather unusual circumstances," and laughed with an infectious chuckle that made even Susan smile and relax a little.

"And . . ?" *BOB* turned her gaze to Carol. "Oh, Carol – Carol Gee," Carol spluttered – "I'm Susan's friend."

BOB nodded a 'hello' to Carol also and purred: "Well I'm sure we're all Susan's friends. Aren't we Michael?"

"You betcha," shot back Michael, taking a slug of his Jack Daniels.

"What's happened to Martin?" Susan, eyes hard against Michael once more, had clearly had enough of the mock pleasantries.

"To be honest, Sweet Cheeks, I don't know. After your little turn, things got a bit . . . confused, as you may have noticed; oh – no – you were out, weren't you?" he grinned, mocking, arrogant. "Looks like he didn't want to hang around to catch up." Twisting the knife a little more.

"Why were you so upset about that boy, sweetie?" asked *BOB* after giving Michael a withering glare that told him to lay off. "That was only a bit of play-acting, you know. Michael had asked us to bring him into the act for a bit of fun as we were doing 'Martin' anyway. What was his name? Martin Dash? What a good looking boy that is, eh?" *BOB* blew out her cheeks to emphasise the point.

Susan felt her cheeks blush and the sheer ignominy of the whole thing suddenly caught up with her. "I don't know," she stuttered "It's all been so upsetting, what's happened . . . and we'd had a lot to drink . . . and . . ." She put her thumb and forefinger to the bridge of her nose, squeezed her eyes shut and her shoulders started to shake involuntarily.

"Oh, darling, don't." *BOB* was off her chair in a moment and wrapped a comforting arm around Susan's shoulder. "It's not worth crying over, believe me, none of these men are." She shot a venomous glance at Michael who was suddenly isolated, Carol also having leaned over to put her hand on Susan's arm. *BOB* was now dispensing a tissue from the box she'd been using.

Michael opened his mouth, raised his eyebrows and turned his palms up in a silent 'What?!'

Carol realised that, if Susan felt anything like herself, she'd still be basically drunk, so it wasn't really surprising to see this second collapse.

However, after some loud snorting into *BOB*s tissues and a long draught of her tea, Susan had nearly recomposed herself and waved her maids away with: "I'm OK. I'm fine. But thank you." And then she mentally girded herself to confront her inscrutable adversary once more.

"All I want to know," she started slowly, deliberately – "All I want to know . . . is what has happened to Martin?" She raised her hand quickly to pre-empt the response that Michael had already told her he didn't know. "What I mean is: what has happened to change Martin from the person he was last week – the quiet, sweet man, struggling with his illness – to what now appears to be some drunken lounge lizard, pawing ageing sluts, out with . . . with *you*."

At this she glared at him and no-one could miss the tone of that. Once again Michael raised his eyebrows as if to appear genuinely hurt.

BOB was trying to catch up – "What illness, dear? What's wrong with Martin?"

Michael leapt at this – "Ah yes, Martin's illness. What indeed is wrong with him? What's he told you at any rate, Susan?" His tone told you that the question might not have been asked in the spirit of genuine enquiry and Susan didn't like it. Didn't like it at all. But she persevered: "Anhedonia. He has anhedonia."

Michael slumped back in his chair with a triumphant air.

"Anhedonia?" piped up *BOB*.

"Yes, it's a mental illness where you don't have any feelings," Susan began explaining but was cut short by *BOB*: "Yes, yes – I know what it is. I had a friend who suffered from that."

Susan wheeled round as if to grab a lifeline – "Really? And what was it like?"

"Well, as you say, a very flat personality. You never got anything from her. Perfectly inoffensive, but perfectly nothing as well. I don't think she was happy. Well, I know she wasn't . . ." *BOB*s account trailed off.

"How do you mean? What happened?" Susan pressed. *BOB* looked at Susan, concerned now, and appeared to be grappling with something and hesitant to speak further. Susan cocked her head to reiterate the question, to which *BOB* replied, reluctantly: "Well, you know – she's . . . not with us anymore."

Susan took the meaning, paused in thought for a moment, and then turned back to Michael.

"What's your connection to Martin, Michael?" She was now impatient to get to the point. "When he saw you in the Tube station, he ran like he was scared to death. Then the next thing I see, he's drinking with you like a long lost brother or something."

The complacent, whimsical look went from Michael's face to be replaced by a hardening of the jaw and a sullen shadow of malevolence passed across his features. "We *were* brothers," he spat out. Then he adjusted himself: "In all but the fact." For a moment he looked vulnerable and Susan (and Carol and *BOB*) were intrigued.

"What's that mean?" Susan suddenly felt she had an advantage to press.

Michael sat further up in his chair again and took another drink before he continued: "I don't suppose our Martin has told you much about his past has he?" – straight back to you, love – "Hmm?"

Susan considered. And replied: "He told me some cock and bull story about moving around a lot and his parents dying. And you stalking him."

Michael let out a gleeful "Ha !" and threw his head back in mirth.

"But I knew that was crap. And I told him so."

"But you got nothing more out of him?"

"No."

"No, I don't suppose you would. Well, for one thing, you need to know that his name isn't Martin Dash."

This was the sort of information that Susan had subconsciously been dreading. That Martin was a conman – a charlatan who'd led everyone, including her, a merry dance these last 14 months. She was now beginning to feel empty. And tearful again. But this time she held it together. She wanted to know the truth.

All of it.

Susan dived straight in: "What is his name then?"

"Martin Dayton."

Michael allowed a dramatic pause for that one to sink in and then continued: "And he grew up in Cornwall with me; with me and Megan." His face had darkened again and Susan could have sworn that she heard his speech crack at the end of that sentence.

It was her turn to wait for a moment.

"Who is Megan?"

Not one bit of Michael moved. Not his hands. Not his feet. Nor his head. Nor his eyes. But Susan could see that beneath the solidified exterior, he was struggling to contain his emotions. And this time there was no doubt that his voice was cracking.

"Megan is – was – my sister."

He looked as though he was about to cry and Susan suddenly saw the other side of Michael Green, a side that appeared hopelessly lost and vulnerable. Quite unlike what she had seen of the man so far. She found that she had connected with some sort of feeling that meant she was hesitant to ask the next question – out of consideration for Michael.

"*Was*..?"

"She was killed," his voice sounded almost hoarse now and he seemed to be breathing more heavily.

Carol and *BOB* had turned themselves into statues.

"– by Martin."

None of them could help it – all three women gasped at once, eyes wide in utter amazement.

A thought popped into Susan's head as to how many more shocks she might be able to take in one night.

"At least that's what the papers said. But I never believed it."

Michael now had his head in his hands, his elbows on his knees. There was ultimately no breakdown like Susan's but she saw a tear drop to the carpet from the shadows of his hands on his cheeks

And then another one.

The three women looked at each other. *BOB* seesawed from Susan to Michael to put a hand on his shoulder but this made him jump up from his chair, in a willed act of reclamation with the words: "Need the loo," and shot off, not to the bathroom behind him but to the ensuite adjoining his own bedroom. When he had passed through the door to the hallway, *BOB* exhaled and asked: "Christ, what have I walked into here?"

"Good question," said Carol, finally daring to move and slumping back into her chair.

Susan didn't speak for a while, giving a cushion on the floor an unusual degree of scrutiny. But, eventually, she asked: "*BOB* – how well do you know Michael?" and then, "if you don't mind me asking."

BOB seemed slightly surprised at this and considered Susan, somewhat warily, before deciding that, no, this wasn't the police, the press or the revenue so she could relax.

She took another sip of tea, looked up at the ceiling for the answer, got it and turned back to Susan. "I've known Michael for about five years, I think. Ever since I started coming over here to do shows."

"You're based in New York, aren't you?"

"That's right, dear, but I do get out now and then," *BOB* shot back and they all laughed. The atmosphere suddenly seemed rather more relaxed with Michael out of the way.

"He owns a lot of properties round here – well, around a lot of places, so I gather – but he used to back another club

I did gigs for now and then: 'The Cross'. Run by Julian Jacobs. Michael would come round after the shows, take me to dinner; put me up; look after me generally, in fact."

"But no, before you're thinking it – nothing like that," they laughed again. "No, he's always been the perfect gentleman. I think he just took a shine to me and we got on. Anyway, I've got my beau back in New York and Michael knows that . . . and I don't think I'm his type !"

The perfect timing of the professional got another laugh out of the girls.

"Now he's opened this place – I think he fancied himself as a bit of a Rick Blaine." She looked at the girls for a sign of recognition.

"Casablanca," from Susan.

BOB nodded – "Well done, sweetie. So I play here and The Cross now. And one or two other places. But I only get over here now and then, as I say. So what I know of Michael is that he's a tough cookie – he can be hard on people. And difficult to read sometimes, but, like I say, I've never had a problem with him. We've always got on."

"Once he decides you're on his side, he's very loyal – he'll look after you. So if your guy, Martin, is in trouble he could have a lot worse of a friend to look out for him than Michael."

"I've always looked after Martin," this from Michael, standing in the doorway, made them all jump.

"Jesus, Michael, why don't you knock?" quipped *BOB*.

Michael grinned and sauntered back into his chair, recomposed. Though Susan noticed he was still sniffing a little. But then again, perhaps he's sought some aid to brighten his mood, thought Susan.

He rubbed his finger across his nose and sniffed again, as if to confirm.

'Didn't think to share with us,' mused Susan. But, then again, perhaps he was being purposely discrete, cautious.

Anyway, he was certainly more voluble now and launched straight back into his story.

"I'm sorry to have shocked you like that, Susan," he started, "but there is a lot to stir up once you get into it, to be honest. Me and Megan knew Martin from when we were kids. We all grew up together in St Ives. Martin was like my brother and he and Megan . . . well" . . . . He looked at Susan from under his eyebrows, she gave him her poker face back and he carried on – "My mum and dad liked Martin too. Looked after him a lot; we all did 'cos of the trouble he had . . . with his own family, you know?"

Susan wasn't sure if he was asking her the question but, in any event, said: "Martin's never told me any of this," and – again – felt a sharp twinge of annoyance. Seeing he'd have to explain, Michael went on: "Martin had a lot of trouble at home with his own mum and dad. Jack Dayton was an artist, part of the colony around St Ives," at this he gave an almost involuntary snort of derision, "and drank a bit – well, a lot, actually. Like all of them. And the rest. But, anyway – his mum was lovely: Sonia. But she battled Jack all the way. Lots of fights. And Martin caught in the middle. Then it started that she'd go off for periods, with the gypsies."

"The gypsies?" this from Susan.

"Yes, gypsies. I know it all sounds a bit . . .," he struggled for the word, ". . . . *exotic* but, yeah, rumour had it that Sonia had a bit of a thing for one of them. But, whatever, she always came back after a while. For Martin really. She loved Martin like you don't know. She actually took Martin with her once or twice. He had a friend amongst them himself, as it happens. Little girl called Molly."

Michael paused, obviously pondering which fork to take next. "But it was hard for her with Jack. Whether he drank because of what she was up to or he drove her away with his drinking and what not . . . I don't know which came first. But, anyway, she always came back, eventually."

"And Martin was in the middle of all this."

"Hmm, it did take its toll, I think. He started going off the rails a bit."

"How do you mean?"

"He was acting strangely. You couldn't talk to him. He was doing various drugs, I know." Michael flicked his gaze up at Susan. She didn't oblige him with a reaction.

"Well, we all were," he conceded, "It all went a bit mental that summer. Martin had actually had some sort of row with his mother. And with Megan."

"Why with Megan?"

Again, Michael looked directly at Susan as he said "Megan loved Martin . . . mightily."

"And did Martin love Megan?"

"Yes," he snapped back, (rather emphatically, Susan thought). "We all loved Martin," (rather obliquely, Susan thought).

"That may have been the problem," he continued, "everyone loved Martin. They all wanted a piece of him. But there was a complication," and here he paused again, apparently unsure of which direction to take. Then finally: "Molly."

"The gypsy girl?" Susan had remembered that bit.

"Yeah, the gypsy girl," the corners of his mouth turned down in an ironic grimace at this. "He seemed to have a thing about her."

"And your sister was none too impressed?"

"No, she was not." Michael gave a short, dry laugh at this and shook his head "Mind you, neither was Sonia, which was a little odd 'cos she wasn't too keen on Megan either."

"Why?" It seemed to Susan that Michael was slowly peeling back the layers of an onion gone bad inside to reveal a whole sorry morass of collapse and resentment and she wondered how much more there was.

Michael looked like he was regretting having said this but then found a way out: "I'm not sure Sonia would have thought anyone good enough for her Martin," and again surveyed Susan for any effect his words were having. But Susan had read the game and resolved to give him nothing. And Michael, in turn, pulled a wry smile at her defiance.

"So . . . what happened?" Susan had to know.

Again, Michael's gaze drifted off elsewhere until he could speak the words. "An accident. Fire. There was a little cottage on the beach at the foot of the cliffs. It was actually my parents' but they didn't use it. It had been left empty for years – I was never sure why. But we had keys, me and Meg. And Martin did too. We used to have some good times there, the three of us. Barbeques out on the beach, got friends round, had some brilliant parties – can you imagine? We were only 18, 19 and it was like our own little home. The three of us."

Susan noted that he's used that phrase more than once and for a little while now she'd wanted to ask whether there was ever a fourth, a girlfriend of Michael's, but something of what she had seen of Michael thus far – as short a time as it had been – suggested to her, somehow, that this wouldn't be a good idea. So she let that one pass. At least for now.

Susan looked to her companions. Both had their attention riveted upon Michael but returned Susan's glance with raised eyebrows and then back to Michael to encourage him to continue the tale. The lights and noise from the street outside had lessened now and it was so quiet in this room that you could hear the low murmur of the fridge in the kitchen.

Michael looked up and seemed to come out of his reverie, realise that they were all staring at him, and decide to finish the story rather peremptorily –

"So, one night the cottage caught fire. Burnt to the ground with my sister in it."

BOB broke the silence that followed this: "How awful, Michael. I am sorry. You weren't there?"

"No. But Martin was."

Susan leaned forward in her chair, resting her elbows on the arms – "And you said that Martin was blamed for it?"

"He was *tried* for it. For her *murder.*"

Just the voicing of the word sent a charge through the group.

It was Susan who spoke the word again but as a question that was evident in the faces of all three of the women.

"Murder .. ? But ... why? ... how?"

Michael blew through his lips as if he needed a breather before starting to explain.

"Well, he was there with her, for a start. That was a clear fact. He came out of the burning house in full view of a group who had been further down the shore and came when they saw the fire. But the real problem was the accelerant."

"The what?"

"Fire accelerant is what the police called it. A big gas cylinder in the house that blew up and did the real damage. They reckoned that it had been doused in petrol to make sure it blew and that meant there was so much more heat; like I say, everything – including my sister – was burnt to ashes. So it looked deliberate."

"They asked me if I'd ever seen the cylinder in the cottage before and I had to say that I hadn't. Martin was put in the frame for it. They said there must have been a row and he'd killed her. It sounded ridiculous to me that Martin would do such a thing and I'm sure now that he didn't do it but at the time I didn't know what to think, I was in shock from losing my sister anyway. And then to have my best friend charged with her murder . . . but Martin's version of events was even crazier – he said that Megan had tried to kill him !"

All three pairs of the women's eyebrows were by now getting tired with being pushed ever higher up their foreheads.

"I know – it was fucking unbelievable. He said they had rowed – about Molly, of course – and that Megan had hit him from behind with something and knocked him out; that the next thing he knew he'd come round, he was lying on the bed and the building was on fire. Just managed to get down the stairs and outside before the beams started collapsing."

"He said he hadn't realised that Megan was lying in the bedroom with him – he'd just come round, thought he'd been left to die and just legged it out of the house to save his life. Said that after knocking him out she must have decided to commit suicide and die with him in the fire."

"To me that was just as crazy a story as Martin killing Meg. Thing is, though – he was acquitted by the jury. In his favour they did find a head injury on him that matched what he'd said; they reckoned that the explosion of the gas canister may have brought him round; and the people on the beach did say he only just got out in time, so if he was trying to kill her it was a hell of a risky way to do it. I didn't know what to think – I was all over the shop."

Susan hesitated before she asked the next question – "So the jury believed Martin's story?" This whipped Michael's head up to meet Susan's gaze. Fiercely. "What? That my sister tried to murder him?" he spat at her.

Susan tried to mollify him, "Well, she wouldn't do that, would she?"

"No, she fucking wouldn't," he replied, in a manner that suggested any further enquiry upon the matter would be unwelcome. Michael lit a cigarette and sank back into his chair.

"So, then he disappeared. And I never saw him again until I came across the two of you at the Tube." Michael's smile now seemed to be as much for his own benefit as Susan's.

This was now where she feared to go but knew she had to: "So what's happened to him? At the start of that day he was suffering from a condition that had robbed him of any personality whatsoever and now – what? You've cured him? What?" She was trying hard to dampen the indignant tone in her voice that even she could hear. Michael's smile broadened as the balance of inconvenient truths had, of course, now shifted.

"Well" – he settled back, taking a moment to blow a couple of imperfect smoke rings towards the lantern – "Martin Dayton's ongoing mental state has always been a thing of wonder, to be honest and, to me, this is just the latest episode."

Susan really was now struggling to keep her indignation in check (simply hearing Martin called by that name sunk her spirits low) and she could see that the bastard was beginning to enjoy this. Through a tight larynx she managed, "How's that?"

It was true that Michael did appear to enjoy having the exclusive hoard of information and familiarity with whole swathes of Martin's life that gave him the clear advantage over Susan.

"He's got the strangest turn of mind of anyone I've come across, quite frankly. He was always different right from when he was a kid. I mean, quite apart from the ... well, you know – good looks." Michael's eyes darted momentarily between Carol and *BOB*. "Well anyone can see he looks a bit different from the norm," he offered, sheepishly.

'Even a red-blooded het like you,' thought Susan. And Carol. And *BOB*.

Michael ploughed on: "You never quite knew where you were with him from one minute to the next. I always thought of him when I heard that Style Council song, 'My Ever Changing Moods'. Always made me chuckle that did. And I told him. And he'd give me 'Fuck off!' back and laugh with me ... " Michael looked wistful for a moment.

It was completely disorientating for Susan to hear this sort of thing about the Martin she knew and she wondered, even at this stage, if they were talking about the same person.

"He was always reading."

Susan's eyebrows did the job of registering surprise and raising the question.

"All sorts of shit," answered Michael. "I can't remember much of it." He struggled and looked to the space above Susan's head for aid. "Kafka – that was one."

'Interesting,' mused Susan.

"Sartre."

'Cool.'

"I had a look at some but it didn't do it for me – and he took the piss out of me for it," Michael didn't seem to be bitter about this but was laughing.

"Oh, Nietzsche !"

Susan smiled inwardly. She'd had a boyfriend at University who was forever quoting Nietzsche and, she found, had been typical of a type of person (usually male) who railed against the restrictions of social norms and would use the philosopher's theories as intellectual cover for the full range of tiresome self-indulgence. Actually it had to be conceded that she had, at one point, entertained some of this herself, but she generally viewed the phenomenon as a necessary and harmless phase that one normally grew out of.

"Whatever doesn't kill you makes you stronger ! – Yes !"

Michael was now laughing uproariously at his own obscure joke. Susan groaned inwardly.

"Oh, and Aleister Crowley, of course" – this offered up more flatly.

"Do what thou wilt shall be the whole of the law," Susan knocked that straight back at Michael and he stopped still; his gaze moved past her left shoulder to the black night sky through the window and she could have sworn that she saw him cock his left ear ever so slightly, as though he had heard the faint call of his name.

"Hmm," was all he said.

Michael's talk was setting Susan's brain jangling. This was exactly the sort of stuff that had filled her adolescent mind at the same age and the name Aleister Crowley always was a sort of covert calling card, brandished to signify that you were one of the initiates who took their transgressions intellectually seriously. Having said that, Susan was fully aware that, in truth, she was a mere dilettante in such matters and that occult sacrifices and drug-fuelled sex rites weren't *really* her bag. But she wondered where it had led these three. And then a moment of recall sprang up from her youthful readings – "Hang on, didn't Aleister Crowley once summon up the Devil in St Ives?" she asked, only a little playfully.

This had an odd effect upon Michael – he jumped slightly, as though pricked with a fork. His eyes darted to Susan and fixed on hers. He took a slow pull on his cigarette and said: "You know about that then?" in a level tone, as though they were talking about the visit of a dignitary opening a new school.

"Well I know the *story*," Susan replied, struck by how seriously Michael appeared to have taken the question.

"It was at Zennor actually," he looked to the ashtray as he flicked the cigarette at it. "Just down the road."

"Well it was only a story, of course," said Susan, hopefully.

Michael snorted. "Hmm."

"Well the Devil didn't *actually* visit Cornwall, did he?" Susan was laughing now.

"P'raps not *then*." Michael returned his gaze to her, still perfectly serious. Susan stopped laughing.

After an awkward silence, she remembered what she really wanted to ask Michael.

"So, he didn't have the anhedonia then?"

"No. Well . . ." He struggled to find the right response. "No, it wasn't like that. He did get depression but that would come and go. He was up and down like a bottle of pop, you know?"

"Bipolar," interjected *BOB* as if, again, she had some personal knowledge of this. Michael looked at *BOB* – "Yeah," clearly surprised and wondering what the personal connection might be. He decided to park that and return to the subject of Martin.

"No, it would come and go but it's now been with him for pretty much the last 10 years. At least that's what he told me."

Susan sat up straight – "You've talked to him about it?"

"Yeah."

"When?"

"Last few days."

"Where?" Susan realised she was beginning to sound like a policeman but her indignation at the preferential access this man appeared to have been granted – *over her* – was subordinating her poise (in reality, already jettisoned – in full view – rather earlier in the evening).

"At my house. Here." Clearly enjoying another round of knife-twisting, savouring the pangs of a jealously that Susan couldn't hide. Almost involuntarily she looked around, piqued by the thought that Martin had been in here. Without her. Acting normal. And then a thought that jabbed her bottom lip out and cast her eyes down: had he been in here earlier . . . with those women . . ?

She drew breath and continued the interrogation: "So when he got out of jail, he went to you?"

"I stood his bail."

The lawyer in her made her ask, "How much was that?"

"One million."

Carol's jaw dropped and *BOB* sat straight up – "Whoah . . . Whoah, what? What jail? What the hell's going on with that boy?"

Susan jumped in before Michael, not wanting to miss the chance to show that, yes, she had some intimacy with Martin and his circumstances herself.

"Martin's been arrested in relation to one of the clients at work. Money laundering. But it's nothing to do with him." She was addressing this to *BOB* but, in the corner of her eye, she saw Michael raise his eyebrows at this.

"What do you mean? – what's your boy do?" asked *BOB*.

"He's a lawyer, like me. And Carol." Susan nodded to Carol, who beamed, having finally got a (small) part in the drama. "We all work together. At the same firm." Susan's mood was brightened slightly, at being able to say that but was quickly punctured by Michael.

"Did."

Susan narrowed her eyes at him.

"What do you mean?"

"Well, I don't think he'll be welcome back there, sweetie."

"No?" As she said this, she wondered if her own days at Stone Rose were also numbered.

"Not after the amount of shit that's hit that fan, no. With the trouble that's going down over this one, I reckon your bosses' first instinct will be to let good old Martin walk the plank. Well, I know so."

"Really?"

"Hmm, seen the statements. A Mr. Gerard Bild for one."

"Fucking Gerry," Susan spat out.

"No – Gerry's fucking Martin . . . " Michael grinned at his own little joke and *BOB* couldn't stifle a wee smirk either.

"But don't worry. I've got some proper lawyers onto it. I'll look after him."

"Oh." Susan was about to issue another barbed rebuke before it came to her that she perhaps ought to be grateful if Michael was actually trying to help Martin. So, hesitantly: "Well, that's . . . that's good of you. Thank you."

BOB nodded.

"Listen Susan – Martin's my oldest friend. There's nothing I wouldn't do for him." Michael looked up at her from stubbing out his cigarette in the ashtray and put on his serious face, wanting to appear emphatic.

Then it hit her. The Google entry from that afternoon. "Hey, it's just dawned on me. I came across your story when I was looking for you on Google earlier. There was a news report about a fire in Cornwall 10 years ago and you were featured as the guy who lost his sister. Your name's not Michael Green – it's Michael Broad !" she concluded, accusingly, triumphantly.

Michael's face reddened and darkened at the same time.

BOB slapped her hand to her forehead and rolled her eyes – "Jesus, how much more?!"

Michael's eyes were now cold and hard.

"Well done Sherlock. No, I'm not Green, I'm Broad. I changed my name when I moved up here. A new start, new name. Leave the old life behind. Same as Martin. Nothing wrong with that," he bristled.

"All of us having something to hide. Something we'd rather not be out, eh, Susan?" This was directed at her with feeling and a twinge of fear rippled through her. She cocked her head to one side but kept her eyes screwed to meet his baleful gaze.

"What's that supposed to mean?"

"It means that this business with Barry Rogers spreads a bit further than just Martin and Stone Rose." Susan's whole body deflated slightly as she realised what was coming and, Michael, being fluent in body language, registered it.

"You know what I'm talking about then?"

BOB and Carol both looked, equally puzzled, at Susan, who guiltily glanced at each of them in turn from under the hand that was now rubbing her eyebrows before returning her gaze to Michael, who had recovered his composure but, to be fair, clearly wasn't going to be any more explicit in front of the other two – whether out of some gentlemanly impulse or a desire to savour the moment, it was difficult to tell. But he did impart, finally: "It's gonna be on the news in the morning, love," and turned the corners of his mouth down, as if in sympathy.

Susan shut her eyes and kneaded her eyebrows harder. Then, defiantly looking straight back at Michael, chin held up: "My father?"

"Your father," he nodded.

Carol really did look puzzled now.

"How do you know it's going to be on the news?"

"I told you – my lawyers are acting for Martin. I know what's happening on the case and the net is widening, believe me. But Martin, by the way, declined to say anything about your father – says he likes the old chap, as it happens."

This was the first utterance to have come out of Michael's mouth all night that made Susan feel good at all.

"However, friend Rogers is not being so discrete, apparently."

"That guy is such a wanker," Susan blurted out, with some vehemence.

"Finally, something we can agree on !" Michael raised his hands to show his palms, apparently delighted. *BOB* laughed and asked: "Who's he? Some greaseball?"

"The prick who's going to drag them all down – I've told my dad time and time again to throw him off. And that bloody creepy sister."

"Ah, the great Joan of Arc. Now there's a fucking case if ever I saw one," Michael caught himself and ducked his head at the assembled ladies.

"Pardon my French."

"Oh please, Michael," drawled *BOB*.

"But seriously, that guy should watch himself. He's been keeping some very bad company. People who won't appreciate him shooting his mouth off."

Susan didn't like the sound of this. "Dare I ask who?"

"Honestly – you don't want to know, believe me. Let's just say 'foreign parties'."

A whole tableau of frightening outcomes danced at the forefront of Susan's imagination but she still thought to ask: "Are these people that you know too, Michael? What exactly is it that you do, by the way? You seem to have a lot of money and know a lot of people, a lot of things. I'm not being unfriendly when I ask that – I do appreciate what you're doing for Martin but I suppose I'm intrigued. What is Mu Productions, for example?"

Michael laughed but then said, rather pointedly: "It doesn't pay to be too nosey, you know, kiddo." This sounded for a moment like a threat but Michael laughed again and continued – "Look, I just got lucky with some property deals. I used my head and parlayed that up, and I get bored, so I try this, I try that; I produce computer games; I open a burlesque club (at this he smiled at *BOB* who shot her arm in the air and called out: 'Hooray !'); and I seem to have stayed lucky so far – most of these things have made money fairly rapidly. And if you're doing all that in a place like London, you do get to know a lot of people. So don't worry – I'm no sort of gangster if that's what you're thinking."

This all sounded a little pat to Susan, like an oft-repeated routine (for the Revenue, say) but she didn't press it.

There was a lull in the talk. Susan caught Carol looking her up and down and followed her line of sight to the appalling state of her own garb. They both started giggling and were soon followed by *BOB* and Michael.

Carol shook her head "Bloody hell, Susan – you certainly know how to show a girl a good time !"

It was as though the recall of each crazy twist and turn rose up in succession like a movie hologram in the space between them, without either speaking a word – their two minds in lockstep – and it seemed that only now did it occur to them how demented each episode had actually been. Each instalment cranked up the gut-bursting hilarity of the whole thing until they were finally hanging over the sides of their chairs, crying with laughter, snot running onto their lips.

A massive release valve had been blown open and it was clearly also a relief to *BOB* and Michael, who chuckled indulgently at the two girls. Finally, when the cacophony of howling had subsided and all were gasping as though they'd run a marathon, *BOB* declared "Jeez – I thought New York was crazy but you guys are fucking nuts !" – this started them all off again and soon they were exhausted from laughing.

At last, Carol said: "Listen Susan, I reckon I'm going to have to get home. I'm done in and I'm supposed to be at work in the morning !" This last comment was conveyed with a level of conviction that suggested that work the next morning was, in reality, no more than a *theoretical* possibility.

Then it occurred to Carol to ask hesitantly: "Will you .. ?" her voice trailed off.

"God, I don't know ... No, I wouldn't have thought so." Susan snorted in reply. "I'll need to see my dad. And Martin." She looked across at Michael, earnestly – "Where is he, Michael?" (She thought she'd try him again now they seemed to be on better terms.)

"I honestly don't know, love," Michael shrugged his shoulders, "I'll see him again soon, no doubt, but I don't know where he is right now."

"What about his mobile? He hasn't answered me but he'll answer you." Susan cocked an eyebrow, thinking: 'There – got you now. This'll test whether you're on side'.

Michael hesitated, apparently unsure for a moment of what to do but then, in an easy-going manner, complied. "Yeah, sure – I'll try him." He tugged his phone from his trouser pocket, prodded the screen with his thumb a couple of times, and held it to his ear while looking at Susan. As if reading her sceptical mind, he rolled his eyes and straightened his arm forwards to show her the screen of his phone, which duly read: 'Martin Dash – calling,' and put it back to his ear.

A ringtone could be heard starting up in the bedroom down the corridor – the standard Nokia ringtone that Martin had never bothered to change.

Susan's whole body suddenly felt warm and her cheeks reddened. She scowled at Michael, jumped up and strode quickly to where the sound came from, through the door into the corridor, past the first bedroom on the left and down to the second at the end of the corridor, where the door was open to let out a pool of gold light. Her heart pounding, Susan swung round into the room with her hand on the left door jamb.

The ringing red phone was lying on the bed of the empty room – she recognised it as Martin's. She picked it up just in time to see the "Michael Green" caller display disappearing and the call go to voicemail. When she took it back into the living room, Michael was ready with the explanation: "He must have left it here, we had a bit of a party earlier..." his voice trailed off at this and the atmosphere reverted to its formerly icy degree. Which was a shame, thought *BOB*.

Michael stood up. "Listen I can get you girls home – you don't need to bother with taxis. Derek, my driver, will take you wherever you need to go. He's a good guy, ex-military; he'll look after you. The car's downstairs."

They all four stood now, rather awkwardly, but The World Famous *BOB* broke the silence, moving first to Carol and then Susan to administer to both a squeeze on the arm and a peck on the cheek.

"Well – good night ladies. That was a hell of an introduction and I expect more of the same next time!" and, to Susan, with a friendly tilt of the head and narrowing of the eyes: "I hope you sort out that fella of yours, darling – he's a real beaut, ain't he?"

BOB didn't seem to be leaving, so the girls gathered up their bags and jackets and were ushered by Michael back out of the flat and downstairs to a now empty club. He diverted them, this time, towards a side exit but at one point they did pass an open door to the club itself. Susan glanced at the cavernous room, which was now entirely dark save for a pale pink light emitted by one of the chiller units behind the bar, just enough to provide a shadowy highlight of the edge of the big stage. Susan shuddered, Michael smirked, and they bustled along towards the street door. But just before that was another door which Michael swung open to reveal the bulky frame of said driver, Derek, sat watching some late night TV, wearing the medium length black leather coat cherished by all true heavies, with matching crew cut.

As the girls clambered into the back of the big Lexus LS outside, Susan offered up her mobile number to Michael with a plea for him to speak to her the next day and to get Martin to contact her.

"Yes of course, darling," he assured her, not entirely convincingly to Carol's mind.

Michael heard Susan and Carol give Derek their addresses to be dropped off in turn before pushing the car door shut and watching the silver sedan glide away from the kerb. Once he'd passed back through the street door into the club, he pulled his mobile out and pressed the contact named 'Martin Dayton'.

23

They drove to Carol's house in Maida Vale first, a journey time of only 15 minutes at one o'clock on a Friday morning. This didn't give much time to talk but they weren't talking much anyway – Carol had tried to initiate a discussion of the Michael and Martin relationship but this had been pretty much shut down when, in response, Susan had touched Carol's forearm to grab her gaze and then flicked her own eyes to the nape of Derek's neck and back again, the meaning being clear: 'Not in front of the servants.'

In any event, Susan didn't want to talk anymore – she'd talked enough and now she was thinking. However, when they pulled up in front of Carol's house in the middle of a curving street of semis, Susan felt bound to say: "Listen Carol, I'm sorry tonight's been so fraught; what, with all that carry-on ... and ... well, you know ... But I just wanted to say you've really been there for me all night and I won't forget it. You've been a proper friend to me. Thank you."

Carol was overjoyed and not bothered about showing it, her grin lighting up the back of the car. "You're joking, aren't you, Susan? That was the best night out I've ever had in my entire life – I wouldn't have missed it for the world!" And then, a little more earnestly: "I'll always be there for you, you know."

It suddenly struck Susan that, amongst all the chaos in her life at the moment, one good thing to have come out of it, at least, was the realisation of what a good friend she could have in Carol Gee. They embraced and squeezed each other tight and, as Carol clomped out of her side of the car, she admonished Susan: "Make sure you call me, yeah?"

"I will."

At that the car door clumped shut and Derek eased away as Carol ambled up the path to her front door, wondering what she would tell her Methodist mother and father of the night . . .

As they reached the end of Carol's road, Derek inclined his head back and slightly to the left: "Queens Gardens then?"

"No, I've changed my mind, I'll go to Valhalla Avenue in Kensington, thanks." Not please but thanks, i.e. a command, not a request.

Their eyes met via Derek's rear view mirror and what little she could see of his expression was enough to tell her that he was more than a little sceptical. But she held his gaze so, ultimately, his eyebrows shrugged and he simply acquiesced.

"Valhalla Avenue it is."

If there had been any problem with this she'd resolved that her next gambit would have been to remind Derek who her father was, and the likely fuss and unwarranted attention that would follow her call to her father's security detail to advise them she was being held against her will by a nightclub owner's bodyguard but, whether or not she had somehow managed to convey any of this – wordlessly – to Derek, she surmised that Derek had calculated that the path of least resistance on this occasion was the easy route to Martin's new flat in Kensington.

Susan had a hunch.

24

As Derek eased them into a space on the opposite side of the road, Susan looked up to the first floor to see a light shining behind the orange canvas blinds hanging in the living room. She suddenly felt the sort of nerves she'd suffered from in her time with the Hampstead Players – only amateur dramatics but, because of its location, often attended by illustrious theatre-goers and 'resting' professionals; her guts would churn and her palms moisten with treacherous sweat in anticipation of an awful humiliation.

She felt that now as she hesitated in the back of Michael's purring status symbol. She realised that she was going to – hoping to – meet a wholly different Martin from the android she had known and she felt almost intimidated by the persona that Michael had described. (This was, of course, always presuming that (a) Martin was in the flat right now and (b) he was going to let her in.)

She looked across to the building's entrance door, painted glossy bright red and now bathed in the soft light of the street lamp just a few yards away; the square gold plate screwed into the brick of the surrounding wall housing the black buttons marked with the flat numbers 1 through 6 and perforated with the small black polka dots of the intercom's speaker grill.

Susan looked forlornly back into the car and Derek's head was turned back to look at her. He raised his eyebrows as if to say, "Stick or twist?" and then his face softened into a surprisingly warm smile. Susan was grateful for that and fortified.

She smiled back, "Thank you, Derek."

"Any time, love," his voice craggy but kind. "I'll just wait to check he's in for you."

"Yes, OK."

Susan click-clacked across the empty road to stand in the pool of light before the red door as though she was stood in the spotlight on the stage back at The Black and Blue Dahlia, facing the unknown. Taking a deep breath, she pressed the button for number 3. Rather quicker than she had expected, she heard a faint click in the intercom's speaker and then Martin's voice transmuted down through the wire, tentative and electric.

"Hello?"

"Hi, Martin – it's Susan."

Just a moment passed before he replied: "Hi, come on up," and the gold plate buzzed and the red door clicked. Susan yanked the handle quickly before the buzzing stopped and turned to give Derek a little wave before pushing her way through the door into the hallway. Derek waved back and smiled but did not appear to be in a hurry to drive off. He was obviously going to wait a while longer, just to make sure, and Susan inwardly thanked him for that.

When she got to the landing on the first floor, Susan could see that the door to Martin's flat was wide open, presumably as an invitation for her to walk in. As she came into the softly-lit living room, she could hear Martin rustling around in the bedroom and he called: "Sorry – I'm just coming." A moment later he appeared wearing faded blue jeans and just pulling down a plain white t-shirt, his blond hair tousled (not long dried after a shower, by the look of it) and his feet bare. Susan couldn't stop an inward pang of disappointment in the realisation that he'd evidently felt the need to make himself decent for her. At the same time she was forcefully confirmed in the notion she'd already grasped, namely that everything had now changed. Martin's whole character, the timbre of his voice, the clothes he was wearing – *the way he looked at her* – represented a wholly different person from the one she had known before.

He looked like nothing more or less than a new James Dean, American-fresh, surprisingly fresh given that he'd been out carousing with Michael Green (*and the rest*) that night. It occurred to Susan that if Martin felt half the burgeoning hangover that had been creeping up on her for some time now, then he was doing a hell of a job concealing it. Conversely, Martin studied Susan and couldn't help but note how the evening's odyssey had left its marks on Susan. On the way, in the car with Derek, she had touched up her makeup and tried to re-arrange her hair but she couldn't do much about the red stains slewed across her white blouse, the pink graze that strafed her left cheek and the general air of a girl who's endured a hard night roistering with the town's rugby team.

Whatever. She was here now and she would have to do. She stood defiantly before Martin Dash (no – Martin *Dayton*), cocked one hip and planted her hand on it.

"Well?" was all she could think to say at that point. To all intents and purposes, she was Kathleen Turner in Body Heat, literally smouldering and goading William Hurt to smash through a glass door to get at her.

The only illumination came from the lamp next to the window so the corners of the room were dark. Light and shade undulated across her face and body. All was silence save for the muffled ignition of a car outside. Martin realised he could actually hear the sound of blood flowing in his ears. The air around them seemed to get heavier and almost claustrophobic. All of a sudden his legs no longer seemed steady and he felt his thigh muscles twitch and his penis press against his jeans.

Their eyes had been locked together for some time and he felt as though he was going to fall.

He had to do something.

He bent to grab the coffee table that sat between them with both hands and flung it like a Frisbee towards the breakfast bar; it clattered against the step that led to the open plan kitchen beyond. Her mouth opened and her eyes widened as he swiftly crossed the space he'd opened up.

He put his hands on her waist and their bodies touched all the way from thigh to chest – he felt her breasts press into him and it made him sigh. She felt his cock hard against her groin and her hands on his buttocks pulled him closer still so that she was now actively rubbing it.

The floor fell away beneath the soles of Martin's feet, he felt like he was shaking but could not be sure that this was actually so. He was alive now. Now. He was exhilarated and frightened. They both looked down at the other's lips as they came together to form a sealed dock, within which there was nothing but sensation and, within that blind void, without warning, the tips of their tongues met. An electric spark.

Martin was running his hands through her thick hair – it was like swimming, his fingers caressed by the vibrant currents. He felt like screaming for joy. His lips were now on her neck, the length of her spine was warm from the inside. Her hand was on his jeans between his legs and she could feel him; she moaned and they had to come off.

In an instant, she had his flies undone and her hand inside, all over the full length of stiff, silky muscle. This was more exciting than anything that had ever happened to her; all those times she had gazed at the beautiful but remote Martin Dash, hoping but hardly able to believe that she would ever get to do what she was now doing to him. Her skin shivered with the pure thrill of it.

Her blouse was now unbuttoned and she threw it to the floor, her white lacy bra after it. Martin caressed her full, right breast with his left hand whilst kissing her passionately on the lips. Her left breast was pressed against his now naked chest, the feel of skin to skin utterly sublime. Finally, she peeled her tight skirt to the floor with her knickers, to be left standing before him in her black stockings, suspenders and heels. Martin's face expressed pure bliss, they pulled close again and looked deep into each other's eyes.

She smiled: "Martin . . ." and they subsided to the carpet right where they stood. As they lay there, his fingers moved slowly up the inside of her thigh and at the top he touched her. Instead of prompting any resistance, this acted as a spring and her legs opened willingly – she wanted him and they both grinned happily. They kissed silently and slowly, their eyes closed, as he carefully massaged her clitoris with his middle finger. Susan moaned with pleasure as her whole vulva was rinsed.

"Please, Martin – please."

He brought himself up to position over her and, as she felt him enter, she screwed her eyelids down and everything was velvet black for a moment. As they began to move together she had the distinct sensation of flight, free from who they were, what they were, and the sordid details of their earthly existence. They were free together and, as she watched his face writhe with so much joy that it looked like anguish, she saw that he had been reborn like a new creature, cracked out of the husk of a chrysalis that had grown around him by accretion over many neglectful years.

She wrapped her legs around his back to pull him ever closer and didn't want it to end. But when they came she was squeezed tight in his arms and they both had to cry out simply to vent the sheer power of what they were experiencing. Martin threw himself to one side, onto his back next to Susan, and they both lay gleaming with sweat, wondering what lay in store for them next.

25

It was now 3:00 a.m. The two young lovers lay naked between the sheets of Martin's king-size bed, Susan's head nestling in the crook of his neck, allowing his arm to encircle her shoulder and his hand to stroke her freshly washed skin. They had showered together and revelled in the discovery of their bodies, uninhibited and shorn of any obligation to behave any way other than as they pleased.

"Well – Jesus Christ, Martin," she had teased as they slipped and squirmed together in the foamy water, "that was worth the wait!" and squealed as he tickled her for her cheek.

As they lay – quieter now – it seemed to her that a thousand questions now needed to be asked and answered but she couldn't find the first one. Martin had been waiting but also wondering if, in fact, the onus wasn't properly upon himself?

Ultimately, Susan sat herself upright, pulling the sheet up to cover her breasts (merely so that he would not be distracted from her questioning . . .), and spoke first but immediately put the ball in Martin's court.

"OK then, where do we start?"

Martin crinkled his forehead, exhaled through his nose and began. The story he told matched the essentials that had been provided by Michael but had rather more detail – and rather more insight – thrown in.

He told her of his early years with Sonia and Jack in St Ives; the picnics on Porthmeor Beach and the walks along the cliffs at Carrick Du; of the evenings spent listening in wonder to his mother sing the old Cornish songs in their little kitchen ('Lamorna' and 'The White Rose'; she had a beautiful voice, according to Martin – strong but soulful –

and would perform in the local pubs) and watching his father paint his haunting landscapes (dark and brooding, Jack said he was trying to show people the hills' memories); of the days occupied with the hunt for Sonia after one of her periodic disappearances inland (onto Bodmin Moor or above the tin mines of Camborne); and the nights endured under the bed sheets, trying to block out the noise of his father raging downstairs after three days on the piss, smashing the cheap crockery and Sonia's teeth.

He described the unusually intimate relationship he enjoyed with the Broad family – Michael, Megan and their parents, Victor and Lucy. Martin's own family environment was clearly bohemian at best, probably dysfunctional and borderline scandalous and he sometimes got the impression that Victor and Lucy (and Michael and Megan, if it came to it) rather enjoyed their self-appointed role as unofficial guardians of the poor boy's moral and material welfare – it sat well with their image of themselves as prominent local dignitaries and benefactors. Victor's family had, in the past, garnered considerable wealth as tin and copper mine owners; much of that wealth had been lost with the decline of those industries and a generation or two of dissolute wastrels but Victor had had the good fortune (or tenacity, if you like) to bag Lucy Hancock as a bride, complete with her share of her family's substantial landholdings.

He recounted the lazy summer afternoons spent playing tennis on the court at the Broads' mansion on the outskirts of the town; sipping lemonade on the wide terrace skirting the front of the house and swimming in the pool that got most of the sun round the back. All like something out of Brideshead Revisited – as undoubtedly intended by 'Viscount Vic' (as Megan sardonically branded her father).

As he told the tale to Susan, it occurred to Martin – not for the first time – how bizarre was the life he'd led thus far. He'd survived a murder trial at 19; spent the next 9 years in a wilderness of oblivion, his mind suspended and numbed, known no longer to his family and former friends; and arrived in London at 28 to become acquainted with the Prime Minister's inner circle, only to find that he was now likely to be tried again in a financial scandal that was, at this very moment, creeping closer to the heart of the country's Government.   Not bad for a lad from a backwater of the country blessed with little more than a brittle psyche and a winning smile.

True, his childhood was, in many ways, not untypical of the experience that many kids had to endure behind closed doors up and down the country but his own always had a peculiar feel to it, somehow, that he could never quite grasp.   Right from his earliest memories, he had been plagued with the nagging feeling that there was something not quite right that he couldn't put his finger on. Thus, the twin torments of self-doubt and paranoia became, in time, his constant companions, to be battled and accommodated and denied.

Into that pot was added the mixed blessing of his looks. Even as a baby, his features were such that passers-by would routinely stop in their tracks and, almost involuntarily, be forced to exclaim: "My goodness, what a beautiful baby !" People seemed to feel that the unique nature of this visitation somehow made the child public property and entitled them to hinder the passage of mother and child while they greedily drank in the full experience of their encounter with what might well turn out to have been an angel. And, whilst there was no doubt that Sonia could – and would – readily feel the pride of any mother who had produced such a specimen, it was equally true that this importunate harrying did ultimately begin to

225

grate on Sonia as she would try to conduct a quiet walk with her son, to be enjoyed by just the two of them together.

His eyes had never really changed colour since then – an electric blue of such an iridescent quality that, when you looked at them, it was all too easy to find yourself entranced, in much the same way that you might lose yourself gazing into the flames of a fire.

Combined with a noble brow, alpine cheekbones, aquiline nose, cherry lips, lean jaw and lustrous pale gold hair, such features meant that he was always doomed to be the centre of attention, whether he wished it or not. Make no mistake, he was human enough to appreciate the gratification that such advantages can bestow but he was also sufficiently intelligent – nay, soulful – to ultimately feel the tedium of people's stock response to such a proposition.

So he and Michael and Megan ran around the streets of St Ives; across the sandy beaches; along the giddying cliff edges; and through the grassy fields stretching back from the coast as they ate together; sang, danced and drank together; and grew together. It was difficult for Martin to describe to Susan exactly what it was that bound the three of them together, particularly considering that he'd often felt confused about the true nature of the relationship himself.

He tried to explain to Susan the difficulties that Michael had with Victor – a vain, capricious man who barely tried to conceal his contempt when Michael failed to attain some arbitrary level of achievement that he'd imposed. In stark contrast to the unfailing indulgence he afforded his favourite, Megan. How that, in turn, fed the crass and heartless persona that Michael too often presented to the world (including Martin). But how Michael had always come through for Martin when it mattered, including the trial, when Michael refused to believe that Martin had killed his own sister against the faces of those in the town who were only too happy for the young Adonis to be brought down to a more earthly level.

And he struggled to relate the true nature of Megan herself – a living, walking, talking contradiction who knew no bounds when it came to satisfying her own mysterious urges but made your heart burst with pride to see her scattering, like skittles, a gang of thugs bullying a younger boy in the fields, armed with nothing but a riding crop and a righteous fury.

"Did you love her?" Susan interjected, not really wanting to ask the question but knowing that she had to.

Martin considered the question, had he loved Megan? For: she had been a fixture in his life throughout childhood and adolescence, the two of them like Bonnie and Clyde (with Michael their Buck Barrow). Against: she had tried to kill him.

They had been drawn to each other from the first moment they ran into each other as kids aged ... Martin couldn't even remember – it must have been 5 or 6. They were both distinctive children – Martin with his angelic looks and magnetic aura and Megan a latter-day Scarlett O'Hara, all flashing temper and coltish allure, wilful and winning. With her midnight black hair, sparkling green eyes and proud bearing, Megan Broad turned nearly as many heads as Martin Dayton and to see the two of them growing up together was to behold a pairing that was generally assumed to be an integral part of the natural order.

As is the way with everyone, Martin always had his own personal agenda – known or unknown – that veered between a sullen, but sincere, loathing of the many and various manifestations of human life and an impulsive delight at the diamonds to be found in the rough and, although there were many times when it seemed to him that Megan's disorder of personalities aligned perfectly with that rosier world view, there were at least as many occasions when he came to view her antics as the epitome of all that he loathed.

And then Molly came along.

Two years younger than Martin, she was the daughter of her mother's friends in the gypsy community that periodically showed itself in the area. Martin had only met her the year before Megan's death, when he had come across his mother and her friends at a game fair in Launceston.

There was something about the young girl with the curly black hair and bright blue eyes that pulled on him. It didn't harm that she was so unlike Megan (quiet and modest against strident and bold) but there was more to it than that and he gradually found that, in many ways, there was more to Molly than met the eye. Unassuming as she was, she knew her own mind and, privately, could be just as trenchant in her judgements as Martin (and Megan, if it came to that); it was just that she tended to keep it all to herself and this made the discovery of the character and intellect that lurked behind the shy demeanour so much the more arresting to Martin.

The more he saw of Molly, the more he could see of a possible future different from that which seemed to be mapped out for him with – and by – Megan Broad. And Molly, in turn, allowed Martin access to her innermost thoughts and feelings in a way that was never afforded to any other.

However, the whole affair had to be conducted with a certain degree of circumspection as Martin had, from the start, surmised that Megan wouldn't have taken too kindly to the appearance of someone that, Martin knew, she would immediately identify as a serious rival. As it happened, his mother also appeared to be firmly in the same camp, her imprimatur solidly behind the Megan candidacy, or, at least definitely against any relationship with Molly and she voiced a complete range of logic for this – Molly was too young; he didn't want to get involved with the traveller lifestyle; he'd known Megan all his life; and, by the way, her family wealth would set him up for life so that he would leave behind the indignities of pauperism that had stained his life thus far.

All this meant was that he and Molly would simply meet where no-one would know.

And Martin tried to explain all of this to Susan. But when he got to the fire, he found that he couldn't explain. As he approached that night in his mind, a feeling of dread came over him, as though a black psychical gangrene was creeping from his fingers and toes, swiftly up his limbs towards his heart, cold as it came. To even turn his inward gaze onto that conflagration was to risk again the panic attacks, the paranoia and the downright fear that had ultimately hobbled his whole consciousness and turned him into the walking zombie that was Martin Dash for 10 years.

This he did not want. He could not face it, so he simply turned away from it. And he struggled to convey this to Susan.

He told Susan that he had never seen Molly again – he believed her parents had whisked her away with them, no doubt from the natural fear of all the gypsies of being too close to the intolerant and vengeful machinations of the authorities.

And how he had finally fled the area for the anonymity of a bedsit in Bristol; got a job in the post room of a legal firm; and, in due course, undertaken the correspondence studies that ultimately led to his qualification as a solicitor, all the time handing off any emotional engagement with those around him, simply keeping his head down and working, just working.

"So, when were you diagnosed with the anhedonia?" asked Susan.

Martin looked rather sheepish; he hesitated but then admitted: "I sort of self-diagnosed, actually."

Susan drew her head back and narrowed her eyes "What?! You mean you made it up? – you were faking it?!" But she instantly regretted blurting that out as Martin's eyes flashed with an anger she didn't like the look of and his cheeks flushed.

"No, I did not fucking fake it !" and he jumped out of the bed to pull on his jeans and then his t-shirt in furious, jerky movements.

In truth, Martin was still feeling wired from the excesses of the night before and, suddenly, what he most craved was a beer and a fag. So he headed to the door out of the bedroom. Having calmed back down again in dressing, he turned to Susan, still sat in the bed with the sheet pulled up to her collarbone, unsure of what to do, and smiled: "Sorry. I'm having a drink if you fancy one."

This struck Susan as, simultaneously, a crazy idea and a great idea and, in any event, she was relieved that she hadn't completely ruined the mood. "Yeah, I'm right behind you," moving to exit the bed herself.

26

Back in the living room, Susan flopped down onto the faded brown leather settee that backed onto to the kitchen area raised above and behind it. She was wearing Martin's dark blue towel robe that she had found on the floor by the bed and smiled lasciviously at Martin, who was carefully reinstating the poor, roughly-treated coffee table to its rightful place at the centre of the action.

Feigning to ignore her creamy white legs stretched out, unabashed, along the settee, Martin strode to the big grey American-style fridge near the breakfast bar and, taking a can of Fosters for himself, asked what she would like, imagining that she might prefer a glass of wine – if, indeed, she wanted anything alcoholic at all. But Susan gave him a look of mock-indignation and shot back: "Same as you, thanks."

Sat in the matching leather chair diagonally across from the soles of Susan's feet, Martin lit up a cigarette from a pack of Silk Cut now retrieved – with an ashtray – from the window sill. Having not smoked a cigarette since a number of years past, Susan had declined to join Michael back in Soho but here in Kensington, with Martin, it seemed perfectly OK – if he was going to be Bogart, she'd be Bacall.

She tasted, with some pleasure and some recoil, the dulling acrid taste that was a reminder of younger years that now seemed an age back and, as the gunmetal blue smoke curled away through her line of sight, she realised that it was silhouetted against a pale morning light that was gingerly creeping into the room from behind the curtains. She glanced at the clock hanging on the wall by the window – 4.13 a.m. – and drank a slug of lager before offering up:

"I'm sorry for saying that about you faking it Martin. I don't think that. It's just seeing you like this, drinking lager, smoking – and *last night*" (the words hung in the air for a moment before she moved swiftly on) – "I don't know what to think. I mean, it's been such a change, hasn't it? What's happened?"

Martin shook his head, "I don't know really. It's not just one thing. But I think seeing Michael out of the blue like that shook something in me and it's been like a rollercoaster ever since. But it was those two nights in the police cells that really did me, really woke me up. It took me right back to the trial in St Ives 10 years ago – especially with Michael being there again. At that time I thought I was going to jail for murder; I thought my life was over – that I was dead before I'd even started."

"While I was waiting for the trial, my state of mind deteriorated badly. The whole scene with me and my parents, me and Molly, me and Megan and Michael, had already gone crazy that summer anyway."

"How do you mean?"

Martin hesitated and cast his eyes down, looking into the past and was away there for a while before he dragged out, slowly, mumbling – "Parties. Drugs. Violence." And then, looking back up at her, warily, self-consciously – "... Witchcraft."

Susan narrowed her eyes, incredulously, "What?"

Martin shook his head and immediately tried to brush it off as if he realised he'd said something stupid. "God, it was all fucking ridiculous. Fucking Megan," he spat the last two words out. "You don't want to know."

'Oh, I do,' thought Susan and she remembered what Michael had said about the Devil being summoned up in Cornwall ... but not by Aleister Crowley ...

But Martin was moving on.

"I'll tell you all about it sometime," and he raised his glass by way of a 'cheers'.

". . . when I'm a bit more pissed," and took another gulp and carried on.

"So everything was twisted already and then the fire and me being charged with it just pushed me over the edge. I spent many weeks before the trial, just on my own, going slowly crazy. I'd had bouts of depression before; seen the doctors about it. But all this sent me off on a whole different level. I'd always been thinking about loads of stuff anyway but now I just sort of got pushed further and further so that I had times when I felt completely out of myself. When I lost myself."

"Thinking about what?" asked Susan. Martin wasn't giving her much to go on and he was clearly struggling to explain himself. Then something came to him and he shot his head up and put his index finger in the air, triumphantly – "I know . . . the book !"

"The book?"

"Yeah, the book," and he jumped up from the chair and into his bedroom. She could hear him rustling about in his drawers before returning with what was obviously 'The Book' in his hand.

He stopped before handing it to her as though wondering whether that was wise and he began flipping through pages at random, as if he was seeing it for the first time. He sat back down without giving it to her, still turning the pages.

"At a certain point, I started writing down what I was thinking." He was speaking carefully now, measuredly.

"And that became something I did all the time until, eventually, I had a small book's worth. I typed it all up, printed it out on A5," he looked up and smiled, abashed, and held it up, "like a proper book."

"The best way to explain is for you to read that," he laughed, "if you can stand to," and leant across the coffee table to pass the book to her. "You can read it at your leisure. It's all in there."

Susan looked at what had been handed to her – just normal, white A5 paper, numbering 100 pages, with ordinary black type on each side, all held together with red plastic ring-binding and a transparent plastic front and back sheet to protect it. It had a front cover – again black lettering on white paper – but here the type was a larger size and a fancier font; the title read: 'Stuff and Things' and, below that, 'Martin Dayton.'

Susan looked up at Martin, who appeared nervous (possibly showing someone his baby for the first time) – "Stuff and Things?"

He smiled and blushed slightly. "Yeah . . . well, you have to read it, really."

"Now?"

Martin thought about this but said, "No, read it later, at your leisure, like I say."

Susan looked inside at the first page which contained just a few lines before the first chapter:-

'All is futile,
But all I hope
Is that you think fondly of me.
All the beauty, grandeur, tragedy, despair and love of Eternity
Burns in and flows through me.
All I hope is that the Nameless One
 – Nowhere in Space and Time –
Recognises me.'

And, below that:-

'*My mind's fucked,*
I'll never have peace and tranquillity now;
Indeed, I've never had it.
I've seen too many things;
I've seen too much of the same things.'

Susan reluctantly closed the book back up again. She really wanted to read it. Now. But Martin was talking again now, apparently wanting to unburden himself of his story to someone, finally.

"You can read it in the book but, ultimately, I'd analysed everything so closely and I'd broken down the reasons for everything so that those reasons no longer meant anything to me – they seemed to be no more than simple mathematical calculations. I looked at everything so closely that, finally, it all fell apart in front of my eyes."

"So, basically, I got myself into a state where I was totally disconnected from the outside world. Yes, I was walking around, I was eating, sleeping, all of that but it was like I was on autopilot. And it just got worse. Even the verdict at the trial didn't seem to make any difference 'cos by that time I was so far gone that nothing really mattered to me anymore. It would have been just the same to me if I'd have been found guilty."

"No !"

"It seemed like that at the time."

"Eventually, I just moved to Bristol. Virtually on an impulse. Lived in a hostel. And then, after a while, it was like I started making decisions simply on a logical basis. Again, virtually on autopilot but, you know: 'I need money' – so I need to get a job. So I got some crappy job in a burger bar. Then I see adverts for this and that, got into the Job Centre and there's a job in an office, a law office, as a paralegal but it needs qualifications – a degree. So, after a while, I realised that I had to get a qualification to get a better job, to get more money, to get a place of my own. So I did a Law degree – correspondence. In a bedsit by then, working in a warehouse, security guard, whatever. And, eventually, I'd got my degree and got a paralegal job with another firm. Did well quickly and then did the Solicitors Finals course – part time – and qualified when I was," he paused to think, "about 25 . . . 26. Then moved up to Leeds to Chard Bone."

"Why was that?"

"That was Cornel. Vine. I was working for him in Bristol; he took a shine to me" – at this Martin flicked a teasing glance at Susan, who wondered – "and he was offered Head of Real Estate at CB and asked if I'd like to go with him. To help him out. I knew it was a good move so I said yes. But – this is the thing – all the time I was doing this I was really just moving through the gears like an automaton. It was just like . . . well, *logic*. I wasn't *feeling* anything. I didn't really want to touch anyone, to have anything to do with anyone. I'd had the sessions with consultants when I was younger and I knew I was bipolar but I read an article by someone explaining their anhedonia and I decided – realised – that was me. And I told people about it."

"I've always wondered why you did that."

"It actually served my purpose – of keeping me apart from people. They knew I was doing the job well, so there was no issue there. And if I had some condition that meant I had no sympathy for people, well that was no major issue for a commercial lawyer !" They both laughed at the commonplace jibe at lawyers in general. "Some even got turned on to the idea."

"Like Barry."

"Exactly. Like fucking Barry."

There was a moment's pause now at the mention of the name that brought them right up to the present; the present where Martin was, again, in danger of going to prison and Susan's father appeared to be at risk of the final disgrace.

"What has happened there, Martin?"

This brought Martin up and the words stopped flowing. He was looking at Susan but his mind was engaged on a calculation of what he might say and what he ought not to say. He was now torn between continuing the flow of self-revelation he had embarked upon, which felt so good, and the desire to not compromise Susan's safety (and, frankly, the embarrassment at how far he had gone with aiding and abetting Barry's nefarious scheming).

He decided that – as much as he didn't want to withhold stuff from her now, to patronise her like that – there was a more critical imperative, outweighing that noble sentiment, to not pass information that would likely bring nothing but trouble for her and her father.

He knew what Barry had done to finance the Crack Harbour development. And others. But here knowledge did not mean power. Having that knowledge simply put him in danger (and not just from the police). And having that knowledge didn't mean that he ought to give it to someone else. Especially a friend. Like Susan. And more than a friend now. No, it was like a disease and he should keep it to himself. Or get rid of it somehow.

"It was like I said – I'd got to a stage where I was making calculations simply on the basis of how to make more money. For myself. I think my underlying rationale was to gather a whole load of money as fast as possible so that, in due course, I could stop working, have my own place, out of sight, and burrow myself away from the world. With no need to come out again. I *think* that was what was going on but, to be honest, everything had become so fucked up with me I'm not entirely sure what I thought I was doing in the end."

"So, anyway, Barry Rogers steps up. Takes a shine to me" – another conspiratorial glance – "and starts talking about all sorts of deals. And commissions. And . . . you know."

"Not really, but do go on."

Careful, Martin.

"The basic allegation, which the press have by now anyway, is big-time money-laundering. Which is obviously a problem. But they're saying it's from Syria as well – fucking definitely a problem. They're on Bush's 'Axis of Evil', Suze. Your dad's mate's mate."

Susan felt suddenly cold and pulled her legs further up under the folds of the dressing gown.

"And is there anything in this?" her voice sounded weak and frightened as the question came out.

Careful, careful, Martin.

"Christ, I don't know," he grabbed the pack of cigarettes off the coffee table in a bid to appear nonchalant. "I don't know. Money arrives from such-and-such bank; I sign off for money to go to this-and-that bank. I know we've been a bit lax with the ID-checking but I don't know who these people are. Honestly."

Martin looks Susan's way again, hopefully. Shrugs his shoulders.

Susan leant forward and stuck out her hand for the cigarette packet to be tossed to her and struck another one up while she mulled this one over. Finally, she blew another cloud of smoke heavenwards, rolled her eyes and exclaimed: "Bloody hell Martin, what a fucking mess. What's happening now, then?"

"I don't know. I've spent two days in Paddington Green being grilled by that bloody Fallon and his mates. And that's what's brought me round by the way. Sitting on my own in that cell for hours. It was like Truro Crown Court all over again. Bloody shocked me right back out of it again, I can tell you. It's like I've been buried alive for years but I've come out to the surface again. Only to find they're going to bury me again . . ."

"Well, how will they if you don't know anything?"

"Well, p'raps so. Michael certainly thinks that's right anyway."

Susan wriggled herself upright, "Yes, now we're on the subject, how does Michael Green – or Broad – come into all this? How come he suddenly appears on the scene?"

"Total coincidence that we ran into Michael when we did" – Susan mentally cocked an eye and she wasn't sure that Martin didn't clock that – "but he's been brilliant, he really has."

"What is his bloody story, Martin?"

Martin took another deep drag from his cigarette and exhaled slowly before kneeling forward to flick it over the ashtray.

"I told you that me and Michael always had a rather intense relationship, a bit love and hate."

"Same as with Megan . . ?!"

"Hmm" – arch look – "Well, having said all that, we did grow up together, like brothers really. And brothers do fight, don't they? But they can still have a strong relationship, can't they?"

"Even if they haven't seen each other for 10 years?"

"Even then, as it appears. He's been great these last few days – got me the best criminal defence team in the country."

"Sparkes Mael; yes, I heard. That doesn't come cheap."

"True. But it appears that Michael has done rather well for himself over the years."

"Yes, I was looking into all that. Where exactly does he get his money from, Martin?"

Martin put his hands up – "Hey, I think he's just done very well out of the investments he's made, worked his way up. He's now got assets all over the place and you know how it works – money begets money? So don't begrudge him what he's built. Anyway, more's to the point, he's on my side. So let's not knock it !" Martin smirked.

Susan shook her head "Jesus Martin. What are you? Michael said you've got a few faces yourself . . ."

"Oh, did he?" Martin wondered what else Michael had said but smiled nevertheless.

"So your *team* is optimistic is it?" she said with only the slightest edge of mockery.

"Well, to a degree. But friend Barry's the ticking bomb. He was held at another station at the same time and we don't know what the hell he's been saying. The police kept telling me he's said this and that and my guys said to ignore it but I don't know. If those Syrians are half as bad as they're made out and they get the idea that Barry's giving everybody up to save his own skin, then the shit will hit the fan."

"Says who?"

"Says Michael, for one."

Susan's expression made the point / asked the question.

Martin, feigning some exasperation, explained patiently: "Michael has been around, Susan.   He knows things, people; he knows what's what – OK? I don't know what's going to happen.   We'll just have to see what the day brings won't we?" and with that he got to his feet and stretched.

"Talking of which, I need to get some shuteye before I have to face it all again.   I'm getting back under for a couple of hours." His face said: "How about you?"

Susan was tempted but she looked at the book lying on the coffee table and decided that what she'd most like now was another beer, another fag, and a bit of a read.

27

4:50 a.m. and Martin was asleep in his bedroom now – if she was very quiet, Susan could just about hear his steady breathing, wheezing softly in and out. What was in his mind now, she wondered? Maybe the book would offer up some clues.

After rereading the poetic preface, she launched into the first pages and what followed, it soon became clear, was basically a conversation Martin was having with an imaginary reader or, rather, a transcribed summary, in prose, of a conversation he'd been having with himself – *in his head* – for some time. Or even, a lecture based on those thoughts. But, in any event, it didn't talk about the traumatic events that had preceded the book and it didn't reveal anything of the personal circumstances of the author at the time of writing. It was, however, organised into general groupings of subject matters with headings such as: 'GREED / CELEBRITY / EGO'; 'PERSONAL / PUBLIC / ARTIST'; and 'CONSCIOUSNESS / GOD / TIME'.

Susan dived in, greedily, and soon became aware that this was a distinctive voice, the like of which she had never really encountered before and, more than once, she involuntarily looked up from the book and across to the half-open bedroom door, beyond which slumbered the tortured author. As she read, she was struck forcibly by the stark dichotomy in the apparent dumbness of the Martin Dash that had presented to herself and her colleagues masking another . . . *being* entirely; and by the thought that, behind that mask, all of *this* was going on – apparently, all of the time. It was unbelievable.

Or had it, in fact, all driven him, ultimately, to the blind alley that had become the Martin Dash automaton? Had he finally thought himself to a standstill where it had started to become repetitive; when there was nothing left to think? Like Nietzsche finally gone mad when he could no longer cope with the horror that his mind had laid bare for him? – this appeared to be confirmed by a line quoted from James Kelman that envisaged a mind so wide and deep that it could countenance *anything and everything*.

She ploughed on into a passage in the 'CONSCIOUSNESS / GOD / TIME' section:

'This is the point really: I believe I'm right in saying that – whether it's a stool, the air, or a politician we're talking about – when you break the components of all matter down to its smallest parts, you reach common denominators: electrons and quarks, i.e. everything is made of the same basic things, the difference being in the way those things are stuck together: their density, speed, etc.

To my mind, this means that, at a certain sub-atomic level, the barriers between things that we perceive – e.g. the border between the back of your hand and the air around it – are not really there. It's in this way that I feel that everything is as one and I sometimes get a sense of this oneness, as though I'm moving underwater, in a thick soup of stuff.

I also get a funny feeling sometimes walking along the streets of the city: that I'm walking along the floors of concrete angular canyons and I see around me blobby sorts of things that are shuffling around too, that have sort-of risen up out of the ground, and that we're all part of the one thing. Try to imagine that you've landed on this planet from elsewhere; that it's all totally unfamiliar to you (you were familiar with a different form of existence); and the sort of impression this alien life would have on you – that's how I often feel.

Sitting talking to someone – often at work this happens, in the middle of a meeting or something – I suddenly get the realisation of the mechanics of what is happening; that we're using a pattern of noises – movements of the air particles between us – that's been developed over centuries to communicate. Two swirling storms of atoms, eyeball to eyeball, trying to communicate; to comprehend each other.

Or ... imagine that your mind has been infiltrated and taken over by the will of another being; that the voice that you commonly hear in your head, that which you take to be 'you' – that which, at this moment is thinking: 'this bloke's a wanker' – is not 'you' but . . . another's voice. That little start, or jump, you may have just felt (if, you were, indeed, thinking: 'this bloke's a wanker') was a recognition (perhaps the first) that all might not be as it previously seemed. That may be a first real look at the reflection in the mirror – your 'self'; the first viewing of that self as something objective.

Just one more trick to persuade you of the strangeness of your life and to get that feeling of alienation from your own body: imagine that 'you' – the person – actually sit (as a small sort of thing) at a concealed vantage point inside the eyes of you, the body – which is actually many, many times bigger than 'you', as is everything around. You're hitching a ride on a huge giant and you look across a great chasm to the person standing closest to your body. And along the street – which is a massive ravine – there are other of these giants lolloping along. Look down at your hands ... they're 60 feet away, at the foot of the hill of your torso.

This can give you an insight into what it is to start casting off your ego, to really start thinking about yourself (and what your life is) objectively.

The ultimate achievement: to lose your ego. As stated bleakly in the conclusion that self-revelation means the annihilation of self at the end of Abel Ferrara's vampire film 'The Addiction'. Which has one of the most frightening scenes in it; or, at least, the most immediate or intense portrayal of fear and horror, when the vampires attack the guests at the party. (It gives me an inward shudder to think about it as I write.) You get a real frisson of dread which recalls those occasions you may have experienced when the violence of life comes right up to your face; everything seems to slow down; and you realise that the ordinary rules governing us have fallen away; the animal is unleashed again and there is nothing to stop it doing what it is going to do to you. You are exposed.

The problem with what's at the end of this, of course, is that you start disengaging from what is commonly known as 'life' so that you start to see other people's concerns and agendas and view of themselves as rather petty and uninteresting. Because, once you've started looking at things like that, the modes of behaviour, the emotions, the quirks, the scams, the routines, the angles, and the games are all demystified and you see them as mechanical, clunking processes.

Just harking back to the idea of our physical selves as towering columns of atoms: that image brings to mind the photographs of nebulae produced by telescopes such as the Hubble (e.g. in the Serpens constellation, p68 Serge Brunier's 'Majestic Universe') and leads on to another preoccupation of mine: that is, the question of scale. Those nebulae are, by the power of the telescopic equipment, brought into vision as almost distinct, concrete shapes or beings but they're millions of miles across. This, to me, is suggestive of 'smaller forms' that we're more familiar with on our 'small' planet.

If we take it as a given that we live in an infinite universe (and it clearly can't be anything else) – that is to say infinitely large and infinitely small – then why should we imagine that our world represents the standard scale by which everything else is compared or measured? Obviously, we measure everything against the scale of our own physical bodies (so that an ocean is big and a pinhead is tiny) but out there in the wider cosmos we are not the be-all and end-all;

far from it. It must be conceived that, in the universes of far greater scale, our world is, quite literally, as an atom is to a galaxy. Surely, we are, on a greater scale, simply a very small part of 'something else', e.g. the forearm of some huge creature, swinging through the vastness of a wider universe. And even when that forearm brushes up against something – a doorjamb – or smashes into the face of an adversary, we don't know any different because we're at atomic level in that scale and set into the cushioned whirl of the astronomical ballet.

And why should it be any different when we start looking at the atoms that make up ourselves and our earthly environment? – infinitely small as well as infinitely large, remember. The fact that our microscopes can only produce definition at a certain scale means nothing; we are as nebulae to our atoms as the Serpens nebulae are to us. So in my forearm is a vast universe of sub-atomic life, that I can't make out but which is infinitely varied and dainty (and, again, cushioned in its own balletic whirl . . .)

As far as my (admittedly limited) reading and comprehension of the state of scientific advancement goes, it's my understanding that the most up-to-the-minute research backs this up – there does not appear to be a solid basic unit of matter.

So, what I'm conceiving here is true infinity in the three dimensions: take your own body as the (arbitrary . . .) starting point and first send your mind outwards through the clouds, the atmosphere, and into the stars; then swing back in a dizzying trajectory straight into your body, down to subatomic level and beyond.

Then we add another ingredient . . . time.

What the hell is that all about? Another dimension that we do experience but which retains considerable mystery for us.

An image of time once took shape in my mind: a long row of square metal plates, each plate the same size, not very thick and all aligned, flat against each other so the effect was of a long accordion, without beginning or end, snaking and twisting its way through black space. Actually, the space it occupied was more like a deep sea space, with grey, ethereal, ghost-like sprays floating around it, and this better fitted the texture and colours of the plates, which were as if made of copper that had long corroded with varying shades of cobalt blue and pistachio green. And it was as if each of these plates was a slice of time, so that each successive plate was the next moment of time, like those old packs of cards you could flick through your fingers, their images creating the illusion of movement, like stop-motion animation.

And this, I reckon, would fit with our actual experience of time: I saw a TV programme which was describing how we see the world – how our eyes and brains interact – and it said that our vision sees individual pictures, thousands a second, like a film reel. And when you think about it this does seem to ring true. Because it does seem to me rather difficult for us to imagine (or experience) seamless movement, or time. I do, however, reckon that the seamlessness is actually there, it's just difficult for us to experience it. It's like what I was saying earlier about the smallest constituent parts of the physical world (the electrons and quarks): as humans we are limited to seeing the 'integral' bits, which we imagine have space – or something – in between them; we have difficulty (for the present?) in imagining, or seeing, seamless matter.

Anyway, this image meant that each of these points in time were fixed, in slices, so that each slice stood still, unmoving . . . always. So that all things in the future as well as the past have already happened; it's all actually stationary. So that it is only the progressive movement of 'us' passing through it that creates the experience – or illusion – of time.

Had a recollection of me playing my electric guitar in my bedroom back at home and my mum shouting at me to not make so much noise – just like the troublesome teenager I once was – and I had a sudden feeling of sadness and my heart swelling, and my feelings cast themselves across the span of the years of my life like a washing-line strung with various dyed garments, some still dripping on the floor of the yard below, some now dried, with a variety of coloured sediment on the tiles below being the only sign of the juice that had once moved through them.

By analogy, what I was saying earlier about there being no standard scale might also apply here. So that there's no fixed starting or middle or end point to this platesnake – it just wreathes around and around so that, from one perspective at least, all time – 'past, present and future' – exists at once and always has done.

Everything that is going to happen has already happened and everything that has happened is going to happen. And it is all sitting suspended in space. Waiting.

Further refinements or aspects of this image that came to me: the platesnake does, I grant you, sound rather linear, one-dimensional; in fact, I also conceived it in infinite dimensions so that for each section of accordion there was – on another plane, only slightly tilted from the first – another section of the same stretch of time but from a slightly different (adjacent) perspective. And then another. And another. And so on. Each lying on top of and through each. Until what you have is a dense (infinitely dense) mass . . . of time and space.

Everyone still with me?! And no – I'm not on my second tab of acid. But I think that your life – my life – is one red line, meandering and weaving; passing through an infinite mass of other possible lines, like a thread of red nylon running through a mass of white cotton wool which expands away, infinitely, all around.

Also, the plates did seem to me like a long row of electroplates. And, being a human, I saw each as distinct from the next. So that there was something between them – what the hell could that be? And I imagined that, every now and again it was possible for there to be a 'short', like an electrical short, between plates. So that whatever the current was – that usually sat stable in the plates – every now and again shorted along a section of plates and suddenly two distant plates were – with a crackle – connected, when they oughtn't to be. (Deja-vu?)

Saw a photo in The Guardian of a black child with AIDS looking at the camera – at me – but at infinity, miles away, and I thought back to the point at which the photo was taken . . . a contact between me and the boy; I was taken to the time when the photo was taken. Did he intend that he was looking, at that point, at the person who would, in due course, look at his photo? A meeting in eternity.'

Susan looked up from the book to the window. The orange of the blind was glowing brighter now that the sun was up and pressing the full weight of its rays upon it. She realised that a tear was running down her cheek and that more might follow if she wasn't careful. She bit her corner lip as if to stem the flow, ran the back of her hand across her eyes and snorted hard through her nostrils.

She tipped her head back onto the soft leather upright of the chair, scrutinised the ceiling and blew a swhoosh of air through her lips. She knew then that she loved Martin; that he wasn't like anyone she had been with before – not easy and not safe but that, amid all the sound and fury of his ravaged mind and soul, there lay a true human heart.

249

She decided to get back into the bed with him and leant forward to place the book on the coffee table. As she did this she noticed, for the first time, a white Samsung mobile, lying next to Martin's keys; obviously another mobile, different from his usual red Nokia that had been left back at Michael's flat. After only the slightest hesitation, she picked it up and pressed the button at the bottom of the device. It wasn't locked and the screen lit up with the various options icons. She pressed 'Calls' to bring up a list of the most recent incoming and outgoing numbers and names. At the top of the list was a call received: 'Michael Broad – Today – 1:02 a.m.' She thought for a moment; curled her lip sardonically; put the phone back down; and rose to pad through into the bedroom, finally exhausted.

28

As usual, the path from unconscious sleep to clear wakefulness had been uncertain and broken. There was a hinterland of dark, rolling shapeshifters and noises off; pull focus into shadowy recesses of the dreamscape, only to kick back in fright once the unknown hove horribly into view. Susan's mind swayed back and forth through jumbled scenes and garbled dialogue, returning all the while to a recurring motif – a deep, slow rhythm like a giant heart beating in the depths of the ocean, heard at several removes in the treacle of the brine. And a visceral pain as her hands – bound behind her back – are wrenched upward so that her exposed neck is thrust down towards the block and her eye catches a glint of light flashing across the edge of the blade held high in the bleak sky that presses down upon all of them the same.

In due course, she came to realise that she had fallen back into the world of primary dreams and was lying, once more, in the same bed from whence she had embarked. As the pieces of her person slipped back into place the obvious question finally set itself: where was Martin? She raised her head slightly from the horizontal – not an easy task with the murderous synapses exacting a spiteful revenge for the previous night's indulgences and impositions.

No sign of him across the crumpled landscape of linen and duvet. She called out 'Martin?' and her voice sounded harsh and disembodied, weak and shocking all at the same time. Still, no reply.

After five more minutes painfully trying to manoeuvre her inner balance to an even keel, and her reluctant fortitude to a state of readiness, she slid her feet off the bed, gathered up the faithful bath robe once more and headed boldly back to the living room.

No sign of the man.

But there were worrying indications – beginning to creep into the edges of her awareness – that the hour of the day might be a shameful something not scaled since the carefree days of her early college career (before the timetable caught her up). She looked to the clock by the window, inwardly wincing.

1:30 p.m.

Bloody hell. It was the afternoon ! She was shocked but, at the same time, couldn't deny herself a rueful grin. The smell of stale smoke and flat beer hung in the air of the flat, the dead cans and full ashtray on the coffee table again redolent of a seemingly distant hedonistic past (how and why had she become so *respectable*?).

Susan hauled the orange blind up its mast and the warm afternoon sun streamed in. She flinched but it was good to see the full-on daylight after the seemingly endless night she'd just endured. After a brief struggle with the catch, she was also able to get the window open and the sound of the city rose up to welcome her.

This building wasn't on the main drag but there were still plenty of cars and vans trundling along the road, folk ambling up and down the pavements, and jazz coming from the open window of an apartment almost directly opposite Susan's position. A disinterested bystander stood across the street would have been treated to the charming cameo of a beautiful young woman in her dressing gown (or her boyfriend's?), dark hair tousled and wrought, blinking for the first time against the light of the day, popping up in the square frame of the window, flat in the high blank wall full of many other identical squares, like an urban advent calendar.

It was a lovely day and, right there and then, Susan decided to enjoy it, hangover or no hangover. She turned back to the interior of Martin's flat and it now appeared so much brighter and starker. She could see more clearly her clothes on the floor (another grin, less rueful). Martin's book on the table where she had left it. The white Samsung had gone but there was a note in its place. Her heart picked up the pace somewhat.

A note.

OK. So read it.

'Susan,

I have some things to sort out today (you can imagine . . .) Didn't want to wake you (I reckoned you'd be glad to catch up on the sleep !)

Should be back early evening but don't let me hold you up if you need to go anywhere. Have left you a spare set of keys.

Love,

Martin X'

She beamed like a fool. *'Love, Martin'* – and a set of keys ! At that moment she was so happy she nearly set into a proper blub. She couldn't quite believe how things had turned around so quickly. All that time spent struggling with Martin the robot – 14 months ! The hours she'd put in, ridiculed – she knew – by many a spiteful tongue. But she'd been right all along – she'd somehow known there was something more behind Martin Dash's blank façade and now she was going to get the reward for her faith.

He was beautiful, he was intelligent, and he was *hers*. She bent to grab the keys – *her* keys – from the table and stuffed them into the dressing gown pocket with the treasured note as she strode to the bathroom for another shower – this time solo.

29

As she chopped the red peppers in Martin's (*their?*) kitchen, Susan sang along lustily to the song playing on Martin's (*their?*) hi-fi radio: Amy Winehouse doing her inimitable thing with 'Tears Dry On Their Own'.

She had already chopped the onions and now pushed the newly made dice into a neat pile next to them so that there now stood two identical mini mountains of soft, edible Lego, one red and one white. The oil had now heated in the pan so she had to wreck the twin peaks, cosying up next to each other, by holding the chopping board over the pan and swooshing the onions – screaming mutely in terror – over the edge with her hand, to drop down into the sizzling pool of death below. Some of the pale, translucent cubes tried to evade their fate by clinging desperately to the skin of her fingers but were mercilessly flicked off to fall in with their fellows.

At a certain point late in the afternoon Susan had decided to go out to buy food so that she could cook some dinner for the two of them that evening. Martin hadn't said exactly what time he'd be back so she figured that she could knock up some of her special chilli and then reheat it when it was needed. She always referred to this dish as her special chilli in a way that might suggest some level of accomplishment in the culinary arts but, in fact, the term was used entirely ironically as her chilli was special only in the sense of being one of just two dishes she actually knew how to cook, the other being spaghetti bolognese (and, if the truth be told, she had seized on the latter only when she discovered that, if you could do the sauce for a chilli, it really wasn't much of a hop and a skip to be able to do a bolognese).

Prior to her grocery trip she had taxied the two miles across to her own flat in Bayswater to get a change of clothes and an overnight bag before she could tidy up the mess she and her beau had made and then settle down to watch an old film on TV.

It was now 6:00 p.m. and she'd started on a bottle of red wine to oil the wheels of this whole cooking malarkey. Amy's lament was building to a climax and Susan bellowed along in sisterly support.

The doorbell buzzed – she only just heard it above the blaring music.

Martin? But he had his own keys. Or had he left them, relying upon Susan to be in?

She came out of the kitchen area and hurried across to turn the radio off before striding to the intercom by the flat's door and grabbing the handset from its cradle on the wall.

"Hello?" she sang out but this was met by silence in response.

"Is that you, Martin?"

Now a man's voice came back – but not Martin's.

"Oh, hi. Erm . . . is that you Susan? It's Danny – Danny Lake." Mediated as it was through the electronic circuitry, Susan could still hear the uneasiness in the voice. Danny Lake was her father's principal parliamentary aide / electoral agent / political fixer / bag man / whatever you might like to call the post but, if Jimmy needed something tricky sorting, it was usually Danny who was entrusted with the job. What the hell was he doing here? Couldn't be good.

Susan hesitated but then asked: "Hi Danny – what's up?"

"Ahm . . . your father's sent me for you Susan. Can I come in?"

It certainly sounded like Danny's unreconstructed Cockney twang but Susan decided to check. "Just hold on a minute please, Danny – I won't be a moment."

She laid the handset down on a small console table that stood next to the door and scurried across to once more open the window that faced onto the street. On poking her head out she saw that it was, indeed, Danny Lake stood before the front door but he was also flanked by another familiar face, George Kay, and they both raised their heads to look at Susan, upon hearing the window click open.

While Danny was the man Jimmy turned to for a fix, Susan had, over the years, worked out (this was never explained or admitted) that the younger, fitter George was the one called in to deal with more . . . *security-related* challenges (that might be considered outwith the normal duties of a Minister's conventional guard).

Danny – hair slicked back, stick thin, in a suit that hung off him – smiled weakly and unconvincingly up at Susan, with a hesitant wave to boot. George (crew-cutted in a dark striped shirt and blue jeans, all straining to hold in the solid bulk that usually only had to be flexed to persuade those who needed persuading) smiled much more cheerily. Whatever Danny was worried about, George wasn't. George didn't really do worrying and, in point of fact, Susan had always found George to be hugely entertaining, with a fund of appallingly sick jokes and startling anecdotes that were even less likely to make you laugh.

But why had Danny obviously thought that he might need back-up on this mission? And why did he appear to be more than his normal jumpy self, anxiously glancing left and right and generally looking as though he would rather be anywhere else than here, stood out on this street, in front of this door?

Susan waved back, with an even weaker smile than Danny's, and called down: "Hi – I'll buzz you in." George gave her the thumbs up. Danny just nodded. And decided to give the street another look up and down.

The older man edged into the main room of the flat and now put his darting eyes to scoping out this new space of potential dangers. George padded behind, doing the same but rather less obviously.

"And to what do I owe the privilege, Danny?" asked Susan, with her arms folded before her, head cocked to one side and an expression that was somehow friendly and dubious at the same time.

Danny turned to George with mock indignation – "Oh, that's lovely, innit George? A real warm welcome !"

They all laughed and Susan relaxed, slightly.

"I'm sorry but you've taken me a bit by surprise. I'm not usually visited in a strange flat to be taken away by my father's ..." and here she hesitated just momentarily ". . . friends."

The two men both raised their eyebrows to register the slight slight but didn't dwell on it. Danny put his hands up: "I know – I know, love. I'm sorry to bust in on you like this, but there's been developments and your father's worried."

Susan braced herself "What developments, Danny?"

Instead of answering straight away, Danny pointed his chin towards the bedroom door and asked: "E's not in then? – Martin."

"No, why?" Susan got the distinct impression from both men that they would really have liked to go into the bedroom to check but were conscious of the offence that would so obviously give.

"Do you know where 'e is?" Danny persisted. Susan realised that, point of fact, she didn't – so again but more forcefully (and slowly) this time: "*No. Why?*"

Danny looked to George, who gave an almost imperceptible shrug, so the explanation was provided:

"Barry Rogers's been murdered."

Susan's jaw actually dropped. Then she suddenly felt herself unsteady and decided that she needed to sit down. Sat on the leather chair where Martin had lounged earlier that morning she looked vacantly at his book lying before her.

Danny indicated the opposite chair with his hand.

"Yes, please do sit, Danny," and Susan looked across to George, who was still standing near the door, "and you George, please."

"I'm OK at the moment, thanks love." George's response was couched in a friendly tone but the fact that he appeared to want to stay by the front door slightly unnerved Susan and Danny spotted this. He developed his explanation – "The thing is, Susan, the police are now gonna be 'unting down a number of possible suspects and friend Martin will be on that list."

Danny's words merely confirmed the fear that had leapt into Susan's thoughts the moment Danny had given her the news: Would they suspect Martin? Why would they suspect Martin? – Why?

Susan started turning this over and the more she did so, the worse things appeared. This was the Martin Dash who had assumed a false identity to hide a previous trial for murder. Who, by his own admission, had been engaged in a massive fraud with the now deceased Barry Rogers (who, according to the testimony of her own father, was the one most likely to bring them all down, with his big mouth).   And this was the Martin Dash / Dayton who appeared to swing in and out of severe mental conditions at the mere drop of a hat.   And who was now in cahoots with a multi-millionaire sleaze merchant for whom the word 'dubious' might have been specially coined.

Susan shut her eyes and put her head in her hands.   Danny turned round in his chair to look again at George, who merely cocked his head towards the door.

"Listen, Susan," Danny, now adopting a caring, protective tone, "Your dad's sent us here to fetch you because 'e wants to protect you, love.   'E wants to 'elp – you and Martin . . . you've no idea where 'e is?"

Susan pulled her head up from her hands to look straight at Danny.

"How can my father help Martin?"

Danny shifted in his seat and moved his lips, momentarily wordlessly, apparently unprepared for that line of inquiry.

"I . . . I imagine 'e'll get 'im a good brief," Danny tried, but not too convincingly.   And then gave up.   "I don't know to be 'onest, love – that's your father's department.   You know 'ow 'e is.   'E's got a lot of influence.   'E can get things done.   All I know is your dad will be Martin's best 'ope."

"But it's your department too, isn't it Danny?"   Susan's view was hardening.   Danny shuffled a bit more and decided to change tack.

"Look, the thing is, the police don't know about this place yet, do they?   Martin gave them the flat in Islington as 'is address."

This was news to Susan but a thought popped up straight away.

"So how do you know?"

Danny grimaced and shrugged and appeared to be in danger of slipping into a total meltdown of ticks and twitches.

"Again – your father... OK, *we*... get to know lots of things. 'Sno big deal."

It was precisely this sort of thing that had always put Susan off delving too deeply into her father's business and, again, she had the powerful feeling that the more she found out, the less she wanted to know.

Danny pressed on – "But they will find out about it soon. Quite soon. We've taken a chance, *your father's* taken a chance sending us 'ere, so we need to get out of 'ere now before anyone else arrives. Your dad wants to talk to you Susan and we can take you to 'im. Where you'll be safe."

"Why doesn't he just phone me?"

Danny shook his head slowly and smiled – no grimaced (as though he'd felt some minor discomfort). "Best not on the phone at the moment."

Again, that all-too-conscious feeling of an unnamed dread inching a little closer toward Susan.

"So where is he now?"

"Well, 'e's actually at Westminster at the moment an' 'e said to bring you there if you were on your own . . ." Danny saw the frown that this produced on Susan's face but tried to make light of it and smirked – "Probably wouldn't be a good idea to parade Mr. Dash – who is quite . . . noticeable – through the 'Ahzes of Parliament as a guest of your father just right now?" He cocked his head by way of suggestion that she might agree. "But you're obviously OK; you've been plenty of times before, 'aven't you? And, as daft as it sounds, it's probably the safest place you could wish for in many ways. Private. Protected . . . privileged. There's no snoopers can get in . . ."

Susan knew that all of this was right. A smell penetrated her senses and Danny obviously caught it at the same time – they both looked to the kitchen area to see little clouds of grey smoke rising happily from the saucepan.

"Shit ! The fucking onions !" she cried and jumped to her feet.

Danny and George grinned. As Susan pulled the pan off the hob and scraped the now blackened mush into the bin (tragic légumes, doomed to be cooked pointlessly), she shot a look at the two men: "Don't you dare tell my father you've heard me curse like that," and they chuckled, relieved.

30

As they glided down Birdcage Walk – George at the wheel of the black Audi, Danny and Susan sat in the back – the sun was only an hour off setting behind them and Susan, now and then, caught flashes of its orange blaze in the rear view mirror.

Tourists and students and office workers were still milling about on the grassy expanse of St James' Park on their left and relaxing on the benches that ran along its perimeter. The evenings were still warm and Susan felt the contrast between the informal, bustling panorama framed in the car's tinted windows and the gloomy, paranoid space she found herself in.

She had decided not to phone Martin in Danny and George's presence and the fact was she'd been directly under their gaze from the moment she'd let them into the flat; wondering whether this had been their intent made her feel even gloomier and caged.

She pushed these thoughts to one side and engaged Danny: "Barry was murdered how?"

Danny looked at her carefully, as though he was considering his answer.

"Shot. In the face."

Susan winced, involuntarily, but did also express a thought: "So he knew his killer."

Danny raised his eyebrows, saw the back of George's head tilt slightly and they both laughed. "Yeah ... very good."

"Where?"

"At 'is place."

"You mean Hadley Wood?"

"Yeah."

"Because he's got the flat in town as well."

Susan noticed George's eyes on her in the mirror.

"No, not the flat," confirmed Danny, flatly.

Silence for a while.

"And when was this?"

"'Bout two o'clock this afternoon."

Both George and Danny were looking at her now, with narrowed eyes.

Susan pushed back – "And how come you boys know before it's on the news?"

Both men smiled again and Danny sighed: "Told you, love – your dad knows a lot of people and gets to hear stuff. First."

They swung into Great George Street and the familiar sight of Big Ben rose up massively against the violet sky.

Even after the many years of visiting her father at Westminster (and on more than one occasion, as children, she and Maria had been paraded before the cameras here, with Jimmy and Rosa, to prove what a wholesome family man the Member was) she still felt a faint quiver of awe each time she came upon the great Gothic pile of the Palace, instantly recognisable the world over as the enduring emblem of British power, imperial and post, like an amber, becrowned crocodile lying in repose – but still menacing – along the edge of the riverbank. And although she didn't care to admit it (even to herself), the fact that her father – *her* father – was one of its most lauded scions also delivered a deliciously guilty nip.

Jimmy's day-to-day office was in the Department's nondescript building on Smith Square, three blocks away but he was currently stuck in the Palace engaged in the urgent business of trying to assess / shore up what personal support he might still have from his comrades in the face of the horrendous shit storm of the Barry Rogers saga that was blowing ever more forcefully the way of himself (and, by association, the Government).

Upon Gordon Brown's ascension as Prime Minister two months previously, Jimmy had, yet again, confounded all expectations by clinging on to his cabinet status, albeit with a slight demotion from Defence to Transport. That Brown had chosen to retain one of the most trusted lieutenants of his arch enemy for the new regime astounded many observers but those with a more archival perspective would point out that Sachs and Brown also went back a long way; that, in truth, Sachs would probably feel more at home, ideologically, in the bosom of the Brown tribe than the Blair creed that he had been obliged to abide these last 10 years; and, most importantly, Brown knew – as Blair had – that Sachs was a big gun best kept in your own service rather than swung back at you; whose loyalty could be relied upon (a valuable rarity in a sea of perfidious sharks, all waiting for their own chance to supplant you), given that Jimmy had long since proved – by word and deed – that he knew his best role was that of trusted wingman rather than the exemplary figurehead, a position to which he was unquestionably unsuited, temperamentally and constitutionally.

So there were obviously many in the new order who were resentful of this turncoat occupying a berth that should clearly have gone to one of their own. So they were obliged to watch and wait for their chance to put the interloper to the sword. And it looked like the opportunity might be arriving rather sooner than they could have dared to hope for.

Danny and George appeared to have the same access as was reserved for their master so that, when they pulled up to the sentry post by an iron-grill gate on the east side of the complex, a quick flash of green and white passes pulled from their jacket pockets and a quick peer by the gate officer through the open rear window at the passless figure of Susan in the back of the car was all it took before they were sliding into the throat of a tunnel that descended down into a car park lying under the building, reserved for ministers of state, senior civil servants and their acolytes.

Up the stairs from the car park the door opened onto a scene familiar to Susan. They stood at the beginning of a long straight corridor that stretched away to a point that you could barely see, even squinting. This was the main committee corridor, the length of which was punctuated by large double doors of solid panelled oak, framed by ornate carved stone and wood, each of which led into one of the 19 committee rooms housed here. The lower half of both side walls of the corridor were covered with the same dark oak panelling out of which jutted benches with the seats upholstered in dark green leather and small tables of the same design ran along in front of just the right-hand row. The upper halves of both walls were plain, painted a light cream and hung here and there with gilt-framed paintings of celebrated alumni. The whole length of the corridor floor was covered in a close-knit carpet design of alternate rows of blue and red and then green and yellow baroque hexagons against a pumpkin orange background, its comforting beauty contrasting with the heavy ceiling that hung directly above it of, yes – dark oak panels.

Susan had been through here a number of times before and it always seemed somehow oppressive to her, redolent of a medieval cloister or a sinister boarding school. Which was, perhaps, how they liked it. In any event, there was quite a bustle about the place and serious types in all sorts of suits pinged in and out of nearly all of the doors as far as she could see, like a Brian Rix farce or one of Kafka's nightmares, she couldn't decide which. They were generally huddled together in twos and threes, always moving – up and down the corridor and in and out of the doors – their discrete chattering producing, in the aggregate, a low murmuring hum, like the bees of a particularly busy hive.

Susan knew where they were headed – the floor above this, which housed more committee rooms but also some more anonymous redoubts that could be misappropriated for occasional use if you knew the right way to go about it. Her father had haunted that floor for many years, she knew; scheming and plotting in those back rooms with all sorts of chancers, corsairs and criminals. Danny knew which room Jimmy was in right now and strode in front, leading George and Susan swiftly over the fancy runner.

As they went, Susan picked up on an air of real excitement about the place, some sort of term-end feeling and wondered what it was all about until she noticed that quite a number of the throng did the double-take when their little group caught the eye – she could feel their heads swivelling round to maintain the scrutiny as they passed – and then a short, rotund figure she thought she recognised as one of the Government Whips reached out to apprehend their leader with the words: "Danny. Danny – what the bloody hell is going on? Where's Jimmy?" Danny never slowed or turned his head but, with a fluid movement, he simply brushed the man's arm aside and called back: "Not now, Brian – sorry."

Then it occurred to Susan that the centre of attention, yet again, was her father and his serial adventurism and that more of the crowd were now spotting them as they passed. Which was why Danny was leading them so fast. And which was why Susan was now blushing and fixing her eyes on the colourful hexagons now blurring into each other as they flashed away under her swinging feet. And why she, once again, felt the paranoia of the hunted. Or at least the daughter of the hunted.

Danny suddenly swung sharp left so that they exited the corridor and came upon the broad staircase leading up to the first floor. As they passed through the white limestone foyer to reach the stair foot, Susan glanced at a painting that filled the whole of one wall – Queen Elizabeth I refusing the Commons' plea for her to marry, with the retort that her coronation ring signified she was already married . . . to her kingdom.

The first floor corridor was a stark contrast to the throng they had just quit. An eerie quiet prevailed with just one man sat staring at his laptop on a bench to their left. To the right, the other end of the corridor was in semi-darkness and it was into this gloom that Danny now led them.

As they neared the end, a dark-suited figure burst out through a door on the left, his oiled black hair fallen in streaks across a face red with what looked like rage. It was David Lamach, Gordon Brown's Director of Communications, and he was obviously in a spin about something. Once out in the corridor he hesitated and glared back into the room he had just departed, clearly asking himself: 'Should I stay or should I go?'

He caught the trio advancing towards him out of the corner of his eye and, just as he turned to face them, the unmistakable roar of The Rt. Hon. James Sachs in full voice bellowed out from within the room: "And you can tell *him* he can go fuck himself as well !"

The simple force of this seemed to rock Lamach's head back and he was briefly stunned. But then his pallor changed from red to white and, for a moment, he seemed ready to strike back until he remembered the group that was now awaiting his next move with no little interest. Not for the first time discretion got the better of valour and, with a lateral wave of the hand (as though to push the snarling Sachs behind him), Lamach approached the reliable consigliere from whom he hoped to get more sense.

He started: "Danny . . ." and then, remembering his manners, nodded, "George," to the burly backup and turned to greet Susan. It seemed it was only at this point that he realised who the men's companion was.

"Ah, Miss Sachs. How are you?" His body moved almost involuntarily (taken by surprise as he was) in what appeared to be a short bow.

As Susan replied, politely, "I'm fine, thank you Mr. Lamach," the spin doctor's eyes narrowed behind his round spectacles as he started to mentally rifle through the scraps of relevant information he held and to try and impose some order upon them. Just for a moment no-one said anything as Lamach stood staring at Susan, clearly lost in his thoughts. Susan decided to break the silence and – tilting her head – asked, smiling: "And how are you?"

"Oh – well . . . well," he replied, distractedly, before finally coming to and remembering the job at hand.

"Sorry. Sorry," he bumbled, "I was just . . ." and trailed off before turning decisively back to his opposite number – "Danny, listen. Listen. Can you make him see sense? You know . . ?"

"How do you mean?" replied Danny, innocently, knowing perfectly well what the sweating Lamach meant but being inclined to enjoy to the full his adversary's discomfort.

"This bloody Rogers affair," Lamach spat out, his temper flaring again before his pretensions to decorum brought him up again; he sheepishly put his hand up to Susan and mouthed: "Sorry," before turning back to Danny and resuming in an altogether more hushed tone as he drew nearer.

"The game's up now, Danny – you know we can't control it anymore." Lamach shot a concerned sideways glance at Susan and now seemed to struggle for the words. "Just speak to him Danny – you know," and then, more hesitantly, with another guilty look, almost whispering now: "We can't allow this to reach the PM . . . you know that." He patted Danny's breast with an almost fatherly air and a pitiful show of benevolence and signed off: "Please, Danny," with the final flourish of his best hangdog expression before nodding to "Miss Sachs" and "George," in turn, and sloping off down the corridor. He turned his head back just the once, as he walked, to see that the three were watching him go. Just to be sure.

As they turned into the door through which David Lamach had just been so rudely expelled, Susan beheld the sight of her father slumped in a deep blood red leather armchair, morosely staring at the whisky in his hand – probably not his first, she thought.

This was not one of the committee rooms but a small, rather homely, study decorated in subdued green and red hues and appointed with expensive Edwardian furniture. Jimmy sat just to one side of an oak-surrounded fireplace in the wall facing them, a heavy mahogany desk over to the left and the right hand wall covered with dark shelf bookcases.

Susan realised that she had been here before – 10 years ago she, her mother and her sister had, together, called in to see Jimmy just after Labour's joyous return to power after 18 years in the wilderness. Then, it had seemed like a new beginning – the loathed Tory rule of cuts and strife were over and her father's tribe looked forward to a different, more progressive era of greater opportunity and justice.

They had clinked champagne glasses happily with Blair and Brown in this very room, assured that these were the men to lead them all up to that glad realm. 10 years later and it all seemed rather more tawdry and drab. The mandate had been tarnished by the exigencies of circumstances – Blair's vanity had dragged the country through the mire and Brown's lust for power had fed the neglect that brought it to its knees.

And her father had supported them throughout, always pleading that it was all justified simply to keep the Tories out but Susan wondered now whether it had, all along, been simply about keeping themselves in; whether that first lethal draught of power hadn't poisoned them all so that staying in office was, by now, the only rationale.

As she looked down at her father, she could see now how much those years had taken their toll on him. The room was lit by just one table lamp on the other side of the fireplace but, even in that gloom, the weariness and sorrow in that tired face were apparent to all.

But Jimmy now looked up to his daughter and smiled; a reaction of simple delight at seeing her, despite the current circumstances, immediately triggering the same emotion in Susan, despite the current circumstances.

"Hi, Darling," his voice raspy; he placed his glass on the side table and jumped to his feet, arms outstretched.

"Hi, Dad," they kissed each other's cheeks and hugged, a moment free of the cares and worries that brought them together this night and that transported them back 20 years, when she would run into his arms to greet his return home and, at that time, he had to bend down to scoop her up. A pair conjoined forever in a feeling.

They moved apart a step while still holding each other's arms, caught in a dance, the better for Jimmy to study his daughter's face. One final broad smile and then to business.

"Sit down, Love," he motioned to the twin of his own chair on the other side of the fireplace, grabbed the whisky decanter and enquired, with a tilt of his head, whether she'd join him? Danny and George left the room without having to be asked, shutting the door behind them. With her glass now poured, Susan kicked off: "I'm sorry to hear about Barry – I know he was your friend."

A pained look shot across Jimmy's face and he took another gulp of whisky. He remained silent for a while, starting at the carpet, evidently striving to formulate his response. "It's a bad job," was all he said, ultimately, placing his glass back on the table and sitting back in his chair to look directly at Susan, his plan seemingly now made.

"Whatever Barry was, he didn't deserve that," was his opening gambit.

"What *was* Barry, Dad?" Susan shot back.

Jimmy thought for just a moment. "Well it turns out that Barry remained just as dodgy as he ever was. I thought – he *told* me – that he'd turned over a new leaf, he'd got legitimate funding lined up; foreign, yes, but not dodgy. I even had it checked out myself. Thought it was kosher . . . but it wasn't . . ."

"Oh, really?" Susan's sarcasm standing in for 'I told you so.'

Jimmy gave her a look that said there was no need for that but then sighed, gave her the point, and continued.

"Hmm . . . turns out that Barry's man – who we checked out – did both sorts of deals, good and bad. I won't give you his name; you don't want that knowledge," at this, Jimmy's face darkened, "but, suffice to say, Barry got the bad stuff."

"For the whole Crack Harbour Development?"

Jimmy nodded: ". . . and the rest."

Susan's eyes narrowed, "What – all of them?"

"There are currently three other major developments on the go with the Grudge Group – as you know," he added, with only the merest hint of irony, before continuing: "They've all had the *benefit,*" he lamented, sardonically ". . . allegedly."

"Unfortunately for all of us," Jimmy then checked himself, "yes, for Barry the most," he conceded, pursing his lips, "this guy was on the radar; both the FCA and SOCA. Turns out the whole operation has been conducted right under their noses." Jimmy paused to consider whether to utter the next comment to his daughter but looked straight at her – "We're fucked."

"Barry's definitely fucked."

Jimmy nearly burst out laughing but, considering they were talking of the cold-blooded murder that day of his long-time friend, caught himself and made do with an ironic shake of the head, silently amazed that he was having such a conversation with his daughter. He allowed himself a moment to scrutinise his progeny and felt a sudden happy wonder and pride that such a magnificent specimen was *his* – his *own* daughter.

He had long since come to realise that she was an independent being, with her own character and foibles, but now he marvelled afresh at the unmitigated verve she brought to the party. Like all parents, he and Rosa had had to learn the trade on the job – there was no manual – and so they had proceeded blindly, stumbling over half-formed and half-baked assumptions, making it up as they went along and, each time they thought they had got somewhere, their children had changed and moved on to a different level in the meantime. And they'd had to relearn again.

Jimmy had been sufficiently arrogant to assume that he would always be superior to his children, that they would always be dependent upon him, that he would always be teaching them. So it had come as something of a shock to realise that, ultimately, they were independent of him, they had their own views, strengths and weaknesses, and their own lives that they didn't need or want him to guide.

And yet he cleaved to the knowledge that his legacy could still be discerned – his instruction, his example, his genes – and the overriding sentiment, finally, was simple delight at having had anything to do with the remarkable person that now sat before him. He allowed himself to believe that he could see, in Susan particularly (Maria, he felt, was ultimately more of her mother), the virtues he liked to think had served himself well – insight, spirit and conscience; for all his repeated transgressions Jimmy still basically viewed himself as a moral man – concerned for the underdog and tilting at the establishment – and, effectively, viewed his occasional deviations from correctitude as the inevitable slips of a fully-rounded man of the world; minor issues, and certainly not to be weighed *that* seriously against him. (In truth, he wasn't entirely displeased at the comparisons with Lloyd George that were frequently levelled at him – again, warts and all.)

And he could see that, in Susan, there was something compelling added to that mix: a kindness, sympathy, generosity, that – he had to accept – must have been borne from elsewhere.

And, in his fondest imaginings, a hope lurked (that barely dared speak its name) that, in due course, Susan would be the one to assume the mantle of the family business – that is to say repaying the debt the family owed to the country that took it in by the devotion of one's life to unstinting public service (preferably in high political office . . .) but he was sufficiently astute to understand that Susan was not a copy of himself; she was her own person, with her own motivations and her own desires, who knew for what? A life with Martin Dash?

At this his mood darkened again.

"Do you know where Martin is, Susan?"

Susan was taken aback by this directness and hesitated.

"Why?"

"What do you mean – why?" Jimmy felt an anger rise up in him and struggled to contain it. "Because I'm asking, that's why !" The air between them changed suddenly and Susan was now on her mettle.

"Well, I'm bloody asking you why !" She felt the words come out, unbidden, and the same fire that burned Jimmy's belly crackled in her too.

Jimmy had spent a lifetime beating up adversaries of all sizes, ranks and hues and his instincts always bade him to attack but this was his beloved daughter, not one of those he was obliged to crush, surely? He was confused and felt vulnerable – truly, for the first time in a long while. Susan pressed the advantage, sensing his weakness, herself feeling no compunction about attacking – after all, he had started it.

"What the hell is going on, Dad? Why are you so interested in where Martin is? So much so that you send your goons out to bring him in?" – a nod to the corridor outside. On the other side of the room's door Danny and George, following every word of the exchange, grinned at each other.

Jimmy was momentarily flustered and he just sat, looking foolish, with his mouth open.

"Who has killed Barry, Dad?" – the, as yet unasked, question now hung in the air.

Jimmy was not helping himself; not having experienced such a level of vehemence from his daughter before, he was floundering and, as he started to mouth, helplessly, "I don't know" – with an injured expression – he merely succeeded in appearing to be evasive.

He attempted an explanation: "Look, Darling – I do not know who killed Barry, believe me, but it's probably not too wild a guess to think that it might have something to do with our friends out East. Those people do not want to be named in a court, believe me, and they'll stop at nothing to prevent it."

"Oh really? And how do you know this? Christ, Dad, listen to yourself – you're a bloody MP, a Government Minister for goodness' sake; you're supposed to be upholding the law – you're a servant of the people. You've told me that often enough yourself and now you sit here talking like a fucking gangster. What the hell has happened to you?"

"I've *told* you" hissed Jimmy through gritted teeth, now getting angrier himself – "I simply put some money into Barry's company myself, thought it was a good investment. That's all I've done. I had no idea all of that rabble were involved, I promise. What on earth do you take me for?"

Good question – Susan studied her father, dubiously.

"OK, so why do you want Martin?"

Jimmy tried to formulate his words: "Susan – you see what has happened to Barry ... I ... I don't want the same to happen to Martin."

275

Susan's head rocked back as if from a blow and she glared, incredulously, at her father. This was undoubtedly a thought that had been lurking somewhere deep down in her but it was only now – when someone else voiced it out loud – that it really hit her, that Martin might suffer the same fate as poor Barry.

She felt like she could no longer keep hold of her mind, as though her thoughts kept slipping out of focus. She should have been able to lean on her father – her *own* father – so why did she get such a bad feeling, observing him, sat here in this gloomy room in the centre of the beast that was the all-powerful British State? Why did she feel so threatened?

As he looked at her now, he appeared not as her father but some alien reptile surveying its prey. Her breathing felt constricted but she managed to croak out – "You want to protect Martin?"

"Yes, of course, Darling – we can help him."

"We?"

"We? Yes, we ... I ... you know what I mean. We – I – can shield him from this. You know I can."

"Or silence him .. ?" Susan felt her pulse banging in her ears. It seemed like the walls of the room were sliding inwards. Her father's face turned a funny colour – she couldn't quite work out why. Was it true indignation or frustration?

"What the fucking hell do you mean by that?" he spat out, leaning forward now. How had it come to this between them, so suddenly? He looked ugly to her and she just wanted to get out of that room now. She stood up but Jimmy did the same. As she moved towards the door, he blocked her way.

"Get out of my way – I'm leaving," she seethed.

Susan could see that Jimmy was now gritting his teeth and his lower jaw jutted forward. He grabbed hold of both her upper arms and she immediately let out a terrifying scream that rent the air like lightning. Jimmy was stunned, his eyes widened. He released his grip and staggered back, horrified.

The door burst open and Danny appeared, hardly daring to look at what he might behold. Susan took her chance and barged past him, now sobbing. As she did so, Danny looked to his boss for instruction. The Secretary of State for Transport slumped back into his chair, defeated. He shook his head, mumbled: "No – leave her," and went for his glass.

As she walked fast back down the corridor, Susan tried hard to resist the urge to run. She just wanted to be away from that scene as quickly as possible but something told her that if she brought attention to herself the opposite result would be more likely.

Before she reached the stairs back down to the busier corridor below, she grabbed a tissue from her bag and wiped her eyes as she walked. Wet black eyeliner stained the white paper so she stopped at the top of the stairs to pull out her compact and do a quick repair job. Seeing her face in the mirror almost started off the crying again; she couldn't understand what had just happened and now felt bereft and frightened. She wanted to call Martin but a sudden rush of paranoia prompted her to wait until she had got out of the range of that oppressive building.

Susan headed straight for the members' entrance, keeping her head down, not meeting anyone's gaze, walking purposefully but not hurriedly. As she brushed past a group in the lobby before the exit, she heard a voice say: "Susan?" but didn't recognise it and didn't pause. Seconds later she was out into the fresh air of the city's bustling evening.

31

Susan stood by the cultivated green lawn of New Palace Yard and turned to look up behind her at the gilded clock face of Big Ben – 7:15. The sun was now low in the sky but it was still warm. Her only thought at this point was to, first, get away so she jogged across Margaret Street and towards the north side of Parliament Square where, she knew, she'd be able to flag down a taxi.

As she approached the blackened bronze statue of Winston Churchill glowering down at his fellows with barely concealed irritation, Susan's eye was caught by a black clad figure standing directly before it, a figure similarly imposing and gruff as though the great man had finally stepped down from the plinth and was pondering his next move. His hands were clasped in front of him and he was staring directly at Susan.

She suddenly realised it was Michael Green's driver, Derek, looking for all the world like a heavyweight Russian hitman, all in black, awaiting his quarry.

Susan instinctively looked behind her but saw nothing and, when she saw that he was smiling and waiting for her to approach him, she remembered his concern for her at Martin's flat (just the night before ! God – how everything had changed since then . . .) and she relaxed and slowed to stand right in front of him.

"Derek, what's . . ?"

He put his finger to his lips to shush her and laughed. "No. No questions just now, please. Martin's asked me to fetch you and we need to get away from here – OK?" He scanned the pavements and Susan shuffled, suddenly nervous. Another courier come to spirit her away – this was getting silly. But all she said was: "Yes."

Derek pulled a mobile from his coat pocket and clamped the device to his ear.

"Where are you now?"

On hearing the reply he turned to look left behind him – "Cool, just pull up there and we'll be with you in a sec." Derek shoved the phone back into his pocket and took Susan's arm with a smile: "Come on, love – just over here."

He led her quickly over the pedestrian crossings off the back of the square and they were then heading along Birdcage Walk. Susan recognised the silver Lexus from last night, now parked – illegally – ten metres in front of them, just as the driver's door swung open and a squat, pasty-faced youth with a crew cut and spectacles jumped out to await them. He and Derek merely nodded to each other. The youth flashed just a quick glance at Susan, expressionless, and Derek held his hand out for the car keys. "I'll take it from here, Bud – you'll get back to base?"

"Yep." Just a nod to Derek and Susan and he was gone, along the pavement and towards the railed entrance down to Westminster Tube station. Derek motioned for Susan to get into the back seat and he pulled the big sedan away from the kerb as quickly as he could.

As they crawled through the evening traffic, stop-starting at all the lights, Susan discerned that they were heading towards the East End and that Derek was continually checking the rear view mirror, his eyes darting across its range. This rendered her correspondingly jumpy and she found herself turning to look out of the rear window too. Derek saw this and laughed: "Don't worry, Susan – everything's OK. No-one's following us."

"You sure?"

"Yeah, yeah. Nothing to worry about."

"Apart from people being murdered?"

Derek rolled his eyes. "Nah, no-one's gonna get murdered."

"Just Barry then?"

Derek shrugged his shoulders, unfazed – "I don't know anything about that. But you're OK. Believe me."

"And Martin?"

"Yeah, yeah – Martin's OK. We're all OK!" He laughed again and put his foot down on a stretch of road that had now become clearer.

"Where are we going, Derek?" asked Susan, finally.

"Ah . . . about 40 minutes," he answered, obliquely.

"No – *where*?" Susan pressed.

"Ah . . . north," Derek ventured, not much more helpfully.

"Jesus," Susan rolled her eyes now and sat back in the seat. "Are you sure you don't want to blindfold me, just to be on the safe side?"

The burly bodyguard burst into booming laughter and slapped the steering wheel; then, after a short pause: "Yeah, perhaps we'd better," and started off chuckling again. Susan shook her head.

Derek glanced in the mirror once more.

They were now going through Stratford on the A12 heading towards the M11 out of London. How far north? she wondered.

Derek called back to Susan: "You all right, love? Hungry? I've got a sandwich you can have," and held up a pre-packed, hopefully.

"No, I'm fine thanks," Susan declined, politely. "How did you know where to pick me up?"

"To be honest, we came for you at the flat. But when we arrived, you were just letting those two fellas in. So we waited."

"What – and you followed us?"

Derek looked a little abashed but answered "Yeah" as if to say "So?"

"When we saw you going into the big house, we thought we'd better not try and follow you in there," a wry grin flashed at her as he enjoyed his little joke. "So Robbie – you just met Robbie – he drove around while I waited to spot you coming out."

"But you didn't know if I would come out. Or when."

"True. I would have phoned you eventually but I preferred not to." Susan wondered why. "Anyway, you weren't in there long, were you?"

Derek watched Susan's face for a reaction. She simply gazed out of the side window, abstractedly – "No."

"Everything OK?"

"No."

"OK," and he drove on.

32

They were soon on the M11 and Derek manoeuvred the sleek machine onto the outside lane so they could gobble up the miles effortlessly. Susan tried to stay her troubled thoughts as the indigo sky, buff fields, green trees, grey tarmac and dirty white barriers flashed by.

She began to question what she was doing. She had just made some sort of break with her father (who she had always loved, nay, adored) in favour of – what? An angelic freak guarded by what appeared to be an underworld gang – Derek seemed nice but she had no doubt that he'd be capable of being very un-nice if the circumstances required it. Or his boss ordered it.

But, then again, what was her father? She did love him but that scene in the upper room had unnerved her and the more she thought about it, the more recollections came to her of incidents in the past – face-offs with colleagues in their home, heated phone calls in the middle of the night, sudden departures and prolonged absences – that seemed now to take on a more sinister turn. Was her father, in reality, just another gangster, albeit licensed?

She suddenly wished she could talk to her mother and thought momentarily of phoning her. But she couldn't have that conversation with Derek listening, so that would have to wait. Then she began to wonder what sort of life Rosa had really spent with Jimmy? What sort of compromises had been demanded and given up?

Ultimately, it all came back to Martin. All the rest of it had been imposed upon her – the gilded childhood in the big house; the private schools moulding the elites of the future; the flat bought by her parents – none of that was her own but Martin was something she had marked out for herself. He had come from such an alien landscape, like nothing she had known before, and yet she had connected right from the off; *she* had recognised his true worth, beyond the mere novelty of such an exotic creature; and she had been there when he emerged, chrysalis-like, from that deep sleep.

Somehow she knew that Martin represented the future for her. She could feel it inside her.

Susan started to take notice of the road signs again. They were now travelling along the M25, eastbound, and when the sign for Junction 28 came into view, Derek indicated to come off. Susan nearly asked where they were going again but decided to save her breath and watch for herself instead.

Through the maze of roads around the interchange, they came out on the A1023 to Brentwood, then quickly turned off left onto what looked like 'Wigley Bush Lane'. Susan couldn't help but childishly smirk at the name. They went through South Weald and past Weald Country Park but from then on it was just a blur of country roads that all looked the same – tarmacked, yes, but nondescript and anonymous with reed-filled ditches on either side at the foot of dense hawthorn hedges screening field after field.

However, after just five minutes, Derek swung the car right onto an unmade lane and Susan realised that she now had no idea at all where they were. The lane was covered merely with rough stone that crunched under the car's tyres like popping bubble wrap. Susan glanced at the dashboard clock – 8:00 p.m. Before them the reddening disc of the sun was now sliding down the back of the horizon settee and the dark ran along behind them. Derek had the headlights on and their mesmerising rays gliding over the pulsing stones brought to mind many a film scene with a crawling vehicle and a bad end for the passengers.

"Derek?" Susan heard how plaintive her little voice sounded but she was, finally, beginning to lose her nerve and she had to ask. A wave of fear had crashed over her and she felt like crying.

Derek's eyes fixed her in the mirror and he furrowed his brow. "It's all right, darling – we're here now. We've just come to see Martin. Don't worry." There was real pity in his voice and for some reason this opened the floodgates. Susan's body shook, her throat gagged and her nose was instantly running. As the car pulled to a stop, she had her face in her hands, sobbing like a child. She knew she was going to die. She didn't look up but simply keened through the cradle of her fingers – "I'm sorry," hardly able to get the words out.

Derek jumped out of the car and spun round to open the right rear door. She flinched.

"Oh no, no – darlin' . . . it's all right. Nothing's going to happen to you." Derek suddenly felt ashamed of his part in bringing her to this and was desperate to redeem himself.

"Look, Martin's here," he indicated with his right hand to the end of the lane. The tall hedges on either side of the lane stopped 20 metres beyond the front of the car and it led onto a wide open space that stretched away before them. Sure enough, from behind the end of the right hand hedge came the unmistakeable figure of Martin Dash, his blonde hair shining like a torch in the deepening gloom. Susan had raised her eyes tentatively from their watery cup just to see him walking cautiously towards the car, caught in the full beam of its bright white lights. He was wearing a denim jacket over a white shirt, black jeans and Timberland boots. He put his hand up in front of his face to shield his eyes from the lights' dazzle and approached warily.

Susan heard the voice of Michael Green coming from behind Martin – "Turn those bloody lights off !"

Derek appeared to be caught in two minds, between returning to the front of the car to turn the lights off – as ordered – and staying at the back to comfort his passenger – as he wanted to do. But now Susan was coming out of the car anyway, pushing past the hapless Derek and running to Martin, who stretched his arms out to pull her in to him, his face now beaming.

The two embraced in the glare of the headlights and their lips locked in an urgent union of love and desire. Derek killed the lights and they were plunged into their own cocoon of darkness that excluded the whole world. Susan gripped her lover's back like the mast of a storm-tossed boat, terrified to let go lest she be swept back into the tumult. Martin felt her tears run down his own cheeks and her chest heaved against him.

"Don't cry, Love – there's no need, really," Martin tried to soothe her as he held her head on his chest and stroked her hair. "What is it?"

As she brought her face up to meet his, Derek slunk past to go to Michael, looking rather sheepish and trying his best not to be there. But Martin nodded to him: "Thanks, mate" – Derek cocked his head up an inch to say 'No problem,' almost apologetically. Susan now let out a sigh that was a mixture of relief and embarrassment, giggled happily at Derek's receding back and shook her head.

"What?" puzzled Martin.

"I can't believe I thought . . ."

"Thought what?"

Susan hesitated and then shook her head again – "Oh nothing, nothing. I'm sorry about this." She indicated her face with her hands, took the hankie Martin now proffered and wiped her eyes. There was, by now, no mascara left on her and her violet eyes sparkled in the fading light, unadorned, the residual splashes of her tears glistening her lashes. "It's been a hell of a few days, to be honest, and it's all suddenly got on top of me. But it's OK. I'm fine now."

She shrugged her shoulders as if to throw it off and now smiled broadly at Martin, her lovely red lips wide open in a cheesy grin of regular pearly whites. With her raven hair cast back off her face, Martin might reasonably have assumed that the Elizabeth Taylor of 'Suddenly, Last Summer' had dropped into his lap.

"But what's going on? What is this place?"

Susan looked past Martin's left shoulder to see where Michael and Derek were talking in hushed tones. Martin turned to look at the pair and then back to Susan, but this was only really to give himself a few more seconds before he had to answer. He hesitated a little more, not really wanting to spoil the moment with what he had to say.

"Believe it or not, it's an airstrip . . . a bit of a makeshift one, as far as I can tell, but there's a small plane behind that hedge," he indicated with a tip of the head past his co-conspirators.

Susan's face darkened as she looked – without looking – and realised what he was talking about.

"A plane?" she said, blankly: "For who?" – slightly dazed, she had probably worked out the answer to the question but it came out anyway.

"It's for me Susan. I've got to get away." A pained expression clung to his face.

"Why?"

"You know why. Barry Rogers has been murdered and apparently I'm the number one suspect. But I'm not going to sit through another murder trial and be fitted up again, Suze. I can't do it. I can't go to prison." He now looked anguished and she held his arms in her hands.

"But you won't, Martin, you won't. I mean, you didn't .. ?" She didn't know whether it was right to enunciate the last words of the sentence or not and, instead, was left staring at Martin in a way she'd not intended.

He screwed his head down into his shoulders and narrowed his eyes "No, of course I bloody didn't . . . Wha?"

"I know. I know you didn't, Love," she assured him. "That's what I mean – you didn't do it and you'll be able to prove that you didn't do it. Look, he was shot at this house this afternoon, so you'll have an alibi, won't you? Where were you?"

Martin shuffled on his feet and involuntarily inclined slightly to his left. Susan's gaze was directed straight past Martin to the ambiguous figure of Michael Green who, just at that moment, happened to be staring straight at her. Could he hear what they were saying?

Susan couldn't help but talk more quietly now, though she wasn't sure why. "You were with Michael?"

Martin nodded.

"Well, that's that then. There's your alibi." Somehow she didn't feel 100% sure when she said this and Martin shuffled a bit more.

"What's wrong with that? Michael will say you were with him, won't he?"

Martin was looking down at the ground. "I don't want to drag Michael into this . . . and . . . there's a danger he wouldn't be believed."

"What do you mean?"

"Well, they'll say he's just doing it out of loyalty to me. Michael might not stand up as a good witness, Susan."

"How's that?"

Martin stretched his lips back across his teeth. "He . . . he's had one or two brushes with . . . well, you know."

Susan said nothing but looked again past Martin to see Michael turn his gaze away from her and say something to Derek, who now looked anxiously across to her himself.

"And . . . ." Martin continued, awkwardly.

Susan looked back at Martin "and what..?" she asked, slowly.

"And we were there this afternoon," Martin looked like he had just been caught stealing from his mother's purse.

"What?" Susan was incredulous – "At Barry's house?!"

"Hmm."

"Jesus, Martin – what were you thinking?"

"I know, I know," he held his hands up, apologetically. "But we needed to get the story straight. Michael took me and I swear that, when we left, Barry was still very much alive."

"Well, was he alone?"

"I'm afraid so. To be honest, there was a bit of a scene and we left in a hurry but I couldn't see any sign of anyone else there."

"No Joan?"

"Not as far as I could tell."

"So, what did he say?"

"I won't bore you with the details but he was all over the shop as it happens – borderline hysterical, actually; making all sorts of threats, crazy. We just got out of it. I was only with Michael all afternoon otherwise and I was for coming home to you." (These words induced a small spasm of pain in Susan's chest, which Martin noticed but he continued.) "But Michael got a call to say that Barry had been shot and it's been panic stations ever since, to tell you the truth."

"That plane is Michael's?"

"Yeah – he's going to get me away somewhere, Susan. The thing is – even aside from me being suspected for Barry's murder – if the real killers are who we think they are, they could well be coming after me next . . ."

Susan couldn't quite believe that they were having a conversation like this at a private airstrip in the middle of nowhere – where had she been all her life while this sort of thing was going on? She was struggling for a moment to deny the logic of what Martin was saying and, just then, a call came from Michael –

"Martin !"

They both looked to see Michael point to his wristwatch, then the darkening sky and mouth: "Sorry."

"Shit, we're going to have to go," Martin was now flustered. "I've made him wait for ages because I wanted to see you before I go but we're losing the light now."

"Wait – I'm coming with you, yes?" Susan grabbed Martin's hand.

Martin just stood and gazed into her pleading eyes. Finally he shook his head and cast his eyes to the ground again.

"No, you can't Susan. I won't do that to you – I can't."

"What?!" Susan was aghast. "You can't go without me. Please don't leave me." She'd known really, as soon as the plane was mentioned, that something of the sort was on the cards but now, when the thing suddenly came into sharp focus, she found that it was too much and she felt again the pressure in her eyes. Her lower lip trembled of its own volition. Martin gazed upon her and never felt so desolate.

He shook his head. "I can't spirit you away just like that, Love. Can you imagine? – Secretary of State's daughter kidnapped by mental killer ! We wouldn't stand a chance. And it's not right to do that to your family. This is the best way, Love, believe me. I won't be gone forever. In a while, I'll get in touch and we'll sort it out. We'll make a plan. We will. Listen, Susan . . . I love you. I really love you. You're the most beautiful, fabulous woman and I want us to be together for the rest of our lives."

"I've been through all sorts of shit in my life and there's more coming now but you're the only one who's ever really understood me, who's ever really loved me for what I am and stuck by me. I can't believe I'm so lucky to have you and I won't let you go now. I have to leave but I'll be back for you, I promise. We will be together." He pulled her to him and kissed her fiercely. They wrapped their arms around each other as though they'd never let go. The tears ran down Susan's cheeks again and, as she ran her fingers through his hair, her whole body seemed ablaze with sensation. She had never felt so alive as she did now and yet she believed she was dying.

"I love you Martin, I love you so much – you don't know. I so wish you weren't going now. I wish we could just go home together and have a normal life like everyone else. But we will, won't we?"

"Yes, we will my darling, we will. I'll be back. And I love you."

"Please call me – please?"

"Yes, I will – don't worry," and he tapped his breast pocket to indicate his mobile.

"Goodbye Susan – for now."

Martin looked to be in torment as he turned and walked towards Michael and Derek, each step a torture and, upon each step, an agonised decision whether to take another one.

Susan felt like she was in some kind of nightmare as she stood alone on the track and even now somehow felt that if she called out it would all stop and she would wake up back in her normal life.

Martin shook hands with Derek and patted him on the shoulder. Just before he disappeared behind the end of the hedgerow, he turned to look at Susan one last time and it was another of those moments that should have been captured. And it was caught, burnt into the retina of Susan's mind's eye – the tragic figure of Martin Dash, only just silhouetted against the darkening sky, his hair falling across his forehead, the gaze of a man in pain, but always in pain, and looking somewhere beyond the pain.

And he turned again and was gone out of sight. Susan stood rooted to the spot and suddenly felt that she could take no more. She slid down to her knees and simply sobbed at the sheer awfulness of it. After all she had been through. After a lifetime of spinning around on the spot, always waiting, waiting for that which she didn't know but knew must be out there. After all that, she had found it – found him. Only to have him snatched from her.

She heard the crunch of Derek's shoes approaching and he knelt to put his arms around her shoulder "Come on, love. It's all right, you'll see him again. I know you will. Come on," and he eased her upright and rubbed her arm to ease the pain.

"Thank you," she sniffed and used the hankie given to her by Martin.

"Can we see it go?" she asked.

"OK, love," and they walked arm in arm along the lane. When they came to the end, Susan could see the extent of what lay beyond: a big, rectangular, close-cropped field sloping slightly from the right down to the left and, just as she looked right to see the little white Cessna, its engine clattered into life. This startled a murder of crows to evacuate a run of trees at the top of the field. As the wrinkled scarf of black birds was dragged along the navy sky, their caws provided an apt accompaniment to the lonely chugging of the plane trundling up to the start of its run.

It was difficult to see in the light that was now left but it looked to Susan that there was no sort of runway here and the choice of location for Martin's getaway had, indeed, been somewhat ad hoc. In any event, the plane now turned at the top end of the field to their right and almost immediately started forward determinedly with much revving and not a little bouncing of the nose. It was at this point that Susan wondered if it was Michael Green in the pilot's seat and, not for the first time, the thought of Martin trusting his fate to that man's hands gave her a nasty shudder of foreboding.

Nevertheless, the plane was now steaming down the field tidily enough, its landing lights showing the way, and, as it came level with she and Derek, Susan could just see a shock of blond hair and a hand waving below it. She waved back but watched, bereft, as the wheels separated from the ground and the dark human moth rose up, floated over the wood at the bottom of the field and melted into the sky. She could still hear the whirr of its engine for a little while after she had lost sight of it but soon that was gone too and they were left standing in a soundless space. Presently the crows returned to float their sinister croak on the currents of warm air lapping over the field.

33

9:00 p.m. and Susan was back in the Kensington flat. She had asked Derek to deliver her there despite his counsel against it. His view was that the police would soon work out that this spot – and not the Islington address – was Martin's actual residence and that she was best staying out of their clutches for as long as possible. But Susan now viewed her own flat – purchased by her father – as enemy territory and really had nowhere else to go: certainly not her parents', for the same reason.

In any case, she now saw this flat as hers and Martin's (and wanted to stay where she could still feel a connection) and, even if the police did arrive, she really didn't have any concrete information as to their suspect's whereabouts anyway. In fact, she realised that she actually had no idea at all where he was headed or when she would see him again, if ever. She now felt utterly washed out and depressed from fatigue and circumstances. But it was too early to try and sleep, her mind was running along a groove and jumping back and over again and again, and she had an idea that it might need an external agent to shut it down. She pulled a cold bottle of white wine from the fridge, poured herself a large glass, slumped onto the settee and clicked on the TV.

Flicking through the channels she finally alighted on the BBC News. The usual tapestry of disasters was being gleefully unfurled – carnage in Iraq, foot and mouth in the UK – and it all seemed strangely of a piece with Susan's mood as she sank slowly into an alcoholic fog.

She was only half awake when a string of words (her eyes had fallen shut by now) pierced her consciousness – '. . . *in a case which, it is alleged, is intimately connected to the embattled Secretary of State for Transport, the Right*

Honourable Jimmy Sachs. The killing of his associate, Mr. Barry Rogers, was reported earlier this evening with apparently no clues as to the identity of the perpetrator. However, in the latest development, his sister – Ms. Joan Rogers – has been taken under arrest after she presented herself at Barnet Police Station with her solicitor, apparently to confess to the murder, for which she has been duly charged. The latest reports suggest that – in a dramatic twist – Ms. Rogers brought a loaded gun to the police station to hand over, identifying it as the murder weapon.'

Susan was fully awake now and sat bolt upright. The story went on to show the blue and white tape around the front of the Rogers' house; a picture of Barry and Joan culled from some society rag showing the happy couple beaming – glasses in hand – with vulgar ostentation at a charity dinner; live footage of her father trying to dodge reporters as he arrived at the Hampstead mansion (thank God she hadn't gone there); and commentary from the show's reporter at the crime scene, trying to explain the twists and turns of the complex affair, which – he opined – was likely to see the final denouement of the colourful career of Mr. Jimmy Sachs, even if he wasn't culpable for any criminal deed.

Joan !

Joan had killed Barry !

She had obviously finally cracked (probably after a bottle or two at lunch); somehow got hold of a gun – in all likelihood, Barry's own, given that he fancied himself as a bit of a gangster and always said (loudly, to anyone who could hear) that he didn't feel safe for himself and Joan without a gun in the home (oh, delicious irony); and delivered the coup de grâce in their own lounge, right in his face.

Susan knew it was wrong to rejoice in such a thing but she couldn't help it. This meant that Martin was no longer a suspect; that the Syrian gangs weren't on the rampage to silence their co-conspirators; that, in fact, Joan had done the job for them, so that the prosecution's chief witness was no more. Martin no longer needed to flee now ! Everything was going to be OK and they would live together, happily ever after ! A hot current of exhilaration flashed through her. She had to speak to him, now. His phone. He'd told Susan that he had his mobile with him – she could call him right now. Nothing was stopping her – she leapt from the settee to grab her bag and rummaged for her phone, her fingers fumbling wildly.

She nearly keyed in the wrong passcode three times to block the phone and had to tell herself to calm down. She scrolled through her Contacts, excitedly, to bring up 'Martin Dash'. With a tumult of thoughts and ideas flooding her brain, she pressed 'Call' and realised she was hopping from foot to foot. She had never felt so happy.

A familiar tone rang out.

She realised that it was coming from within the room.

All the breath seemed to be sucked out of her as she moved to where the sound was coming from – Martin's black jacket on the chair by the window with the orange blind. In some confusion she reached in the pocket and pulled out Martin's Nokia – buzzing, with her name flashing on the screen.

Time stood still for a moment.

The red plastic device hit the wood-panelled floor at exactly the same time as the first tear.

THE END

10134548R00160

Printed in Great Britain
by Amazon